THE

Eden ⟶ !2

Bill Kitson

Published by Accent Press Ltd 2014

ISBN 9781783753512

Copyright © Bill Kitson 2014

The right of Bill Kitson to be identified as the author of this work has been asserted by him in accordance with the Copyright, Designs and Patents Act 1988.

The story contained within this book is a work of fiction. Names and characters are the product of the author's imagination and any resemblance to actual persons, living or dead, is entirely coincidental.

All rights reserved. No part of this book may be reproduced, stored in a retrieval system, or transmitted in any form or by any means, electronic, electrostatic, magnetic tape, mechanical, photocopying, recording or otherwise, without the written permission of the publishers: Accent Press Ltd, Ty Cynon House, Navigation Park, Abercynon, CF45 4SN

Acknowledgments

My thanks to Hazel Cushion and the team at Accent Press for their hard work and professionalism, especially to Greg Rees, whose meticulous editing went far beyond correcting my punctuation and grammar.

Finally, to my wife Val, for the countless hours she spent getting the manuscript into order.

For Val.

Proof-reader, copy-editor, unpaid agent, publicist, events manager, wife, lover and best friend, with all my love and admiration.

Chapter One

November 1980

I was asleep, and so for some time didn't hear the phone. Eventually, the persistent ringing roused me and I staggered downstairs, shivering in the chill November night air. I wondered sleepily who could be calling me in the middle of the night. If it was some drunk who had dialled the wrong number I would be less than happy; and keen to let them know it.

It wasn't a drunk, and it wasn't a wrong number. It was far more serious.

'Hello,' I began cautiously.

'Adam, oh, Adam, I need you ... I need help. I think I've killed someone!'

My brain cleared, the last fog of sleep lifting instantly. 'Eve? Where are you? What happened?'

'I'm at Barbara's house. She's away. I ... Adam, please ... can you come?'

'Calm down, Eve. Tell me what happened.'

I heard her take a deep breath. 'Barbara had to take two horses to Fontwell Park races. She won't be back until tomorrow, I'm here alone. I woke up and heard a noise outside. I went out and saw someone in the stables. It was dark. I ... I hit him – with a baseball bat.'

I wondered briefly where she'd got a baseball bat from, but this was not the time to ask. 'What happened then?'

'He fell on the floor of the loose box. When I touched him he didn't move. I shut him in then ran back to the house. I rang you straight away.'

'OK, give me time to get dressed and I'll be on my way.'

I covered the fifteen miles between Laithbrigg, where I live, and the village of Rowandale, where Barbara Lewis's racing stables were, in record time. As it was dark, the country road was empty of traffic, and the one perilous moment came when a startled fallow deer dashed across in front of my car.

As I drove, I wondered what sort of a mess Eve had got herself into this time. We had met almost a year ago, as guests of her sister and brother-in-law, a visit that had almost cost both of us our lives at the hands of a crazed killer. It had also been when I fell in love with Eve. Falling for her was the easy part. Persuading her to give up her successful career and leave London for the tranquillity of the Yorkshire Dales to live with me was far more difficult.

Eve hadn't turned me down flat, not in so many words, but she had made it abundantly clear that she wasn't ready to commit to a relationship yet. In the months since, encouraged by the support of her older sister Harriet, I had continued my long-distance courtship of Eve. I was beginning to believe I was making some headway when she announced that she intended to visit her old schoolfriend Barbara Lewis who, fortunately for me, happened to live in the next village. Her intention would also be spend a few days at Dene Cottage with me. Now, it appeared that I would see Eve earlier than anticipated, but hardly in an ideal situation. I was still wondering what I would find there when I pulled up outside Linden House Stables, on the outskirts of Rowandale village.

Eve had obviously been on the lookout for the car's headlights, because she was already by the gate when I got out of the car. I hugged her, and as she clung to me, reflected wryly that I'd dreamed of this embrace, but in vastly different circumstances. She led me past the house towards the quadrangle of brick-built, single-storey loose boxes that formed the stable block. She pointed to the first door. 'He's in there.'

Apart from the clothing I'd put on hurriedly, the only item I'd taken from Dene Cottage was my torch, and I shone this on the door. It was locked. I glanced back. Eve was waiting a few yards away, obviously fearful of what I would find inside. 'Did you lock the door?'

She looked puzzled. 'I thought the key was in the lock but look, it's on that nail where it's kept.' She pointed upwards to the right of the entrance.

'But you didn't put it there?'

'Not that I remember.'

As I took down the key, Eve told me where to find the light switch. I took a deep breath, opened the door, and reached for the light. I stepped inside. 'Eve,' I called to her, 'are you certain you locked the door?'

'I think I did, but now I can't be sure, why?'

'Well, either your victim became a ghost and passed through the wall, or you didn't lock it. I think he must have recovered and walked out of here.' Even as I spoke I wondered what sort of burglar would lock the door behind him, replacing the key on the hook. And how did he know where to find it?

Eve hurried forward and joined me in the entrance. 'Look, you can see blood on the floor.'

'I didn't doubt that you hit him, or that he bled. I think you might have intended to lock the door, but because you were so upset you panicked and ran.'

'I still don't understand. If he came round and I hadn't locked him in, why didn't he just scarper? Why did he lock the door behind him? He must have done, because I've just watched you unlock it. What sort of burglar does that make him?'

'Exactly what I was thinking. Perhaps he wasn't a burglar. Perhaps he was sent to tamper with one of Barbara's horses. To nobble it, I think the expression is.

Has she any horses running in important races, do you know?'

'I'm not sure. Apart from the two she took to Fontwell today she only has one or two runners in the next few weeks, and I don't know if they're entered in any of the big races.'

Another, far darker motive occurred to me as Eve was speaking, but I decided this wasn't the time to voice it. If the motive wasn't robbery or to get at one of her horses then it was possible that the intruder's target had been Barbara. 'Would you like me to stay?'

'Oh, Adam, yes please. I wouldn't feel safe on my own here tonight.'

We locked up, hung the key back on the nail, and as we turned to go towards the house I switched my torch on. We had almost reached the door when I saw movement in my peripheral vision. 'Who is it?' I demanded, my voice loud and confident, although I felt far less than so. 'Who's there? Come on, show yourself. Now!'

My torch beam illuminated the figure of a man standing close to the high brick wall alongside the loose boxes. I stared at him in surprise. He was, I guessed, somewhere between thirty and fifty years old, of medium height and build. Whether he was ugly or good-looking was impossible to determine, for his shoulder-length hair and an abundant beard any Santa would have envied concealed almost all of his features. His forehead was disfigured by an ugly bruise and a gash from which blood had seeped. This, I guessed to be the result of Eve's handiwork. I assumed him to be a tramp, and repeated my question. 'What are you doing here?'

He frowned, as if the simple question puzzled us. His reply certainly baffled us. 'I was sent here, I guess. Yes, sir, that's correct; I had to deliver the warning. I had to tell someone I'd seen them. They were by the bell ...' he hesitated. 'But I don't think it was you I had to see. The trouble is I get very confused.'

You and me both, I thought. Eve spoke for the first time, anticipating my question by a short head, to use local parlance. 'Seen what, or who?'

'Shouldn't that be whom?' His English was immaculate, although there was a trace of an accent, but I was unable to determine where from. 'I meant the children, but of course if the warning wasn't for you, that wouldn't mean anything. They were just like the rhyme, all covered with blood.'

I felt certain by now that the man was suffering from concussion, for none of what he was saying made the slightest bit of sense. 'You've had a nasty bump on the head. Why not come inside and let us attend to it. We can have a nice cup of tea. I'm sure that'll make you feel better.'

I saw Eve staring at me, her doubts as to the wisdom of allowing the intruder into Barbara's house plain. Nevertheless, she went ahead and opened the back door. The vagrant stood on the threshold, blinking in the bright light of the neon tubes, before I ushered him to the table and made him sit down on one of the chairs.

As I'd escorted him inside, I'd noticed no body odour and I was interested to see that both the hair and beard were well-combed and clean, as were his fingernails. His clothing, although obviously far from new, was also neat and tidy. If this man was indeed a tramp, he still retained a measure of pride in his appearance. I felt it was time to try and draw him out; to obtain some identification. 'My name's Adam,' I told him, 'Adam Bailey; and this is my girlfriend Eve Samuels. What's your name?'

He smiled. 'Adam and Eve? That sounds right and proper.' The smile faded. 'I don't know … I have trouble remembering … simple things like my name, or where I come from. People ask, and they don't seem to understand that I can't recall who I am.'

'This isn't recent then? Not since you were hit on the head?'

'I don't believe so. I think it's been going on for a long time, but I can't be sure. I have a feeling that coming here was important, but don't ask me why.'

He looked up as Eve came across with a small bowl and a couple of cloths. 'Put your head back, please. I'm going to bathe your wound. The water has some antiseptic in, so it will sting, I'm afraid.'

He leaned back in the chair, waiting for Eve to apply the cloth, and his eyes concentrated on the wall opposite. 'Oh, you've moved the clock,' he said.

Eve paused, her hand in mid air, water dripping onto the table. 'Have you been in this room before?'

He frowned, as if the question was a strange one. 'I guess so, ma'am.'

As he was being tended, I asked again about the weird statement he'd made outside. 'What did you mean about the children? Something about a rhyme; and them being covered with blood?'

'Don't you know it?' He seemed surprised by our ignorance, and began to recite something that might have been a nursery rhyme.

'Babes in the wood, babes in the wood, how did you get to be covered with blood?' Even his voice changed as he chanted, to one that sounded almost childlike.

'What does it mean?' Eve asked.

'I don't know. I don't think anyone does. I believe it's a warning, but that may be only my imagination. Things get muddled up and I can never be sure what's real and what isn't.'

Eve had completed her ministrations. 'I don't think it needs stitching,' she told him.

He drained the last of his tea and stood up. 'I should go,' he told us. 'I have to find the person who needs to be warned. I thought if I came here I could deliver it, but it seems I can't, because it isn't for you.'

'What is this warning?' I asked. 'You've mentioned it before.

'It's to do with the children. They only come out when someone has to be warned.'

'Warned? What about?'

'Warned that someone is going to die, of course.' He looked at each of us in turn. 'That's good, isn't it? The fact that the warning isn't for you, I mean?'

He turned away and moved towards the door, but had only taken a couple of paces before his knees gave way and he leant heavily against the wall. I rushed over. 'Perhaps we ought to get him to hospital,' I told Eve.

'No, we can't do that, Adam. Please. I'll explain later, but things are really bad for Barbara at the moment. Any whiff of scandal or strange goings-on could mean her losing everything. Can't we look after him here?'

I agreed, although it was against my better judgement. It took a while and more cups of tea before we convinced our visitor we would be happier knowing he was safe with us.

'OK, I'll stay,' he agreed. He stood and headed for the hall. 'I'll stay in the blue room, shall I?' And with that he headed upstairs.

Eve and I stared after him, more confused than ever.

'The blue room?' I looked at Eve.

Eve shrugged her shoulders. 'There's a single room at the back of the house. It has blue wallpaper.'

Moments later, we headed after him. I carried his overcoat which had been left on the kitchen chair. As I went to fold it, something in the pocket bumped against my arm. Caution warred with curiosity, before I dipped my hand in to remove the object. I stared at it in some surprise. Whatever I might have been expecting him to carry, a book of poetry was way down the list. Eve's expression was as puzzled as mine.

I tapped gently on the bedroom door Eve had indicated, and pushed it slowly open. The tramp had removed his shirt and I saw his back reflected in the dressing table mirror. I tried hard not to gasp. His skin was tanned, deeply, as if he had spent a long time in far warmer climates than ours. However, his back was criss-crossed with a series of white diagonal stripes that the tan could not touch. Somewhere, at some point in the past he was unable to remember, this man had been whipped unmercifully, flogged to within an inch of his life. He must have a constitution like iron to have survived such an ordeal. 'You left your overcoat in the kitchen,' I stammered. 'I didn't want you to wonder where it was.' I bade him goodnight and hurried downstairs to find Eve.

'I'm not surprised he can't remember anything,' I told her. 'His mind has probably shut the memory out because it's too traumatic.' Although it was by now the early hours of Sunday morning, neither of us was in the least sleepy. 'What do you make of your victim?' I asked her.

'Don't call him that, even as a joke. I'm so worried I might have caused him real harm.'

'I don't think you did. Admittedly hitting someone over the head with a baseball bat isn't conducive to improving their health, but he was mobile, conscious, and lucid, even if we couldn't make head nor tail of what he was talking about. And why were you reluctant to call the police or ambulance? You muttered something about Barbara being in trouble. What did you mean by that?'

'Barbara made me promise not to say anything about it to anyone, so please don't repeat a word of what I'm about to tell you. What about the man upstairs, though? Do you think delaying treatment might make his condition worse?'

It wouldn't do it any good, I thought, but seeing the anguished expression on Eve's face, I refrained from telling her so. 'Why don't you make us a coffee and you can explain what you meant about Barbara.'

Chapter Two

The distraction was welcome and after she put the coffee mugs on the table, Eve told me what she'd heard from her old schoolfriend. 'Babs is in the middle of a very messy and acrimonious divorce. Her husband ran up a load of debt and then scarpered to go live with a woman from where he works. Babs filed for divorce, but he's employed a solicitor who has lodged an enormous counter-claim. It alleges that she mistreated him, citing physical abuse and mental cruelty, plus denying him his conjugal rights for almost all the duration of the marriage.'

'If they've cited physical abuse they would need eyewitnesses to make that stick.'

'Unfortunately, they do. Two of them, to be precise; plus some very ugly photos. When Babs found out he was having an affair, she confronted him and during the argument struck him across the face with her riding crop before throwing him out. He had the photos taken a couple of days later when the bruising on his face was at its worst.'

'That's bad. What about the witnesses?'

'It's all part of the same sorry tale. The confrontation took place in the stable yard, in front of Barbara's head lad and the feed merchant she used.'

'And they're willing to give evidence for her husband?'

Eve grimaced. 'That's where it gets worse. Soon after she threw her husband out, Babs noticed discrepancies on the feed bills. Items she hadn't ordered. She challenged the merchant, and found out the head lad and her husband had been taking backhanders and the merchant invoiced nonexistent items to pay for the bribes. Babs sacked the head lad and changed her supplier, so they're both bitter and vindictive enough to do all they can to harm her.'

'I can understand that. So how much has the solicitor claimed on behalf of her husband?'

'Half the value of the business and the property. That's the house, the yard, and the land beyond where she grazes the horses.'

'I didn't realize she owns the property. He's not going to do badly out of it, for someone who is being accused of infidelity. What does he do for a living?'

'He works for the County Council. Something to do with the Highways Department, or Planning, I'm not sure which.'

'I can't see either of those places as hotbeds of illicit passion, somehow. You surprised me when you said Barbara owns Linden House, though. I thought it was part of the Rowandale Hall estate, like all the other land round here.'

'That's another story, quite an intriguing one, in fact. Barbara's father and grandfather worked for the estate. Linden House was a tied cottage and became the family home, but when mechanization did away with the need for heavy horses her grandfather rented the stables from the hall and took out a racing trainer's licence. About eighteen months ago the last member of the Latimer family, who own Rowandale Hall, died, and Babs found out that shortly before his death, old Mr Latimer had added a codicil to his will bequeathing Linden House and the stables to her. So once probate is granted, she will become the owner. Hence her ex-husband's sudden interest.'

'That bequest is unusual. Any particular reason for it, or was it pure generosity?'

'I'm not sure about this, but I believe if things had turned out different, Babs might have married into the Latimer family.'

'But I thought you said the man who died was the last of them?'

'There was a son. And from what Babs told me, I think she was in love with him, but he fell out with his father and went abroad. He died a few years ago, in Mexico.'

'That can't have any bearing on why Barbara is having all this trouble, though.'

'No, but the racing authorities are a bit sticky when it comes to scandal and Barbara is terrified all this animosity might lead to someone trying to object to her licence renewal. Added to that, Rowandale Hall and the rest of the estate is up for sale and the head of the syndicate that rents the shooting rights has put a bid in for it. His gamekeeper has been actively hostile. He stopped Babs from taking her horses across the estate to the gallops. They're on the other side of the village, and it was always understood that they could walk the horses along the edge of Rowandale Forest. However, he's put a stop to that, and even threatened to shoot any of the horses he found there.'

'I'm not sure how the law stands on it, but I have a feeling that if a path has been used for some years, it might be classed as a public bridleway, in which case the gamekeeper couldn't stop her. He certainly couldn't shoot any of her horses. Apart from the legal aspect, knowing the locals, they'd string him up from the nearest tree if he did anything like that.'

'I suppose you're right, but Babs isn't exactly thinking straight at the moment, and most of that stems from the divorce.'

Eventually, Eve said, 'I must get some sleep. I'm tired out. But I don't much like the thought of going to sleep with that man still in the house.'

'How about if I was to stay in your room in case he wakes up and starts wandering around?'

Eve eyed me suspiciously. 'Is that a case of frying pan or fire?'

'I wasn't suggesting going to bed with you. I thought I could sit on a chair until morning. Like you did for me when I was ill last Christmas.'

'Oh, all right.'

There was a note in Eve's voice that I didn't understand. It might have been disappointment, but I dismissed the idea as wishful thinking. Before we went upstairs I looked in Barbara's sitting room and inspected her collection of books. I would need something to keep me awake – and to distract me from being so close to Eve. I chose a thriller that had been published the previous year, entitled *Whip Hand* by the racing legend turned author, Dick Francis. I'd admired his work for a long time, and the subject seemed appropriate for our surroundings.

I tried to immerse myself in the opening chapter to avoid watching Eve undress. It didn't work, nor did it go unnoticed. 'Pervert,' she muttered, but didn't seem overly concerned at my voyeurism. She certainly didn't hurry to get beneath the concealment of the sheets. Having been caught in the act, I had no compunction in staring in admiration at her superb figure as she carefully folded the clothes she had been wearing. Once she was in bed, Eve turned and smiled at me. 'Thank you for coming to my rescue, Adam, and for being here with me. Are you sure you'll be OK in the chair?'

'I'll be fine. Sleep well.' I watched her for a few moments until her breathing suggested she had dozed off, and then turned my attention to the book. The story was exciting enough to keep me awake, and I was pleased to see that when I glanced towards the bed from time to time, Eve was having no trouble sleeping.

Although it was still dark, a pale half-light was beginning to show around the edges of the bedroom curtains when I heard noises from outside. I peered out in time to see two diminutive figures ambling towards the stable block.

'That'll be Barbara's stable lads,' a sleepy voice from the bed informed me. 'Barbara left them instructions about the morning routine as she won't be back for a few hours.'

I turned and smiled at Eve. Despite having just woken up, she looked radiantly beautiful, her flame-red hair fanning out on the white pillow, framing the perfect oval of her face. 'You look lovely,' I said.

'You need your eyes testing.'

'Shall I go and put the kettle on?'

'Adam, you are an angel.'

'I'll look in on the lodger as I go downstairs; see if he's back in the land of the living.'

I returned moments later with news that was startling enough to make Eve sit bolt upright in bed – which did my blood pressure no good. 'He's gone.'

'Gone? Gone where?'

'No idea. The bed hasn't been slept in. By the look of it, he slept on the floor. The pillow and one of the blankets are on the rug alongside the bed, but other than that, there's no trace of him. I checked the other bedrooms, plus the bathroom, and took a quick look round downstairs, but there's no sign he was ever in the house. He's quite simply vanished.'

'When did he do that, I wonder?' She eyed me suspiciously. 'Did you fall asleep?'

'No, definitely not. I've almost finished that book. What surprises me is how he managed it. I've been up and down those stairs a few times in the last few hours, and they creak and groan every time. I would have heard any sound such as that, but there was nothing.'

I could see Eve was unconvinced, and felt sure that in spite of my denial, she believed I had fallen asleep at my post. After she had dressed, she insisted on checking the house once again, to be sure nothing else apart from the tramp was missing. After we'd drunk our coffee, Eve said she would go and talk to the stable lads to make sure that everything was OK. 'At the same time I'm going to ask them about the tramp. They both live in the village, so it's possible they might have seen him, or know who he is.'

Whilst she was doing that, I decided to check the loose box where Eve had discovered the man. I was prompted more by curiosity than anything else. Of course, the man might have been looking for nothing more than somewhere warm and dry to pass the night. Alternatively, he may have thought there was something inside that might be worth stealing, but somehow I wasn't convinced by that idea. Despite his weird utterances and strange appearance, he seemed to have retained a sense of pride. It showed in his manner, and suggested to me that he wouldn't stoop to theft.

I had no real expectation of finding a clue as to his motive, and sure enough when I opened the door, even in the stronger light of day, the only indication that he'd been in there was the small patch of dried blood that discoloured the loose straw on the floor, where I guessed that bales had been stacked before being used. Or so I thought, until I turned to leave, and my foot caught on something that rolled across the floor, to strike one of the tines of a pitchfork that was leaning against the wall. The chink of metal on metal attracted my attention, and I stooped to pick the object up. I inspected it with growing astonishment. 'How the hell did that get here?' I muttered.

There is nothing wrong with my imagination, but even by stretching it to the limit, I couldn't work out how the small disc in my hand had come to be on the floor of a loose box in a racing stable in North Yorkshire.

I was still trying to make sense of my discovery as I locked the door. I was about to walk down the yard to show Eve what I had found, when I heard the sound of a vehicle coming down the drive. Without thinking, I slipped the object into my pocket as a horse box pulled to a halt opposite the end of the stable block.

The young woman who emerged from the driver's seat of the cab was small, slender, and extremely attractive. She had close-cropped blonde hair and lovely features, the beauty of which was marred at that moment by a ferocious scowl. If the frown didn't provide a strong enough clue as to her mood, the greeting she gave me certainly left me in no doubt. 'Who the bloody hell are you? And what are you doing on my property?'

I hoped my smile would placate her. It didn't. 'And good morning to you, Barbara,' I replied. That didn't work either. She looked to be in danger of exploding, so I hastily added, 'I'm Adam Bailey. Eve asked me to come over.'

Barbara's features relaxed slightly, and she came close to smiling. Not too close, but it was a vast improvement. She held her hand out, and as I shook it, she apologized. 'Sorry, Adam, but I've had a lousy weekend. Damned owner insisted I took both his horses to Fontwell, which is the other side of the moon from here, even though I told him they hadn't a cat in hell's chance of winning. Turns out he was using the race meeting as an excuse for a dirty weekend with his secretary. Added to that, the bloody horse box wouldn't start. I had to enlist the help of someone with a pair of jump leads. On reflection I should have used them on the horses, they might have run better. The result was I dare not stop on the way back in case I couldn't get the bloody thing going again. I'm knackered, and dying for a pee and a cup of coffee.'

The significance of my presence dawned on her, and she looked at me keenly. 'You said Eve asked you over. Was that social, or has there been some sort of emergency?'

'There was a spot of bother last night, but nothing to be concerned about.' I was about to explain when Eve came out of the yard.

'Hi, Babs, I thought I heard the van. The lads have finished the morning work and mucked out. They're grooming now, so I've left them to it. They said to tell you everything's OK. I take it you and Adam have introduced yourselves?'

Barbara gave me a wry smile. 'That's one way of putting it. What was the problem last night?'

'Why don't I ask the lads to unload the horses and we can explain over a coffee?'

'Good idea. I need something to keep me awake. I've been driving all night.'

Eve began by giving her account of her encounter with the intruder. I remember thinking, as she was speaking, had this really only happened a few hours ago?

As she listened; Barbara's eyes widened with amazement. When Eve explained that she'd armed herself with the baseball bat she'd seen in the cloaks cupboard to confront the intruder, and that she'd used it to fell him, Barbara responded, 'Blimey, Eve, you were useless at rounders when we were at school.'

Eve ignored the jibe. 'That was when I phoned Adam for help.' Eve looked at me and the warmth of her smile got my heart racing again. 'He came galloping over like a knight in shining armour to rescue his damsel in distress.'

I didn't allow myself to dwell on the phrase 'his damsel'. Instead, I took Eve's remark as a signal for me to tell the rest of the story. Eve is no fool, and she knew my previous career as a reporter and foreign correspondent had trained me to pick up on snippets and minute details others might have missed or forgotten.

If Eve's part of the story surprised Barbara, my account of the tramp and his strange behaviour left her both baffled and astounded. However, when I mentioned what the man had said about the children who were 'covered with blood' and recited the rhyme as he'd spoken it, there was no doubt that Barbara knew exactly to what the odd rhyme referred. Her face drained of all colour and I saw her hands tremble. Was that fear, I wondered, and if so, fear of what?

It was equally clear that Eve had also noticed her friend's reaction and challenged Barbara about it. 'What is it? Are you all right?'

'Yes, yes, I'm fine.' She was obviously disturbed by the mention of the rhyme.

'You know something about it, don't you, Babs?' Eve encouraged her.

Barbara hesitated then cleared her throat nervously. 'It's known as the Rowandale Skipping Rhyme. Kids have chanted it ever since I can remember. We all used to sing it when I was young.' Her voice was like that of a child as she began to chant.

'Babes in the wood, babes in the wood,
Why did you go in that cold, dark wood?
Babes in the wood, babes in the wood,
What did you see in that cold, dark wood?
Babes in the wood, babes in the wood,
How did you get to be covered in blood?
Babes in the wood, babes in the wood,
Who will be next to be covered in blood?'

Eve shivered. 'That's spooky. But what does it mean? Things like that, nursery rhymes and fairy tales, usually have some foundation in fact, don't they?' She looked at me for confirmation.

I nodded.

'Nobody is really sure,' Barbara told us. 'Some people believe the story behind it goes back as long ago as Viking times, and that it's a relic from some unspeakable atrocity they committed. There is a legend that once over, the marauders entered the village, slaughtered all the old folk, the men, and the children, and carried off all the women apart from those who were too long in the tooth to be used for sex. Others are of the opinion that it might be to do with the War of the Roses, because there were lots of skirmishes around here at the time. Then there are a few who think it has to do with some dark deeds perpetrated by the people at Rowandale Hall. They were a fairly dissolute lot. The Hall's empty now. The last surviving member of the family died a while ago.' She looked at Eve. 'I told you about him, didn't I?'

Eve nodded, and before Barbara continued, I asked, 'There's more to this than just an old nursery rhyme, though, isn't there?'

It seemed for a moment or two as if Barbara wasn't going to answer my question, and when she did speak, it was with obvious reluctance. 'If that man wasn't making it up and he really did see the children; then that's bad news for someone.'

'Why?' Eve and I asked in unison.

'Because the other story concerning the babes is an even grimmer one, if that's possible. They have only appeared a few times that I know of, but local legend is that the children are a premonition of death. If the legend is to be believed, every time they are seen, someone dies suddenly and violently shortly afterwards. And I know that part to be true.'

'How can you be sure of it?' Eve beat me to it that time.

'In the parish records there is the account of one sighting in the middle of the last century. A man from Knaresborough was out riding in the grounds when he came across one of the villagers. The local man saw the children standing alongside the path, pointing at the rider. He warned the man to turn round and go home because if he continued, he'd be killed. The rider ignored him, and fifteen minutes later, his horse put a foot down a rabbit hole, unseated the rider, fell on him, and broke the man's neck. That's one example. The other is from within my own family. My great-grandfather was killed in the First World War. His commanding officer wrote to my great-grandmother, telling her that he had been delirious for several days after being wounded by shrapnel. An hour before he died, he sat up in the bed and stared straight across the ward. He told everyone about the children who were standing there covered in blood, but of course no one else could see them.'

Barbara looked at us in turn. 'I think I'll have to go for a few hours' kip, I'm absolutely bushed.'

'Before you do, there's one more thing I must tell you. Just before you came back this morning I went into that loose box where Eve saw the tramp and I found this.' I took the find from my pocket and handed it to Barbara. Eve peered over her shoulder. The both looked bewildered, staring at the small gold-coloured coin.

Barbara looked at me. 'What is it, do you know, Adam?'

'I do, but I was hoping you would recognize it. The fact that you don't, that you haven't seen it before leads me to think the tramp may have dropped it, but where he got it from is anybody's guess.'

'Adam, don't be so provoking, tell us what it is,' Eve demanded.

I couldn't resist her, even had I wanted to. 'The metal is gold, and the coin is a German twenty-mark piece. It dates from 1912. Fortunately, when I was at school we were taught nineteenth- and early twentieth-century European history, so I recognized the figure represented on it. The face is that of Kaiser Wilhelm II. Now you can understand why I'm puzzled as to how it got here.'

Although Barbara was clearly shocked and bewildered by what we had told her, she took the disturbing news better than I had expected. I had already reached the conclusion that there was a core of steel running through her slender frame. Judging by what Eve had said about Barbara's current situation, she was going to need all that mental strength.

After she went upstairs for her much-needed sleep, Eve and I discussed the position. 'I can't leave her, the way things are,' Eve said. 'I know I was going to visit you, but I'd never forgive myself if anything happened to her that I could prevent.'

She looked at me, as if expecting resistance, but I hadn't even considered the notion. 'Of course you can't desert her, I understand that. Even if it means you don't get to come to Dene Cottage at all, it would be selfish of me to insist in the circumstances.'

'It might not mean cancelling the visit altogether. I said I would go back to work next week, but that was purely my decision. As I get paid on commission only, I can choose my working schedule to suit, all it means is that I don't get paid.'

Later, when Barbara returned downstairs, we explained the change in Eve's plans and I could see that the trainer was relieved that she would not be left alone. I set off home for Laithbrigg, having been thanked profusely by Barbara and kissed gratefully by Eve.

Although I was comforted by the knowledge that I was doing the right thing, I felt sure that the memory of that kiss would make Dene Cottage seem a cold and lonelier place over the coming days.

I drove slowly, turning over the bizarre events in my mind. After driving through Rowandale village and out on the other side, the woodland that comprised Rowandale Forest gave way to moorland as I climbed up the dale. I negotiated a particularly tricky bend and was surprised to see two cars parked by the roadside where the heather almost encroaches onto the narrow grass verge. The vehicles were dissimilar in many ways. One was a Mercedes sports car that looked as if it had emerged from the dealer's showroom only minutes earlier, the other a Land Rover that had the appearance of being very long in the tooth, and having led a very tough life.

Neither driver was in their car, they were standing close to the Mercedes, deep in conversation. I wondered if there had been some sort of accident, as the conversation was clearly heated, being accompanied by much arm-waving and finger-pointing. The men reflected their vehicles in both clothing and demeanour. One wore an expensive-looking suit with highly polished shoes. He looked as if he would have been more at home in a city centre than on a country lane in North Yorkshire. He was clearly the Mercedes owner. The other man, by contrast, was clad in moleskin plus fours and wearing an olive green sweater, apt attire when driving a Land Rover. They gave me no more than a cursory glance as I passed, and apart from wondering briefly who they were, and what two such dissimilar characters could have been arguing about, I soon forgot them.

I'd asked Eve to phone each day to reassure me that everything was OK at Linden House. She did so, with no startling developments to report over the next three days. When she called on Friday morning, she told me she and Barbara had discussed the situation, and that as things appeared to have returned to normal Barbara had said she would be quite content on her own. Would I please go and collect her so we could spend the next few days together as planned.

I resisted the temptation to put the phone down, snatch the car keys and set off for Rowandale immediately. 'Are you certain that's wise?' I asked.

'Barbara is sure, so will you come for me this afternoon, if it's convenient?'

'Of course I will.'

I reached Linden House soon after 3 p.m., not wanting to appear over eager. As I was putting Eve's cases in the car, Barbara, who had joined us by the vehicle, asked me a very strange question. 'When that man recited the rhyme about the children, can you remember his exact words? I asked Eve, but she isn't sure, but she said you'd know because you were trained to recall such minute details.'

I thought for a moment; then repeated the rhyme as requested. Barbara looked at me keenly. 'Are you absolutely certain you've got the wording one hundred per cent accurate?' she asked.

'I am, because it was so bizarre. I committed it to memory there and then.'

Barbara looked puzzled. 'You are sure?'

'Of course.' Now I was puzzled. 'Is everything OK, Barbara?'

'Yes, er, yes. Thank you,' she replied, doing little to quell my curiosity.

I was still puzzling over her reaction when Eve and I drove out of the yard. Why should my repetition of the rhyme cause such interest, I wondered?

Chapter Three

Over dinner that evening I decided to test a theory held by Eve's older sister, Harriet. Harriet had been my ardent supporter and confidante during the months since Eve and I had met, encouraging me to continue my pursuit of her.

I was by no means confident enough to adopt the technique suggested by Harriet. 'Adam, for goodness' sake, stop messing about. Tell Eve how much you love her; then take her to bed and prove it.'

'I'm not at all sure that would work,' I told her doubtfully.

'Why not? It did for me.'

Years earlier, when we had been students at Leeds University, Harriet and I had been lovers. Even after all these years, I still found it bizarre that she was encouraging me to seduce her sister.

I took a deep breath and dived in. 'Eve, I was hoping this visit might persuade you to take things a little further,' I suggested.

Eve's reply, although non-committal, was more promising than I'd hoped for. 'Let's see how things develop, shall we? Spending a few days alone together will be an interesting test. If you can still bear the sight of me at the other side of the weekend, who knows?'

'Does that mean you might be prepared to reconsider your earlier decision?'

'You're very sharp, Adam. Sometimes too sharp for your own good. It can get you into trouble, as you should remember.'

I winced, recognizing her allusion. It had been a bright

idea of mine that had almost got us both killed a year ago.

Later, as I escorted her upstairs, she stopped on the landing outside her room and turned to face me. 'It's good to be here, Adam. You've a lovely house, in a delightful setting.'

Then she leaned forward and kissed me, lighting the fires of passion that had been smouldering for months. 'I'd forgotten how nice that was,' she whispered. 'And the best part of being here is seeing you again.' She pushed me gently towards my room. 'Now, go to sleep and dream of me.'

I was already sure I would be a good husband for Eve. That night merely reinforced my certainty, because I did exactly as she instructed.

The following morning I was up and about early, but it was only minutes later that Eve joined me in the kitchen. I offered her tea or coffee. She opted for tea, and as we sat at the small table with our drinks I asked how she'd slept. 'I had a really good night,' she told me. 'I didn't wake up until I heard you going downstairs.' She grinned wickedly. 'How about you?'

'I did as I was told. I had a great time. How was it for you?'

Eve blushed and changed the subject abruptly. She turned her head away as if to look out of the window. 'I envy you living here. It's so quiet and peaceful, even more so than at Linden House. Such a contrast to London.'

We spent a long, lazy morning chatting, and for a large time I answered Eve's searching questions about the plot for the current novel I was working on. Shortly after lunchtime I suggested we go for a walk. It felt good to be out in the open air. It felt even better to stroll down the hill towards the village with Eve alongside me. The village was deserted, a fact which puzzled Eve. 'Where is everyone? Have they all been abducted by Martians?'

'I don't think so. There are reports of little green men

having been seen in the village, but usually by one of the locals who has staggered out of the pub after closing time. At a guess, I'd say everyone is at the football field.'

'Are they so keen on football?'

'No, but everyone is keen on beer, and it's a good excuse to get an early start because the landlord of the local pub sponsors the soccer team and opens up as soon as the match is over.'

'And there I was thinking we had the place to ourselves.' Eve slipped her hand into the crook of my elbow. It felt so good that I decided not to protest.

'Why choose here?' she asked suddenly.

'I was brought up near here and I've always loved this area. When I was looking for somewhere to live I saw Dene Cottage in an estate agent's window and that was it. My mind was made up.'

'What does Laithbrigg mean? There are a lot of strange place names around here.'

'It means a barn or shed close to a bridge.'

'How very prosaic. I was hoping for something far more romantic.'

'Well, you can have that with Rowandale, if you want? The rowan tree was said to ward off witches and afford protection.'

We reached the bottom of the hill and without conscious thought turned left to go over the bridge that spanned Thorsgill Beck. Eve pointed to the stone barn alongside the riverbank. 'Is that your agricultural building by a bridge?'

'Possibly, although I don't think it's the original one. Laithbrigg is mentioned in the Domesday Book, and that barn looks a lot more recent than 1086 AD.'

'You're a mine of useful information. Is that really when it was written?'

'Yes, although recorded would probably be a more accurate description. I suppose you could describe it as the forerunner of the modern census.'

We stopped in the middle of the bridge, where Eve looked down into the sparkling clear water of the beck, before lifting her head and staring upstream towards the head of the dale. She listened for a moment. 'Can you hear that?'

'Hear what? All I can hear is the sound of the stream and a curlew somewhere up on the moors calling to his mate.'

'Exactly, it's so peaceful here. A tonic for eardrums battered by the sound of London traffic, jet planes, and the like. You have such beautiful scenery and so tranquil a lifestyle. I envy you it. Have I said that before?'

'A couple of times.' I couldn't resist teasing her. 'I can see I had a narrow escape. If you'd accepted my proposal I would have always wondered if you'd only married me for my scenery.'

I got a gentle slap for my cheeky remark. It was more of a caress, given the power with which I knew Eve could hit. I'd had firsthand experience of Eve's punching power. 'I don't think you need to worry.'

'Because you've no intention of marrying me?'

'That's not what I meant at all, Adam. If I do change my mind, it certainly won't be because I love the scenery or the tranquillity of where you live.'

I was at a loss, not for the first time, by Eve's sudden change of mood. Being at a disadvantage, I changed the topic of conversation. 'Do you want to walk over to watch the football for a while? The view is even better there.'

The football ground at Laithbrigg is at the end of a long farm track. We had almost reached the turning when the first sign of trouble came. There was a sudden stirring among the few leaves still clinging to the trees, and at the same time I felt something cold and wet splash on the back of my hand. We glanced back, to see that where only minutes before there had been clear blue skies, the horizon was filled with dirty-looking black clouds, etched at the leading edge into shapes that always remind me of giant cauliflower florets.

'Trouble,' I muttered. 'It looks as if we're in for a storm.'

'Those clouds appeared from nowhere,' Eve said. 'I can't believe the change since we were at the bridge. What shall we do?'

I thought for a moment. 'I think we should set off home. We don't know how long this storm will last. If we're lucky we might get indoors before it starts raining.'

My theory was good, but it failed to take into account how fast the storm was travelling. We had only just reached the bridge when I felt further heavy splashes of rain or sleet on my arms and head. 'Here it comes. We'd better hurry.'

The sky was darker now, and the rain was falling heavier. We were both wearing trainers, ideal for jogging, which became more necessary as the rain started to come down heavier. I glanced at Eve and took her hand. 'Come on, Evie, let's run for it.' By the time we reached the cottage we were both absolutely soaked through; even our trainers squelched with every step we took. Eve's beautiful red-gold hair was a dripping tangle of matted, flattened curls that clung to her face and head. I felt raindrops coursing down my nose, my cheeks, and dripping from my ears. I fumbled with the key under the partial shelter of the lintel before opening the front door. As I ushered Eve inside, I noticed two puddles where we had been standing, albeit momentarily.

Once inside, we kicked our footwear off and peeled off our socks. 'Upstairs, and let's get out of these sodden clothes.'

Eve looked at me for a moment before smiling. It was that secretive smile I loved so much. On this occasion, the reason for her smile didn't remain secret for long. I had just removed my clothes and was standing holding them, deciding where to put them when my bedroom door opened. 'Give those to me; I'll dump them in the bath with mine for now.'

I handed Eve the clothing, momentarily embarrassed, until I remembered that she had seen me naked before. I was still standing there, bemused, when she returned. She handed me a towel. 'Dry my hair for me please, Adam. I can't reach the back properly.'

I took the towel, my brain dizzy from this unexpected development. Eve seemed totally unconcerned by the fact that we were both naked. I began to rub her hair with the towel, and after a few seconds she leaned back against me. The touch of her skin against mine had an electrifying effect that was as powerful as the storm raging outside. My rubbing turned into a caress, which Eve was obviously enjoying, to go by the contented purr that issued from her throat. I was about to tell her that her hair was dry when she turned suddenly and put her hand on the middle of my chest, pushing me gently away. I backed off until my legs came into contact with the end of the bed. Eve pushed hard, and I was forced to sit down. She stood directly in front of me, her breasts inches away from my face. She put her arm around my neck and pulled me gently forward. For one brief, glorious moment she held my head between her breasts. Then, in what seemed like one movement, she thrust me back onto the bed. As soon as I was in a prone position, she climbed astride me. 'I can think of a better way to get warm and dry than messing about with towels, can't you?'

A long time later, Eve sat up, propping herself with one elbow. The sheet dropped away, I felt desire rekindling. I thought of looking away; then dismissed the idea as stupid. 'Are you hungry?' I asked.

'Not very, although we haven't eaten since breakfast. Perhaps a snack just to keep our strength up.' Eve gave me a salacious grin that promised much.

'I've bought one of those gizmos that makes toasted sandwiches. How about a cheese and ham toastie?'

'That sounds ideal; then we can come back to bed.'

After we ate, we talked, whispering our thoughts to one another. Why we whispered, I've never figured out. The nearest house was half a mile away. However, it seemed right at the time.

'I still can't believe my luck. Did I dream it, or did this really happen.'

Eve tightened her grip on me. 'It happened. So, no more landlord's daughter from now on.'

'What are you talking about? What landlord's daughter?'

'You know well enough. The one from the village pub.'

'You mean the Admiral Nelson?'

'Whatever it's called, yes.'

'Who told you about the landlord's daughter?' Realization began to dawn. 'Was it Harriet, by any chance?'

'Yes, she said you'd told her you'd taken this girl to the pictures a couple of times. A "luscious blonde" is how she told me you described her. That was when she advised me to get myself up here and seduce you before it was too late. She said if I didn't make a move I'd lose you, because you're too much of a gentleman to take advantage of me.'

'A couple of hundred years ago your sister would have been burned at the stake as a witch. The landlord of the Admiral Nelson has two children. Both of them are blond, but I wouldn't describe either of them as luscious. They're both good footballers, and if it hadn't been for the rain we'd have seen both boys playing this afternoon. Whilst Harriet was making up the fictitious account of my behaviour, she was advising me to take you to bed the minute you got here and make love to you, tell you how much I adore you, and make you promise to marry me. In other words, Harriet has been playing both of us for suckers.'

Eve seemed far from unhappy at the news of her sister's duplicity. She stretched; a languorous movement that brought her foot into contact with my shin. At the same time her breast brushed against my arm. It might have been accidental, but I doubt it.

I had a sudden, belated, and worrying thought. 'Evie, darling, I'm sorry, I never realized. What about protection?'

Eve began to caress me. 'It doesn't matter, Adam. Not to me, anyway. Does it worry you?'

I hadn't given any thought to the possibility. 'No, I don't think so.'

'Then we'll let nature take its course, shall we?'

Chapter Four

It was late Sunday morning before we got up and even then I was reluctant to break the spell. I knew that before long we would have to discuss the future, but for the moment I was deliriously happy that Eve had demonstrated her love for me.

The soaking we'd received the previous afternoon meant that both of us required a complete change of clothing. In the haste of our need for one another, any thought of the sodden garments Eve had dumped in the bath had been completely ignored. It was only when Eve opened her suitcase to select replacement items that she discovered a snag. 'Damn!' she exclaimed.

I was still in bed, resting on one elbow, taking in the view as Eve rummaged inside the case. 'What's wrong?'

'I put my underwear in Barbara's washing machine along with her stuff. When I was packing Friday I forgot them. The only pair I have is those that got drenched and I can't put them on.'

'Well, if you can't get dressed, why not stick them on a radiator and come back to bed until they're dry?' I patted the duvet invitingly.

Eve stuck her tongue out. 'Don't be greedy, Adam. I will put them on the radiator and I'll manage without until they're dry.'

'If you want, I'll drive you across to Rowandale this afternoon, then you can collect your smalls and we can check that Barbara's OK. Killing two birds with one stone.'

Eve turned and blew me a kiss. 'Thanks, Adam, I'll go

put the coffee on while you get dressed, shall I?'

With the cabaret over I got dressed and followed her. My contentment must have been obvious when I entered the kitchen, because Eve looked at me and commented, 'That's an extremely smug expression on your face, Mr Bailey.'

I put my arms around her waist and kissed her lightly. 'Of course it is. You have given me the most precious gift a woman could give a man.'

Eve considered this for a moment. 'I suppose that's true, but I didn't think of it that way. Not at the time. For one thing it was so natural and right between us –' she paused and gave me another salacious grin, '– and besides, I was enjoying myself too much.'

When we had eaten brunch, which consisted of toast and more coffee, we set off for Rowandale to retrieve the missing lingerie. What had been intended to be no more than a flying visit was extended, in the first instance, because when we arrived at Linden House, there was no one around. The house doors were locked, and I could tell Eve was worried. I looked across towards the far wall, where Barbara's Mini Cooper was dwarfed by the horse box. 'She obviously hasn't driven anywhere. Maybe someone collected her and took her out for Sunday lunch.'

Eve's concern for her friend was contagious, and although both of us were reluctant to give voice to our fear, thoughts of the recent intrusion and the possibility that Barbara might have come to some harm were in our minds. I suggested we check the stables. All the horses were securely in their boxes, except one. Eve sighed with relief. 'The grey from that end box is her horse. She likes to exercise it when she can.'

With no sign of Barbara, we waited; our indecision and unease mounting, until Eve, who could see the open country beyond the stables, pointed towards the edge of Rowandale Forest. 'There she is. How odd, I wonder what made her choose to go in that direction.'

I moved to one side so I could get a better view. The tiny figure on the large grey in the far distance was definitely that of the trainer, and it looked as if she had just emerged from the dense woodland. 'Why do you say that?'

'Barbara told me the forest has a bad reputation amongst the locals. It's very dark and dense, and there are parts of it that no one has ventured into for years and years. Even the owners of the estate haven't been into more than a quarter of it. She told me it's huge, over ten thousand acres.'

'It certainly covers a big area, not only on this side of the dale, but on the far side as well, reaching right up to the high moors. And I guess it only stops there because it's above the tree line. Why the evil reputation, though?'

'Apparently, the locals reckon it was all to do with terrible things that had happened in the past, but nobody is sure whether that's true or legend. You remember, she mentioned that skipping rhyme and where that might have originated?'

I nodded, and Eve continued, 'Barbara said that although nobody knows the origin, the rumours continued until recently, when they had all but died down and people were beginning to forget, until the past few months, when there have been a few strange sightings, and more than one person has reported having been in the edge of the forest and sensed that they were not alone. So naturally, the whispers have all started again.'

'How fascinating, a haunted forest. Sounds like something by the Brothers Grimm. I don't suppose there's a gingerbread house in the middle, is there?' I was treated to one of Eve's withering glances. She does those very well. Fortunately for our harmony, Barbara's approach stopped further discussion. It was almost as if her return acted as the signal to kick off a series of events that none of us could have foreseen.

The horse had been stabled and Eve was in the middle of explaining the reason for our unannounced visit when I heard the sound of several vehicles approaching.

There were three cars, and they came down the drive to Linden House as if the drivers thought they owned the place. Which, as we soon discovered, one of them believed he did. The first was a Mercedes sports car, identical to the one I'd seen the previous week parked on the edge of the moor. As the driver emerged, or rather exploded from the vehicle, I recognized him as the man I'd seen. Given the tenor of their discussion that day, I was mildly surprised to see the Land Rover driver emerge from the back-marker of the trio of vehicles. Sandwiched between them was a new-looking BMW, whose owner I'd never seen before.

I had little time to inspect him, though, because my attention was on the Mercedes owner, who was approaching me at speed, his face a purple mask of rage. He marched up to me and reached forward to grasp my sweater. The attempt failed, because I stepped back smartly and his fist closed on thin air, causing him to stumble. My suspicion that he'd been drinking was confirmed as he shouted, 'Who the hell are you?'

Ignoring as best I could, the foul blast of whisky-laden breath that accompanied his words, I looked at Barbara. 'Do you know this man?'

'Unfortunately, I do. That is my soon to be ex-husband. Not soon enough for my liking. Ignore him; I've been trying to do it for years. His name, for what it's worth, which I admit isn't much, is Charles Lewis.'

Lewis spun round, but the whisky caused him to stumble again. He moved towards Barbara, gesturing back towards me. 'Is that the bastard who's been warming your bed, you filthy slut?'

Eve interrupted, her tone several degrees below icy. 'How dare you? Kindly don't refer to my fiancé in such disgusting terms. And, though it's absolutely none of your business, the only bed he's been warming is mine.'

Her words did nothing to appease Lewis's rage; in fact they seemed only to add fuel to the fire. He looked at Eve for a second before returning his gaze to Barbara. I was still dwelling on the notion that I'd been promoted to the status of fiancé, when Lewis returned to the attack. All the while the interchange was being watched with interest by the two other new arrivals.

'Listen to me, bitch, I want these people off my property at once, do you hear me?' He gestured towards us.

'It would be difficult not to hear you – you're shouting. You're also drunk. And you have absolutely no right to demand anything of me; you forfeited your rights long ago. If you want to play the big man, why not go do your pathetic posturing in front of that stupid whore you've shacked up with.'

'Don't you talk to me about rights; I'll tell *you* what you can and can't do,' he bawled. 'I'm going to make you live to regret crossing me. If you hadn't been so frigid I might still be here. But now I know I have it in my power to ruin you. I'm going to ensure you lose everything; the house, the stables, even your licence. I'll have it all and you'll finish up penniless, on the street. Not that you'd earn much there, you're too cold.'

'And just how do you propose to do that, you pathetic little worm? Let me remind you that you're the one who's been screwing around, not me. Although, from what I hear she's not too choosy about who she sleeps with. She can't be, come to think of it, or she'd never have taken up with you. I only hope she changed the sheets and got herself checked over. You wouldn't want to go catching some unpleasant disease. Mind you, that would be fairly apt, because you *are* an unpleasant disease.'

Lewis looked round for support and his gaze settled on

the BMW driver, who, like his companion, had been silent up to then. 'Tell her, Matthews,' Lewis shouted, 'tell her what you told me. Let's see what the bitch has to say about it then.'

Trevor Matthews stepped forward, his eyes fixed on Barbara with the cold venom of a snake. 'I have to inform you that, as the representative of the new owners of Rowandale Hall, I shall be applying to the court to have the terms of Rupert Latimer's will revoked. I don't know what undue influence you brought to bear on the senile old man, whether it was sexual favours or some other service, or whether you simply instructed him to change the will whilst his mind was confused by dementia, but we will argue that he was of unsound mind when he added that codicil. We will demand that the provision be struck through and that the property represented within be taken back into the estate as part of the purchase agreement.'

The Land Rover driver then delivered a chilling postscript to the message. 'I have to inform you that henceforth the gallops on Rowandale Moor will be closed to you. If you attempt to exercise your horses there, I will not be responsible for the consequences.'

I saw Barbara's face turn ashen, and for a moment thought she was about to faint, but it was fury, not fear that fuelled her. She fixed her gaze on her ex-husband. 'This is all your doing,' she hissed. 'Get off my land now, and take these two with you. You were no use as a husband, either in bed or out of it, and now you've proved you're equally useless as a human being. I hope you can keep your new lady friend happier than you kept me; although I doubt it.' She glanced downwards. 'Yes, I doubt it very much, because even that limp little article doesn't work properly, like the rest of you.'

Lewis stepped forward. One hand gripped Barbara's throat, whilst the other was raised, fist clenched. I was about to intervene, but before I could move, before Lewis could deliver the threatened punch, his head was yanked violently back.

The tramp had appeared as if from nowhere. As we watched, powerless to move, he took hold of Lewis's wrist and jerked it rigid, at the same time twisting it violently enough for his victim to open his mouth. The scream wasn't uttered though, because the sharp-bladed knife against his throat acted as an effective silencer. 'I guess it's time you left.' The tramp's tone was calm, conversational. 'And take your friends with you. Don't think of coming back. If you ever set foot on this property again I'll stain this knife with your blood.'

Even as he was speaking, the tramp hustled Lewis towards his car. Matthews was already inside the BMW, his hand reaching to lock the doors.

The Land Rover driver was the only one to stand his ground. He stared at the tramp, his hand firmly holding a thumb-stick. 'Who the hell are you, to give orders here?' he demanded, shaking the stick at him.

The tramp appeared to notice him for the first time. Having thrust Lewis, a quivering jelly, into the Mercedes, he turned towards the third intruder. Once again I was startled by the vagrant's speed of movement. He took three steps forward, making a sweeping downward movement with the knife, as he neared his target. Enough was enough. The thumb-stick fell to the ground, split lengthways to give the appearance of twin garden canes. Its terrified owner turned and ran for his car.

There was only one minor accident as the vehicles reversed out of the drive, although such was the drivers' panic there could well have been more. I noticed with satisfaction that Lewis clipped the gatepost in his haste to escape, creasing the wing of the Mercedes with an ugly dent.

Barbara turned to where the tramp had been standing only seconds before. 'Where is he? I want to talk to him.'

She looked confused. 'I need to thank him. Did either of you see which way he went?'

Eve and I looked round. Sure enough, the tramp had vanished as quickly and silently as he'd appeared. Barbara and Eve went down the stable yard, whilst I headed up the drive to check out the front of the house and the lane beyond. Five minutes later we met by the back door of the house. 'There's no sign of him round the front,' I told the girls.

Barbara gestured towards the fields beyond the stables. 'Unless he's turned himself into a sheep, we couldn't see him.'

The fields, bordered with drystone walls, sloped towards the river on one side, the shoulder of the hill being thickly wooded where Rowandale Forest began. I stared at the sheep grazing contentedly in the middle of the first field. 'I doubt he went that way.' I pointed towards the flock. 'No way would they have stayed there if someone had walked or run past close to them.'

'How strange. Then he must have gone up the drive. Are you certain that he wasn't hiding somewhere around the front?' Eve asked.

'Absolutely; it's more open there, all the way up to the crest of the moors.'

'There is one positive result from that confrontation, though,' Eve pointed out to Barbara. 'Whatever happened to him, this mystery man doesn't appear to pose a threat to you. Quite the opposite, from what we saw today, he seems intent on protecting you.'

'Eve's right,' I added, 'and when we encountered him last week, he said he was here to warn someone. What if that someone was you? Perhaps even then he was trying to protect you from something, whether it was real or imaginary.'

Barbara thought about what we'd said for a short while. 'I suppose you're right,' she sighed. 'However, it is a little unnerving when a complete stranger appears like that and then vanishes just as rapidly, even if he means well.'

Eve took hold of Barbara's arm. 'I think from what we've just heard and seen you're in more danger from the others than the tramp. What do you make of those threats about the house and the stables?'

'I don't know, Eve. I haven't had time to take in what Matthews said yet. My immediate concern is what Armstrong said about the gallops.'

'Armstrong? Is he the one with the Land Rover? Who is he?'

'His name's Walter Armstrong; he's the new gamekeeper appointed by the shooting syndicate. They sacked Ezekiel Calvert, who had been employed by the Latimer family for many years, and brought this Armstrong in to replace him. Armstrong isn't well liked in the village, mostly because of Ezekiel.'

'What about the other man, Matthews, I think you said his name was. Who is he?'

'Trevor Matthews, he's the shoot secretary. I think there are about ten permanent members of the syndicate. The rights on the Rowandale estate are very expensive, and when the old man decided to rent the shooting out, this lot stepped in. Matthews is one of the leading lights. He's a property developer from Leeds with a less than savoury reputation. He and one or two of his cronies are the ones who put up most of the money for the shoot.'

What had been planned as a flying visit ended up with us staying for tea, which enabled us to help Barbara formulate a strategy to counter the twin dangers she faced. Before these could be put into operation, however, matters took a dramatic and violent turn for the worse.

Chapter Five

We returned to Dene Cottage in the early part of the evening. The momentous change in our relationship had been all but overshadowed by the events of that afternoon. I was conscious of the fact that we needed to discuss the future, but in the event, that too had to be delayed.

'At least you remembered your underwear this time,' I joked as I unlocked the front door.

'Wise guy! I don't suppose you've ever forgotten anything important, have you?'

I was about to admit my frailties in that department, but something in Eve's words drew my attention. I stopped in the act of turning the key. Eve, who was becoming uncomfortably proficient at reading my thoughts, asked, 'What is it, Adam?'

'Something you said just now put me in mind of the tramp. Ever since that night we encountered him I've been conscious about something in his speech. There's a trace of an accent, and the way he phrases things sometimes isn't local. I admit it's barely noticeable, but once I spotted it, I've been trying to place where he's from, and now I think I've worked it out.'

Like falling dominoes, my thoughts collided, sending me from one aspect of the man to another. It wasn't only his accent, or his manner of speech, but the distinctive appearance of the knife he had brandished at Lewis that convinced me I wasn't wrong. I shook my head in surprise at where my thoughts had led me.

Eve took my hand as I closed the door. 'Tell me about it.'

'This is pure speculation, with very little to back it up, but I may know where the tramp hails from, or where he's spent a lot of time. And I can also guess how he came by those terrible injuries on his back.'

'I've had experience of your speculation before, and it can be surprisingly accurate. Run it past me, and I'll give you my opinion.'

I explained the first part, which took Eve by surprise. 'American?' She looked and sounded less than convinced. 'How do you come by that idea?'

'The first time we met him, almost the first thing he said was, "I was sent here, I guess. Yes, sir, that's correct." Do you remember?'

'I do; what of it?'

'The wording is more American than English. The "sir" for one thing. He also called you ma'am, which no Englishman would do. Then this afternoon, he told Lewis, "I guess it's time you left". Someone from around here would say I think, rather than I guess.'

'That's only a minute scrap of evidence. Have you anything else with which to convince the jury?'

'Yes, there was the knife he brandished at Lewis. I recognized it immediately, but because there was so much going on, I failed to grasp the significance. It's known as a Ka-Bar, and they have been carried by American soldiers since the Second World War.'

'Are you certain that was what it was?'

'Yes, I've seen a few on my travels.'

'OK, so the tramp was carrying an American army knife. I still don't see how that explains the marks on his back.'

'Think back a few years, Evie. What's been the major conflict American troops have been involved in over the past fifteen years?'

'You're talking about the Vietnam War?'

'Exactly, and when I was working in the States I heard

some terrible stories about the way the North Vietnamese treated prisoners. If he was captured and tortured, that would be the most likely cause of those injuries. It might also explain why he can't remember things like his own name.'

'Because he doesn't want to? Is that what you're getting at? The memories are so painful his mind has shut them and everything else about his past out?'

'I'm no psychiatrist, but it does seem the most logical explanation of his amnesia. However, even if my speculation turns out to be accurate, nothing about his past gives us a clue as to what he's doing around here, or why he's interested in Barbara.'

'Do you honestly believe he's American? He might have picked up the speech pattern from films, or TV. I certainly didn't detect any accent, nor did I spot the phrases until you pointed them out.'

'I'm not saying he is American, only that there's a possibility he spent some time in the States. It would tie in with the knife, and those injuries. There is one other thing, that poetry book I found in his coat pocket. It's a very old book, entitled *Mountain Interval.*'

'Why is that significant?'

'*Mountain Interval* is a collection by the American poet Robert Frost. He is revered in America, rightly so, but all but unknown in this country. I'd never heard of him until I went to work in New York.'

'The name means nothing to me,' Eve agreed. 'As to the other part of your theory, I didn't know there were any British soldiers involved in Vietnam. I thought it was mostly Americans, Canadians, and Australians.'

'I don't believe there were any British troops, at least not officially. I think there might have been a few "observers", which is polite code for Special Forces such as the SAS, but I also think there could have been some who joined as mercenaries, or because they believed in the cause. If our tramp was living in America at the time, he might have considered it his duty to volunteer. I suppose I could call an ex-colleague of mine in New York. He's now working for NBC, and he might have access to someone at the Department of Defense in Washington who could tell him, but we'd need more clues as to the man's identity first.'

'It sounds like a vicious circle to me.'

'Another thing that occurred to me after today's confrontation is that car Lewis was driving. I can't believe our County Council is so lavish with their salaries that he can afford to go swanning around in an expensive piece of metal like that Merc. Given the state of their marriage, I can't imagine Barbara buying him a bicycle, let alone something that costs as much as that sports car; even as a leaving present.'

'Maybe he bought it on hire-purchase.'

'He'd still have to have a chunk of money to put down as deposit. I suppose his bit on the side might have bought him it. Wealthy women often buy their boyfriends expensive presents, or so I'm told.' I stared at Eve meaningfully. Her father had left Eve and her sister a sizeable fortune each.

She responded to my sly comment with a stony glare. 'Consider yourself lucky you got me: with or without a dowry.'

I hastened to assure her just how fortunate I felt.

Later that evening, having had tea with Barbara at Linden House, we ate a supper consisting of pâté, cheese, and biscuits, accompanied by a glass of claret. I'd been on the point of broaching the subject of our future, but was still undecided how to begin, when, as we dined, Eve made her great announcement. 'I'm thinking of returning to London tomorrow. Will you give me a lift to the station?'

My dismay must have been apparent, because she smiled placatingly and added, 'I'm only talking about being away for a few days. I should be back next weekend.'

'It seems like a lot of expense for such a short time. Can't you deal with whatever you have to do over the phone?'

'Not really. I suppose I could give my notice in at work by phone, but that would be a bit unfair. They've always treated me well, it would be churlish to tell them I was quitting without doing it in person. And even if I was prepared to do that, I certainly can't arrange to put my flat up for sale by telephone.'

I stared at Eve, the penny only dropping extremely slowly. 'You mean …'

'I mean that I've decided that London is far too boring compared with the pace of life and excitement here in the Yorkshire Dales. So, if you still want me to, I'd rather like to come and live with you in this darling little cottage.'

I pulled her to her feet and held her close. Having demonstrated that her plan met with my complete approval, I walked over to the dresser and took a small box out of a drawer. I held it for a moment before I turned and handed it to Eve. 'This belonged to my mother. It was never off her finger from the day she and Dad got engaged until she died. Would you like it? Or would you prefer me to buy you a new one?' I added, unsure of her reaction.

Eve opened the case and looked at the solitaire diamond ring. With tears in her eyes she turned to me and smiled before she handed it back. 'You should do this, Adam.' She held out her left hand for me to place the ring on her third finger, which I duly did. 'Look,' she exclaimed, 'it's a perfect fit.'

'What made you decide?' I asked a while later. 'Was it last night?'

'No, I was already certain. Why do you think I came up to Yorkshire? I had to think up a good excuse, and when I talked to Barbara and she told me how things were at

Linden House, it fitted perfectly, like the ring. Last night only confirmed it.'

She paused and gripped my hand tighter. 'I realized what a mistake I'd made when I said no earlier this year, and it was making me miserable. Then, when you refused to give up, I knew I had to grasp this chance or risk losing you forever.' She grinned wickedly. 'That storm on Saturday night gave me the perfect opportunity to seduce you.'

The following morning I drove Eve across to York in time to catch the London train. I'd dreaded the thought of that journey, but Eve's decision the previous night changed all that. The knowledge that we would only be apart for a short time was enhanced by the thrill of looking forward to a lifetime spent together.

Not unnaturally, when I returned to Laithbrigg, I was unable to settle to work. Before entering the house, I sat in the car staring at the building. Eve had said how much she adored the cottage, but I was aware that although the accommodation had been ideal for my solitary existence, when Eve joined me, and with the added prospect of us starting a family, it would be far too small.

The choices were simple. We either had to move, or make some changes. As I looked at the weather-beaten shingle alongside the door, I smiled. That could be the first change. A simple transposition of the letters would do the trick. There was ample room to the side and rear of the building, so when the cottage became a house by the addition of an L-shaped extension we would have ample family accommodation, and we could then rename it Eden House.

My inability to concentrate meant that I also got little work done on the Tuesday. As I'd promised Eve, I phoned Barbara Lewis that evening to check she was OK. There was no reply, and I was extremely concerned, but on

Wednesday morning, after several attempts, I managed to contact her. 'Yes, I'm fine, Adam.' She told me. 'I went to Wetherby races and got back late.' She then explained how she had been trying all morning to make headway over the sale of Rowandale Hall and seemed as if she was about to say more, but then said, 'Sorry, I'll have to dash, one of the owners has just arrived to watch his horse exercise.'

I promised to call her again the following evening; and turned my attention to writing. By Friday morning, the characters in my plot were still demonstrating their unwillingness to cooperate, so by late morning I decided to abandon work for the time being and take a walk. It was a cold, fresh, clear day, which might go some way to clearing the fog in my brain Eve had created.

Laithbrigg is unlike many villages in England, and certainly unlike Hollywood portrayals, in that it isn't built around a village green. The houses form a single row facing Thorsgill Beck, with the church at one end; the pub and village shop at the other, and the packhorse bridge somewhere in the middle. Apart from the bridge there is another way of crossing the beck, but that way isn't available all year round. A short distance beyond the pub, opposite the last house in the village, is a set of stepping stones. These are often covered in water, but I decided to risk them. If they were impassable I could always retire to the bridge.

I strolled in somewhat leisurely fashion along the street, my mind still preoccupied with what to do about the fault in my plot when I noticed the pickup truck belonging to our milkman parked at the side of the street ahead of me. It was long past the time when he delivered, and I realized this must be his wife, who collected money from customers on Friday. I'd not left mine out as I usually did, and decided to wait for her to come back to the truck so I could pay her then and there.

I didn't have long to wait. As I stood for a moment

watching the stream gliding smoothly by, I noticed movement out of my eye corner. I looked down the street to see the woman emerging from beyond the pub. The lady was built on generous lines, but despite her size she was moving like Sebastian Coe when he'd won his Olympic Gold Medal earlier that year. She obviously saw me but by the time she reached the pickup her pace had slackened considerably, probably because she was out of breath. I noted the expression on her face, which seemed to be a combination of fear and horror.

'Something wrong, Mrs Price?' I asked. I can be pretty good at stating the obvious.

She gasped in an effort to breathe and speak, but found the twin tasks impossible. After three or four failed attempts to communicate, she managed to convey her message, albeit with great difficulty. At the same time she was waving her arm in the direction of the far side of the village.

'Body … there … body in the … beck … body … by the stones.'

'Body? Whose body?'

'No … idea …'

'Good God! Wait there. I'll go look.' I sprinted the couple of hundred yards until I was past the pub. I wouldn't have challenged Coe, but then he wasn't weighed down with heavy clothing and walking boots. Sure enough, exactly where Mrs Price had said, I could see a body wedged against the stepping stones, partly obscured from all but the closest inspection by the nearer bend of the beck. The victim was a man. His features were distorted; by fear of what had been coming or by pain preceding death, I wasn't sure which. Not that he'd been particularly handsome in the first place.

Recognition came quickly, not only via his face but by his clothing, clothing that bore holes where a knife had been used. There are very few people in Laithbrigg or the surrounding villages who wear suits except for parties, weddings, and funerals, or to attend church. Certainly not as a matter of course during the week.

It is an unfortunate fact that, as an ambulance man once told me, a way of dealing with terrible scenes is through a form of gallows humour. My immediate thought, as I stared at Charles Lewis's body, was that at least Barbara no longer had to worry about the terms of a divorce settlement. Then a darker thought intruded. Although Lewis's death might have solved one problem for her, it had undoubtedly created another, in that given the acrimonious state of her relationship with the deceased and the fact that their differences were common knowledge, Barbara would be high on the police list of suspects.

I returned to the pickup, where Mrs Price was half-sitting, half-leaning on the tailgate of the vehicle. 'You're right,' I told her. 'We'd better phone the police and get them out here before anyone else sees the corpse. It would hardly be nice for the children returning from school to witness something like that. Do you want me to make the call?'

Although she had recovered her breath, Mrs Price appeared to have lost the power of speech. She stared at me for a long, silent moment as if I was a complete stranger then nodded. My first attempt, using the public phone box opposite the bridge, met with failure. The device was out of order, signalled by the lack of dialling tone. I looked around for an alternative and settled on the pub. Inside, a couple of villagers who I recognized were seated on bar stools chatting to the landlord. Conversation died as I entered the bar and all three inspected me as if I'd that minute landed from Mars. Deciding that I was not an alien, which in fact they already knew because, although I was by no means the most frequent visitor, I had been in the pub many times since moving into the village, they lost interest. I only got their attention back when I asked to use the phone, adding that I needed to contact the police. 'I tried the kiosk, but the phone there seems to be out of order.'

'Has been for weeks,' one of the locals told me, morosely. 'They've been told about it a few times.'

'Why do you need the police?' the landlord asked.

'We've found a dead body in the stream. Or rather, Mrs Price has.'

The open-mouthed silence that followed my statement told me that I hadn't lost my talent as a conversation stopper. I picked up the phone passed from behind the bar and amid total silence, dialled 999.

Both the customers and landlord listened intently to my end of the conversation, and I guessed that there would be only one talking point in the bar that night; probably for weeks to come, given the lack of competing excitement in the village. When I'd finished, I sank onto the nearest stool and looked along the counter. 'Would one of you mind fetching Mrs Price inside, please? She's had a terrible shock and she's in a bit of a state.'

To be honest, I wasn't exactly feeling on top form myself. No matter how many acts of violence you witness, the sight of a corpse mutilated as badly as Lewis's is unnerving, to put it mildly. One of the locals dismounted from his barstool and hurried outside. I guessed that he was both keen to hear her story and equally anxious not to miss anything that might be said inside during his absence. The landlord placed a tumbler of whisky on the bar in front of me.

'Drink that, it's on the house,' he told me. I noticed he hadn't put ice or water in it, presumably because there wasn't room for any. A couple of minutes later, without being asked, he prescribed and dispensed a similar dose for Mrs Price. None of the locals seemed tempted to go inspect the body; presumably my description of the corpse to the police deterred them. I can't say I blamed the drinkers; these were devoted disciples of Bacchus and there can be few things more likely to put you off your beer than the sight of a badly mutilated body.

Chapter Six

The police didn't arrive in the manner portrayed in films or on TV. There was no sudden invasion of a host of cars, no influx of flashing lights, no blaring sirens, no team of detectives with their back-up squads of coroner's officers or pathologist. Rather, they turned up in dribs and drabs. First on the scene was the constable whose duty it was to cover the twin villages and several others in the surrounding area. PC John Pickersgill was nearing the tail-end of his career. Overweight, a heavy smoker who was fond of his food, and, as I knew from my occasional visits to the Admiral Nelson, not averse to the odd pint or two. He was a fine example of old-fashioned, no-nonsense community policing. Pickersgill was the sort of local bobby who would not hesitate to deliver instant justice via a clip around the ear to youngsters committing minor acts of misbehaviour. Such treatment, frowned upon though it might be by so-called advanced thinkers who considered it barbaric, nevertheless prevented more serious offences from occurring. As far as I knew there was little, if any yobbish behaviour within Pickersgill's patch.

He strolled into the bar of the Admiral Nelson as if he was merely another customer about to order a pint. He nodded to the landlord and locals before focusing his attention on Mrs Price and me. 'Hello, Mary, you've had a bit of a shock, I hear. Stay there and finish your drink. You'll need it when CID turn up and start pestering you with daft questions.'

He turned to me. 'Morning, Adam.' I nodded. 'Having seen some of your reports from war zones, I'm aware that you're no stranger to scenes of violence, so perhaps you wouldn't mind showing me the body?'

I finished my whisky and followed him out of the bar.

'The report I had of your phone call didn't mention an identity, do you know who the body is?'

'I deliberately didn't say anything over the phone because the landlord and locals were listening in, but I did recognize him. His name is Charles Lewis.' I explained how I knew the dead man.

'Try and keep quiet about the fact that you recognized him, otherwise most of the county will know by closing time tonight. That lot will get the information out of you faster than the KGB or the Spanish Inquisition could. This will keep the rumour factory busy for months.'

We reached the stepping stones and Pickersgill gave a sharp exhalation of breath as he looked at the corpse. 'Very messy,' he said after a couple of minutes. He looked closely at the crime scene. 'It's a good job the body got wedged in the stones, I reckon, otherwise he'd have gone all the way to the river. That would have given folk in their narrowboats a nasty shock if he'd drifted past whilst they were eating their toast and marmalade.'

It seemed that black humour was Pickersgill's way of dealing with trauma as well as mine. He stared at the deceased for a while longer; then turned to me. 'What do you think? You've a bit of a reputation in these matters. You sorted out that business at Mulgrave Castle last year, didn't you?'

My liking for Pickersgill was turning rapidly to respect. 'You know I did.'

'Ah, well, I make it my business to know as much as I can about anyone who moves into my patch. You were dead easy by comparison with some.'

The fact that he and I had sunk many a pint together did go some way to him knowing my history.

'So what about it, O Great Detective?' He invested the

title with ironic capitals, but I regarded it as a challenge.

'One question I would ask is, where's his car? He has a flash-looking Mercedes sports job.' I gestured around. 'I don't see it anywhere, and from what little I know or have been told about him, I don't think Lewis was the keenest hiker in the area. Added to which he isn't dressed for it. That would suggest he might have been killed elsewhere. I guess if he's floated downstream the priority ought to be searching the bank further up Thorsgill Beck. It might be easier to locate the car and that should give you the place where the murder was committed, unless the motive was car theft.'

'That was pretty good considering you've had little time to think about it. Let me know if you've any more bright ideas on the subject. Now you'd better go wait inside. The super-sleuths will no doubt want to ask you a load of meaningless questions when they arrive. I'll have to stay here and guard the corpse.' Pickersgill smiled ironically. 'Not that the poor bloke is going anywhere, but it might stop anyone getting frightened by it.'

With the arrival of CID and their attendant services, the constable was relegated to the task of crowd control. As there were no crowds to control, merely three or four villagers who had emerged from their cottages on seeing and hearing the police cars, ambulance, and other vehicles that were arriving in a constant stream, Pickersgill's task was little more than a sinecure. Or rather, it would have been, but for him having to sort out the traffic jam caused by too many cars occupying a narrow village street that had been constructed when a horse and cart were the standard means of transport.

Inside the pub, a corner of the bar had been commandeered for interviewing witnesses. As the only witnesses were Mary Price and me this seemed to be a singularly futile example of overkill. Once the detective in charge, an inspector by the name of Ogden, had finished with Mrs Price, he turned his attention on me. What he imagined I could tell him, that he didn't already know, I had no idea, nor did his subsequent questions leave me any the wiser. There seemed little point to them, but Ogden ploughed on, as if working from a manual, while a detective constable, who looked as if it would be a few years before he started shaving, dutifully recorded my answers in his notebook. The interrogation reached the extreme of banality when Ogden asked, 'Was the body in the same position when you found it as it is now?'

'Yes,' I replied, keeping my face straight with an effort, 'he hasn't moved a muscle.' I resisted the alternative answer of, 'apart from when he got up and danced a couple of Irish jigs,' but the temptation was great. Eventually, Ogden seemed to realize the futility of asking me any more pointless questions and abandoned the interview, having first warned me that they might wish to speak to me again.

'Oh good,' I told them as I stood up to leave, 'I'll really look forward to that.' It was quite apparent that the sarcasm was lost on both men.

When I emerged from the Admiral Nelson, Pickersgill was leaning against the low drystone wall opposite the inn, his boredom apparent. 'How did you get on with the great brains of CID?'

'I take it you don't have much time for Detective Inspector Ogden?'

'Did you say detective or defective? I read an article recently that implied the standard of examination questions was getting easier. The fact that Ogden has reached the rank of inspector would tend to suggest that theory is accurate. Did he check your watch?'

'No, why would he do that?'

'Because he doesn't know what time of day it is without someone to tell him. I bet he asked you what your relationship with Mrs Lewis is, though.'

'I don't have a relationship with Mrs Lewis. She's a friend, that's all.'

'I know that, and you know that, but I bet Ogden doesn't. To him the term "friend" would imply that she was your mistress. Don't kid yourself; it won't be long before he gets round to asking if you're sleeping with her. It's a standard line of questioning for him. The fact that you're already spoken for won't even enter his thinking.'

I looked at Pickersgill; my astonishment obviously apparent, because he explained, 'I saw you walking through the village last weekend holding hands with a lovely young woman. I assume her to be your friend from London you told me about. I also recognized her from the photos that appeared in the press at the time of the Mulgrave Castle affair, and more recently when the two of you were star witnesses at the trial. Miss Samuels, isn't it?'

I realized it was impossible to conceal anything from Pickersgill. 'That's correct; we're engaged to be married.'

'You're a lucky man, Adam, but I think I ought to warn you that it is rather hazardous not to keep your attention on your driving around here. The country lanes can be very tricky, especially when you're gazing admiringly at your passenger instead of watching the road.'

He relented from teasing me, and added, 'I saw you driving with Miss Samuels on Monday morning.'

'I was taking her to York to catch the London train. She's gone to give her notice in at work and put her flat on the market so she can move here to live with me.' I realized for the first time what a thrill it was to tell someone what Eve and I were planning.

'Congratulations, I'm sure you'll be very happy, and I think Miss Samuels will be very welcome here. When will she be back?'

'I'm not sure, hopefully sometime this weekend.'

'Perhaps you could phone me once she's returned. I'd like to meet her.'

I looked at him suspiciously. 'Have you any specific reason? I don't remember you rushing to be introduced to me when I moved into the area. You waited until I was in the pub.'

'Given your background in investigations, I thought you and Miss Samuels might want to get involved in finding out who did this.' He gestured towards the stepping stones where someone I assumed to be the pathologist was supervising the removal of Lewis's body.

Pickersgill's question took me by surprise. 'I don't know, Johnny. I haven't had time to think about it, to be honest.'

'Please do; I don't want to have to rely on that lot.' He pointed towards the pub. 'If I leave it to Sherlock Ogden and his boy blunder of a sidekick I'll end my career with an unsolved murder on my patch, and I wouldn't want that.'

When I returned home, I tried Barbara's number, but there was no reply. I wondered if she might be attending another race meeting, and even went to the trouble of checking the morning paper, only to discover that there was no racing scheduled for that day.

I was still trying to decide whether to drive across to Rowandale to see if she was all right and to tell her the shocking news about Lewis's demise, when Eve rang. 'I've got everything sorted out here,' she told me cheerfully, 'so I'll be home tomorrow.'

I felt a warm glow at hearing Eve refer to Dene Cottage as home, and that distracted me momentarily from telling her my news. 'What time is your train due at York?'

I noted the details on a corner of the paper; then said, 'Eve, I've something to tell you. Something serious. I found a body this morning. Or at least the milklady did.'

'What! Where? Whose body was it? And what's that

about a milklady?'

I explained who Mrs Price was, and of finding the corpse by the stepping stones. 'The thing is, Eve, I recognized him straight away. It was Charles Lewis.'

'Good Lord! Are you certain? How did he die? Was he drowned?'

'No, he was stabbed over and over again, by the look of it, and at a guess I'd say the killer used a very sharp knife.'

Eve jumped to the same conclusion that had been troubling me ever since I saw the dead man's wounds. 'A knife such the one the tramp was carrying, you mean?'

'Exactly.'

'Do you think he did it? Have you told the police about him?'

'I haven't mentioned it, so far. Although I certainly believe he might be capable of it if Lewis provoked him, or attacked Barbara. I'm not saying he isn't right in the head, but you have to admit his behaviour is somewhat eccentric, to put it mildly, and he did issue that fairly bloodcurdling threat.'

'That still doesn't mean he killed Lewis.'

'No, but there were witnesses to the encounter, and two of them can have no reason to like the tramp. If they tell Ogden what they saw and heard last Sunday, I'm sure he will assume that the tramp carried out his threat and not bother to look for anyone else.'

'Who is Ogden?'

'The detective in charge, I met him after we found the body. He's a bit of a dope; asked me a string of futile questions. Even our local bobby, John Pickersgill, is very scathing about him.' I told her what Pickersgill had said, before adding, 'By the way, he knows all about us.'

'The village policeman knows we're engaged? How did he find that out? Did you tell him?'

'I didn't need to. He saw us together at the weekend and again on Monday morning and put two and two together.'

'He sounds very astute. Perhaps he ought to be the one to investigate the murder, rather than this Ogden chap?'

'I think he's planning to, by proxy, so to speak.'

'What on earth does that mean?'

'He asked me to phone him as soon as you're back. He's going to ask us, off the record, to have a look into Lewis's death because he doesn't trust the local CID; and Ogden in particular, to get it right.'

'Oh Lord, here we go again. I obviously can't leave you alone for five minutes without you getting into trouble.'

'All the more reason for you to hurry back home.'

'It sounds nice, when you refer to Dene Cottage as home. Seriously, though, Adam, are you sure we ought to get involved in this? Apart from the police politics, think of what happened before. I wouldn't want us to end up in the same sort of danger. We only just escaped with our lives then. This time we might not be so lucky.'

Chapter Seven

'The problem is, I think we're already involved in this case, to some extent, given that it was Barbara's husband who was murdered.' I continued to try and convince Eve we should try and help Johnny Pickersgill.

'Have you told Barbara about what happened to Charles?'

'Not yet; I did try her number a bit earlier, but there was no reply.'

'Leave it to me; I'll call her. The news might come better from me, although I doubt whether she'll grieve too much.'

'I would have thought the police will already have told her, but she may want someone to talk to. What concerns me is that apart from the tramp, the person with the greatest motive to kill Lewis is Barbara. Not only was there the acrimony of the divorce, but if he was claiming half the property, there's the financial angle to consider.'

'You don't honestly believe that of Barbara, do you?'

'No, not for one minute, but I'm prepared to bet that Ogden will. Don't forget, I've seen the way his mind works.'

'Yes, I got that impression, and I haven't even met the man.'

'I forgot to tell you, but when I last spoke to Barbara, she told me she was having great difficulty getting an appointment with the solicitor handling the Rowandale Hall estate. I'm not sure whether she was being a touch paranoid, but she said she'd got the impression that the man was being deliberately evasive.'

There was a pause while Eve considered what I'd told her. 'Does she have the right to demand an interview?'

'I feel sure she must have; after all she is a beneficiary in Rupert Latimer's will, and a major one at that. As such I reckon she could demand to see any or all documents relative to the disposal of his estate. But there again, I'm no legal expert, and from what I gather, wills and probate law are a bit of a minefield.'

'Isn't there a time limit before you have to apply for probate, or whatever it's called? I seem to remember after my father died we had to sign things before a certain date.'

Eve's father had been a very successful and extremely wealthy businessman, and when he and her mother died, Eve and her sister Harriet both inherited a large fortune. 'I wouldn't know; my family has never had enough money to be kept awake at night by problems such as that.'

Eve made a sound that, when I was living in New York, I heard described as a 'Bronx cheer'; elsewhere it was known as blowing a raspberry. I grinned and then answered her seriously, 'I would imagine that if there is an issue or dispute over one of the bequests, or if someone challenges the will, that would delay applying for probate until the matter was resolved. I wouldn't suppose anyone would want to hurry the process in such a situation, because as soon as they have probate, the Inland Revenue will be round with their begging bowl.'

'Tut-tut, Mr Bailey, such cynicism. Do you really think this solicitor might be in collusion with Matthews?'

'Now you're getting to sound as paranoid as Barbara. I suppose it is just possible, but I very much doubt it. For one thing, if he did anything like that and it all went wrong, he'd risk losing far too much. I think it's far more likely that he's simply being extremely cautious.'

'Of course, none of this would have happened if Brian was still alive.'

Eve's statement confused me. 'Brian? Who's Brian?'

'I'm sorry, I was assuming you knew. I forgot you weren't there when Barbara told me about him. You remember I told you about Rupert Latimer's only child that died in Mexico? His name was Brian. Barbara talked about him whilst I was staying with her. She'd had a little too much wine one evening and that loosened her tongue. It's a rather sad story. He fell out with his father after the old man accused him of stealing some valuable pieces of silverware and jewellery from the Hall. It seems they were sold to a jeweller in Leeds and when Rupert Latimer traced one of the items and went to see the jeweller, he identified Brian from a photo the old man showed him. When Rupert confronted Brian with it, the boy took offence and walked out, swearing never to return. He had money in his own right, so he was never going to be destitute.'

'How old was he?'

'I'm not sure, twenty-one or so, I think. Anyway, about a year later, police raided the jeweller's in Leeds and arrested the jeweller, plus a man who was trying to dispose of more of the Latimer collection. It turned out he was the butler at the Hall, and the two men had been robbing Rupert blind for ages.'

'You said that Brian Latimer died. What happened to him?'

'Nobody heard from him for years, and then his body was discovered in an abandoned mine somewhere in Mexico. He'd been shot several times, and police there reckoned it might have had something to do with drugs. Barbara told me they identified him via his British driving licence. It was when she was telling me this bit that she got really upset. That's when I gathered Brian Latimer meant more to her than just a friend or neighbour. Whether it ever came to anything, I'm not sure.'

'As you say; a very sad story. And if your intuition is right, and things had turned out different, Barbara might have been the mistress of Rowandale Hall now.'

'I agree. I could never understand why she married a waster like Lewis, but if she was still recovering from Brian's death, that would explain a lot. Anyway, she's rid of him now, and all the problems he caused.'

'Except that his death could give her even worse problems by the sound of it, both from Matthews and the police.'

'You're right. I think the sooner I'm back; the better.'

'Now that, I totally agree with, and it has nothing to do with the murder.'

'I'd better phone Barbara. I'll see you in the morning, Adam.'

'Let me know if you get hold of her.'

We exchanged loving messages before she agreed. My concern over Barbara was in no way assuaged by Eve's call. I roamed the house that evening, restless and unable to settle. I was concerned about the murder and I missed Eve more than ever. When it got to midnight, and I still hadn't heard from Eve, I went to bed. I was unable to sleep, however. I was plagued by the persistent memory of the tramp, his seeming fixation on Barbara, and most of all, the knife he carried. This, allied to the assault on Lewis, led me down the path of supposition into an extremely unsavoury area. Had he seen Lewis as a rival, tracked him down, and killed him? And, having done so, had he descended on Linden House to claim his prize? The stables were extremely isolated, and the fact that Barbara was alone there, without even the stable lads to call on for help, left her highly vulnerable.

It wasn't only the tramp who posed a potential danger. She had been threatened by the gamekeeper, Armstrong, by his employer, Matthews, and by Lewis. Although Lewis no longer posed a threat, the manner of his death was even more disquieting. Eventually, I did doze off, but kept waking up at regular intervals. Each time I woke, I peered at the bedside clock. After this had happened three or four times I decided it needed a new battery, because it appeared to have stopped. It wasn't until almost daylight that I remembered it was plugged into the mains.

Next morning I set off for York early. I could buy some much needed stationery supplies before meeting Eve's train. I reached the station just as her train was pulling in, and was by the barrier to greet her. We walked back to the car, followed by a porter whose trolley contained a small mountain of suitcases. I glanced back at the man. 'Are all those cases yours?'

Eve nodded.

'You should have warned me. If I'd known, I'd have borrowed a removals van.'

Eve looked surprised. 'Why, won't they fit in your car?'

'I'm not sure they'll fit in the house, let alone the car. Anyway, did you get hold of Barbara?'

'No, I tried several times, right up until midnight, but there was no answer. I wondered if you wouldn't mind if we go via Rowandale on the way home.'

'I'll certainly do that; in fact I was going to suggest it.' I started to ram suitcases into the back of the car. 'I just hope the rear axle holds out.'

When we reached Linden House, the gates to the drive were open. I drove in, parking behind Barbara's car, which was alongside the horsebox. The yard was deserted, and I got no response to my knock on the door.

'I'll go check the stable block.'

'OK, I'll keep trying the door. If she got back late she might be having a lie in.' Even as I said it, I didn't believe it, nor do I think I convinced Eve. It was almost noon, and Barbara would be used to rising early to look after the horses that were in her care. Sure enough, there was no response to my continued assault on the door panels, but it gave me something to do whilst I was waiting. Five minutes later, Eve returned, and I could tell from the frown on her face that she'd been no more successful than I had.

'The horses are all in their boxes, and by the look of them, the boxes have been cleaned out and the horses groomed, but that doesn't mean anything. The stable lads would do that as a matter of routine without having to be told what to do, whether Barbara was there to supervise them or not.'

Eve looked at me appealingly. 'What do you think we should do, Adam? I'm really worried.'

So was I, but I dare not give voice to each one of my fears. Added to the other concerns was the thought that Barbara might be with the police. Although I kept trying to dismiss it, the phrase 'helping with their enquiries' kept returning to mind. 'If I knew where one of the stable lads lives, I'd go ask them, but I think our best bet would be to go to Dene Cottage. Once we're there I'll phone John Pickersgill. He might have some news.'

'That's your policeman friend, isn't it? What sort of news do you think he might …?' Eve stopped speaking as the implication of what I'd said struck her. 'You don't think they've arrested Barbara? Surely nobody would believe she was capable of murder?'

'You haven't met Inspector Ogden. You and I might not suspect her, but with him it's more than a distinct possibility.'

There was no need for me to ring Pickersgill. As we approached Dene Cottage I could see his patrol car parked close to the end of the drive. John emerged from under the canopy of the open porch as I pulled in.

'Good afternoon, Adam,' he greeted me, before turning to smile at Eve. 'And you must be Miss Samuels. Pleased to meet you; I understand congratulations are in order.'
Having disposed of the pleasantries, he looked at each of us in turn. 'Now, would one of you mind telling me where we can find Mrs Lewis?'

I saw Eve flinch at his question. One theory as to

Barbara's whereabouts was discounted, but that was by no means good news. 'Actually, I was going to phone you as soon as we got in the house to ask if she was with you, or Inspector Ogden. I had the idea he might have pulled her in for questioning about her husband's murder, detained her even. We've both been trying to contact her, but without success. We even stopped by the house on the way here, and there was no sign of life. The house was locked and the horses had been seen to, but there was no one around.'

'That's down to the stable lads. I saw them at work first thing this morning. They've no idea where Mrs Lewis is either. We found the same as you. Everything in order, but the house all locked up. Of course, Inspector Ogden finds the fact that Mrs Lewis has gone missing extremely suspicious. He's put an alert out for anyone who might have seen her, which is why I was sent to ask you.'

Pickersgill glanced towards the house. 'It's been very hectic this morning. Perhaps we could go inside and I'll allow you to make me a cup of tea, whilst I tell you about the other developments. One of which is that you're not in Ogden's good books, Adam.'

'That's hardly going to keep me awake at night. Come on, then, we'll put the kettle on and you can tell me what I've done to upset the inspector.'

We settled in the lounge with our drinks, and John looked at me sternly. 'It seems you were less than forthcoming in the statement you gave to Ogden. He thinks that's highly suspicious. He even suggested you and Mrs Lewis might have something to hide. I told you he'd jump to that conclusion, didn't I?' He grinned at Eve. 'But then, he doesn't know about Miss Samuels.'

'What do you mean by "less than forthcoming"? I answered every question Ogden asked.'

'You failed to mention what happened at Linden House last Sunday.'

'That's because he never asked me about it. All he asked me about was the body; who found it and how come I was able to identify it. I take it one of the other witnesses of the events of Sunday afternoon has come forward.'

'Both of them have, actually. Matthews and Armstrong both visited the police station late yesterday afternoon of their own accord to volunteer information. They told us everything that happened.'

I failed to respond, so after a moment Pickersgill asked, 'What can you tell us about the tramp who threatened Lewis?'

I left it to Eve to answer him. As she related what she knew, she glanced at me a couple of times for confirmation, but my mind was elsewhere. I knew Eve wouldn't have noticed anything amiss, but I was slightly surprised that Pickersgill had failed to grasp the significance of what he'd said.

Pickersgill finished making notes and then looked at me. 'Over the past few months I've received several reports of this wild man of the woods, but until now nobody has actually confirmed that they've not only seen him, but spoken to him as well. You may not place much significance on his assault on Lewis, but I have to tell you that following our conversation, I drove around looking for Lewis's Mercedes. I found it, several miles upstream from here, close to where Rowandale Forest comes down to the banks of Thorsgill Beck. The car was unlocked, with the keys in the ignition. Nearby I could see the marks of two sets of feet in the mud. One was made by those fancy Italian shoes Lewis was wearing. The others looked like walking boot prints. Close to the riverbank I also found what looks like blood on rocks close to the water's edge. The place where the car was abandoned is very near where the wild man has been spotted on at least three occasions.'

Pickersgill paused before continuing. 'I think you can understand that we're very keen to interview him; and Mrs

Lewis too. We want to know what their relationship is.' He saw Eve was about to protest and held up a warning hand. 'Please don't say there is no relationship, because that obviously isn't the case, otherwise why did he spring to her defence when he thought Lewis was threatening her? And, I might add, he did so with a knife that according to the description I read bears a striking resemblance to the one used to stab Lewis. The need to speak to them is being treated as extremely urgent, so much so that Inspector Ogden has said that if we don't speak to either or both of them by daylight tomorrow, he's going to order officers to conduct a search of Rowandale Forest.'

I stared at Pickersgill in surprise, biting my lip to avoid laughing out loud. He must have sensed my amusement, because he held up one hand. 'Yes, Adam, I know it's a daft idea. You could send a couple of regiments of soldiers into the forest and they wouldn't find anyone who was determined to avoid detection, let alone doing it with a couple of dozen policemen. You may know that, and I may know it, but try telling Inspector Ogden.'

After Pickersgill left, Eve confronted me. 'What happened there? I was beginning to think you'd gone into a trance. Why did you switch off suddenly and leave me to do all the explaining to Pickersgill?'

'I was concentrating on something he said. He told us that Armstrong and Matthews had gone to see Ogden yesterday afternoon to tell him what they'd witnessed last Sunday.'

'Yes, I heard that clear enough, but why did you think it was important?'

'They could only have done that if they knew that Lewis was dead.'

'I still don't see the relevance.'

'I was trying to work out how they found out that

Lewis was the murder victim. Or, how they found out that he was dead, let alone murdered.'

'Sorry, Adam, I still don't get it.'

'I switched the radio and TV on when I came home, and listened to virtually every news bulletin. There was no mention of the body found in Thorsgill Beck until late evening; no indication if the body was that of a man, a woman, or a child, and no reference to how they died, let alone the victim's identity.'

'Right; I'm with you now. If they didn't hear about it via the media, how did they know to visit Ogden and tell him what they'd seen?'

'Exactly, and that means they either have a contact within the police force, or someone else told them. In which case I'd be interested to learn who that was. Because if neither heard anything via a leak, that means they either witnessed the murder, or they killed Lewis themselves, or they know who did. I'm not sure which of those options I prefer.'

My final sentences met with no response. I glanced at Eve, and could tell by her abstract expression that her thoughts were elsewhere. I waited, and after a moment, she looked up. 'You know what, Adam? Maybe the tramp wasn't as weird as we thought.'

'In what way?'

'That night; when we thought he was rambling with concussion, and he mentioned that rhyme. We were under the impression that he was talking nonsense because of the blow to the head, but perhaps the injury had nothing to do with it. He told us he'd seen the blood-covered children, remember? Then he said he'd gone to Linden House to warn someone. We dismissed it at the time, but perhaps he did go to warn Barbara that someone she knew was going to be killed. Let's be fair, his description of the children, and from your account of the state Lewis's body was in, well that must have made a bit of a mess, sounds pretty much identical to me.'

I felt a sudden frisson of fear. Fear of the unknown; of what we cannot readily explain. I'm no great believer in second sight, or the supernatural in any form, but I was unable to shake off the feeling that the prophecy from beyond the grave had turned out to be uncannily accurate.

Chapter Eight

Neither of us slept well, concern over Barbara's disappearance putting paid to our chances of a good night's rest. By mutual consent we were up, dressed, and on the road to Rowandale before first light. The fact that the consent was unspoken said a lot for how quickly our relationship was developing. However, any hope that our dawn raid might yield positive results, was soon dashed.

We questioned the stable lads, who told us they had neither seen nor heard from their employer since the day before Lewis's body had been found. I could see by the way they avoided eye contact with us that the men were placing the worst possible construction on Barbara's absence. If her own employees believed her to be responsible for her husband's murder, I thought, what must someone like Inspector Ogden, who didn't know her, be thinking?

'I don't suppose you've seen a tramp hanging around, have you?' Eve asked.

I knew she was concerned for Barbara's safety more than any though that she might be guilty of murder. The lads shook their heads in reply.

As I was watching one of them bring a sleek, muscular thoroughbred from its box, I wondered if Barbara's disappearance might have other, thus far unforeseen consequences. 'Are any of these horses entered in races in the near future?'

The senior of the stable lads answered, 'Mrs Lewis doesn't have another runner for another ten days or so.'

'That's fortunate; there must be penalties for not

running a horse without going through the proper withdrawal procedure, I suppose.'

'There most certainly are. Apart from the fines that would accrue, the trainer would have to appear before the stewards to provide an explanation.'

We waited until they had exercised the horses and completed the grooming, feeding, and mucking-out procedures before returning to Laithbrigg. I left my phone number with the senior lad, with instructions for him to phone me if he saw or heard from Barbara.

We ate a leisurely breakfast, and although we talked over the situation at some length, neither of us could come up with an idea as to how to solve the problem, or indeed explain it.

'It makes everything so much more difficult not having spoken to Barbara since the murder,' Eve said. 'If we'd been able to; at least we might have some clue as to her intentions, or at the very least, her state of mind.'

'I hardly think we need worry on that score. The way things were between them, I reckon Lewis's death would be more a cause for celebration than mourning.'

The unsatisfactory state of affairs and our inability to do anything was frustrating, and we were at somewhat of a loose end. Matters changed, early that afternoon, however, although I would normally not class a visit from Inspector Ogden as light relief.

Eve had declared her intention to go for a long soak in the bath. Normally, this would have provoked a racy or suggestive comment from me, something on the lines of volunteering to wash her back, for example, but somehow, the mood didn't seem right.

After she went upstairs I went through into the study and picked up the Saturday evening paper, as yet unread. Although it mentioned the murder, there were few details; certainly none that I didn't already know. I switched my attention to other news, and had all but finished reading when I heard a knock at the door. The paper had held my attention for long enough. Several minutes earlier I had heard the sound of bathwater flowing down the outlet pipe.

As I walked down the hall I heard Eve moving around upstairs. I wondered who the visitor was. I didn't get many. I opened the door, and was surprised to see Ogden standing there, accompanied by the juvenile detective constable. I was about to greet them when Ogden pushed past me into the house.

'Where is she?' he demanded; his tone curt.

'First of all, good afternoon, Inspector.' I paused, before continuing. 'Now it's your turn. You have to say, good afternoon, Mr Bailey. Then I ask you if you'd like to come in, and follow that up by enquiring as to the reason for your visit. It's called having a conversation.'

'Never mind that rubbish.' His tone and the gesture that accompanied it were dismissive. 'Where's Barbara Lewis? I believe you are hiding her and I need to speak to her as a matter of urgency.'

'Of course you do, Inspector. Why didn't you say so earlier?' I pointed to the oak dresser. 'She's in there. Third drawer. I hid her under the cutlery.'

'Don't play games with me.' Ogden's face was red with anger. 'Do you think I'm stupid?'

It was too good an opportunity to miss. 'Yes, as a matter of fact I do.'

For one moment, I thought I'd pushed him too far. He looked to be on the verge of apoplexy, or a heart attack. His face was the colour of an over-ripe beetroot. When he spoke, it was in a shout that would have been heard by the neighbours, but for Dene Cottage's isolated position. 'I have to tell you that I also believe you are conducting an extra-marital affair with Mrs Lewis, and that when her husband confronted the pair of you about it, one or both of you murdered him.'

'I think that should be ex-husband, Inspector,' I pointed

out, 'but if that's what you believe, I'm surprised you haven't come armed with a search warrant.'

Ogden's sour expression melted into one of malicious triumph. With a flourish, he produced a sheet of paper from his pocket and waved it in mid air. 'That is exactly what we do have.'

He turned to his subordinate. 'Go check upstairs. I'll look around down here. That way I can keep my eye on Bailey.'

I was about to warn the young DC about what he would find upstairs, but some imp of mischief caused me to keep silent. By now, I guessed Eve would be dressed and on the point of returning downstairs. I'd shown Ogden the study and lounge and we had just stepped into the dining room when I heard a high-pitched scream.

'So I was right all along,' Ogden gloated.

I heard the sound of footsteps coming down the flight of steps in what I can best describe as a panic-stricken gallop, and the young detective appeared, his complexion equally as red as his superior's had been seconds earlier.

'I … er … Inspector … there's a lady … a lady upstairs. She isn't dressed. She's in her underwear. I walked in and there she was.'

Eve, I thought, you little minx. No wonder I love you so much.

'Of course there's a lady upstairs. I hope you told her to get dressed immediately so she can answer our questions about her husband's murder?'

'Er … no … Sir, I … er … that is, she isn't –'

Before he could say anything meaningful, the dining room door was thrust wide open, catching the inspector between the shoulder-blades. Eve didn't walk into the room; she marched. 'Adam, what the hell is going on? Who are these men? How could you allow him –' she pointed to the hapless young detective, who was now cowering behind Ogden '– to burst in on me as I was dressing?'

The wink she gave me as she spoke nearly caused me to laugh aloud, but I bit my lip and replied. 'I'm sorry, darling, I couldn't prevent them.'

She now turned on the young constable. 'Who the hell are you?'

'Never mind that. Who are you?' Ogden demanded.

'What business is it of yours?' Eve snapped.

'I am Detective Inspector Ogden. I'm investigating the murder of Charles Lewis, and I believe this man,' he waved his hand in my general direction, 'has been having an extra-marital affair with Mrs Lewis and may have conspired to murder her husband.'

'I never heard such poppycock in all my life.' Eve's tone was withering. She took a couple of steps towards Ogden, the menace in her eyes plain. 'Adam has only met Barbara twice, both times when I was present. In fact he only met her because of me.'

'Then who are you?' Ogden was nothing if not persistent.

'My name is Eve Samuels. I'm Adam's fiancée. Both of which you could have found out for yourself if you'd bothered to ask PC Pickersgill. But I suppose that would have been too much like detective work. Now, I'll trouble you to leave, and take that little pervert with you, before I call the chief constable, who is a close friend of my brother-in-law, to complain about your conduct.'

'I was in the process of executing a search warrant,' Ogden remained stubborn.

'And I don't care. Now I'm going to phone Mulgrave Castle. You'll be lucky if you're still in a job come Monday morning.'

Eve turned to walk towards the phone before Ogden finally admitted defeat. He headed for the door, but as the DC opened it for him; he had one last try. 'I still need to ask if either of you know where Mrs Lewis is hiding.'

Eve was remorseless. 'No, we don't. Now out!' she thundered.

As we watched their car pull away, my arm was around Eve's waist, and I could feel her shaking with suppressed laughter. Once they were out of sight she gave into it.

'Oh, I did enjoy that,' she said after she recovered. 'I was about to come down when the bell rang. Ogden has a very loud voice, so when I heard him order the boy upstairs and you didn't object, I knew you were up to some mischief, so I took my blouse and jeans off and waited, ready to scream.'

She paused and looked at me. 'You were dead right, Adam, the man's an idiot.'

'It'll be interesting to hear what John Pickersgill makes of this fiasco. I only hope Ogden doesn't blame him for it.'

Although the episode with Ogden had been entertaining, it did nothing to advance our knowledge of the case. 'As the police obviously haven't a clue what's going on, I reckon we should try and find out by other means. Do you fancy dining out tonight? The Admiral Nelson has a good restaurant, and they do an excellent steak.'

'How will that help us? Not that I'm averse to you buying me dinner.'

'If anyone knows what's going on around here, it'll be the locals in the pub. John Pickersgill reckons they're better than the KGB at obtaining secret information.'

'OK, why not.' She glanced at me slyly, 'Is this just an excuse for you to show me off?'

'There is that as well. Then they can all see how lucky I am.'

At the time, it seemed that the plan was little more than a long shot, but as it transpired, visiting the pub proved to be a momentous decision.

It was only a few minutes after seven o'clock when we

entered the bar of the Admiral Nelson, but although the pub had only been open a short while, the room was already busy. The locals, many of whom had undergone years of training to become seasoned drinkers, had been augmented by a sizeable contingent of new recruits, almost all of whose faces were unfamiliar to me.

As we waited by the bar for service, I got into conversation with Henry Price, our local milkman, whose wife had discovered Lewis's body. Naturally, I enquired about her wellbeing after such a shock.

'Aye, she were right shaken up by it, I can tell you,' Price replied. He shook his head, 'Couldn't get a word out of her all that day and t' next as well. I were beginning to think I'd gone deaf.' He paused and added, 'Anyroad, she's back to normal now; talking t' hind leg off a donkey. I reckon she's making up for lost time.'

'Who are all these people?' I gestured to the far end of the room, where the strangers had congregated. They had formed a defensive, tight-knit circle. It reminded me of how the wagon trains protected themselves from Red Indian attacks in the westerns I'd watched as a boy.

'Shooting syndicate from t' Hall,' Price replied succinctly. 'Although judging by what Zeke Calvert says, maybe missing syndicate would be nearer t' mark. He reckons wildlife around here is safe from extinction as long as that lot are their only threat.'

'Do you know any of them?' By now I'd recognized two of them: Walter Armstrong and Trevor Matthews, both of whom we'd encountered at Linden House. I mentioned this to Price and was rewarded by a scornful laugh from my right.

'Armstrong! Calls hissen a keeper? That idle sod couldn't keep hens, let alone pheasants.'

I turned, to find Ezekiel Calvert standing alongside me, an empty pint glass in his hand. I'd just succeeded in attracting the barmaid's attention, so out of courtesy; I offered to buy them both a drink. Neither refused, and as the girl filled our glasses I introduced Eve to them. I added an explanation for her benefit. 'Ezekiel used to be keeper on the Rowandale Hall estate, but he was replaced by Armstrong, hence his jaundiced opinion.'

Calvert's eyes gleamed appreciatively as he shook Eve's hand. 'Nowt jaundiced about it. Armstrong knows bugger-all about gamekeeping. He has no idea how to raise pheasant poults, or how to incubate the eggs. And hasn't a clue how to manage release pens, or keep the young birds safe from foxes and other predators. He doesn't know the first thing about vermin control or woodland management, and his knowledge of fieldcraft wouldn't cover my thumbnail. Even if you wrote it in massive letters,' he added.

Calvert paused, but only to take a sip from his newly replenished pint. 'Mind you, it doesn't matter to that lot if the pheasant stock has gone down by nearly half. It just means they get to spend less on cartridges. The reason for the decline in pheasant numbers has nowt to do with their supreme marksmanship.'

'They're not very good shots, then?' Eve enquired.

'You're joking, Miss Eve. Most of them couldn't hit a barn door with a twelve-bore, even if they were leaning on it. The only two amongst them who are half-decent shots are that tall bloke in the corner and the slip of a lass standing alongside him.'

Calvert gave us a sly grin. 'Shooting isn't the only thing they have in common, either. Luckily, I don't think his wife knows owt about the cottage on Rowandale Moor. Tucked away down a little lane; out of sight of prying eyes. A right cosy little love nest.'

I could tell Eve was fascinated by this glimpse into local scandal and gossip, so I asked, 'Who are they?'

'His name's Derek Bartlett. He's got summat to do with property in Leeds. Her name is Ursula Moore. She's a solicitor. You wouldn't think so to look at her, but they reckon she's a holy terror in court. You want to hear what Johnny Pickersgill has to say about her – if you can put up with the swearing.'

'Zeke's right about the cottage,' Price confirmed. 'She phones me whenever they're about to use it, which is most weekends during the winter, whether there's a shoot on or not. I have to deliver milk from the Friday right through to the Monday. There's always just the two cars parked outside, his and hers, but the curtains are kept drawn and there's never a sign of life. I collect the empties on Tuesday and the money is always there, plus a bit of a tip. To this day I've never seen either of them at the cottage; but for the cars, I wouldn't know they were there.'

Calvert sniggered. 'Well, I have. Seen them, I mean. When folk want to be private, they should shut curtains at t' back of t' house as well as t' front. They must think nobody ever goes up on t' high moor.'

'And what were you doing up there?' Price asked.

'Poaching, of course. A man's got to feed hissen and his family. The wife's partial to a bit of grouse. I were that distracted I nearly went home wi' an empty game bag. I'll tell thee summat, the way those two were going at it they could teach rabbits hereabouts a trick or two.'

'What about Armstrong, then? If he's as useless as you say, how did he get the job? Surely they must have asked for references before they took him on.'

'I don't know.' Calvert shook his head. 'I've never heard of probation officers providing references.'

Price took issue with him. 'Now, Zeke, you know that isn't true.'

'Ah, well, he's from Manchester, so it might be. One thing I do know, there's no pheasants around there.' Calvert paused, 'Or maybe his fancy bit of stuff got him the job.'

'Who might that be?' Price got his question in before I

had chance.

'I've no idea what her name is. Quite a glamourpuss though, and she drives a fancy sports car.'

'What, like that one Lewis had?'

Calvert shook his head in reply to my question. 'No, a smaller one, with a lower body. Can't remember the name.'

'Why did they replace you?' Eve changed the subject.

As we waited for Calvert to respond, I noticed Price wince slightly, but the reply was understated, calm even. 'They reckoned I wasn't presenting enough birds for their liking. I could have done, but the truth was I couldn't be bothered. I did the first couple of times, but when they came back empty-handed I lost interest. Everything was different in the old days. The men Mr Rupert invited could shoot. In the height of the season we'd usually have more than a hundred birds in the bag by the end of the morning drives. This lot were lucky if they managed a dozen. Those birds were the unlucky ones. By the time it came to the afternoon session, a lot of birds were queuing up to fly over them because they knew they were safe. The others couldn't take off because they were too weak from laughing.'

'That's hardly Armstrong's fault, though, is it?' As she spoke, I wondered if she was provoking Calvert on purpose. His comments were certainly entertaining.

'It is if he's not prepared to walk through the forest. The birds will soon learn they're safe so long as they don't venture too near the edge. I don't think he's walked all the way through since the day he started.'

'Why not? I thought that was part of his job.'

'It should be, Miss Eve, but I guess he's frightened. That forest is a bit scary. Who knows, maybe he's worried that the babes will get him. Sometimes, I wish they would.'

'The babes?' Eve asked, her face a mask of innocence.

Calvert looked at her for a second; then glanced at me. 'Haven't you told her about the babes?'

'I didn't know about them. I only heard about them a few days ago. And I did tell her.' I nudged Eve in the ribs to make her behave herself.

'I forgot you're not locals. What did you think when you heard the tale? Do you reckon it's just a fairy story, like some people round here believe?'

'I'm not sure; it certainly sounds unlikely.'

'Aye, well, unlikely or not, there are plenty believe in the babes, and are less than keen to catch sight of them.'

'What's your opinion?' Eve asked.

'It isn't an opinion. I know the babes are real. I've seen them.'

Even Price was startled by Calvert's admission. He looked at the keeper accusingly. 'Are you making this up, Zeke? Fancy yourself guiding ghost hunters through the forest, do you?'

'It's true, I tell you.'

'Then why haven't you said anything before now?'

'For the very reason that you doubt me now, Henry. If I went around telling folk I'd seen three children covered in blood, children that disappeared into thin air as I got close to them, folk would think I was off my rocker.'

'When did you see them; or think you saw them?' Price persisted.

Calvert was silent for a moment. 'It'd be five, maybe six years ago. Two days after I saw the babes, I got a letter from my nephew in New Zealand, telling me my sister and her husband had been killed in a road accident.'

Once again, I felt a cold shiver run down my spine. There was a long silence before Price asked, 'Whereabouts did you see them, Zeke?'

The tone of Price's question had changed, the disbelief now absent, reflecting the legend that the babes foretold bad tidings.

'In the forest, of course, they were standing by the edge of one of them coal pits near the Silent Lady.' Calvert saw my puzzled expression. 'The Silent Lady is a waterfall. It's where Thorsgill Beck tumbles off the high moor and runs through Rowandale Forest. Nearby there they used to dig for coal and stuff in ancient times. Because the waterfall is right in the heart of the forest, the vegetation is dense, muffling the sound of the water, hence the name, the Silent Lady.'

'It's very unusual to have a waterfall where you can't hear the sound of the water,' I commented. 'I've stood near Niagara Falls and almost been deafened by the noise.'

'Aye, well maybe it's because it's unusual to find a silent lady that they gave it the name.'

At that moment, we heard Calvert's name called. He looked round towards the corner where the dartboard was. 'I'll have to go. I'm next up on the oche. Nice to meet you, Miss Eve.'

When Calvert was out of earshot, I asked Price, 'What do you make of that?'

'I'm astonished on two counts. First off, I'm staggered that Zeke came out with that tale about the babes. Second, I've not heard him talk so much in front of strangers before. I think that might be Miss Samuels' doing. Zeke always did have an eye for beautiful ladies.'

Eve laughed. 'Especially the silent ones, it seems.'

Chapter Nine

We were called through to the dining room, where the shooting party was already occupying a long table across the French windows at the rear of the building. I'd been a little dubious about sitting in close proximity to a group that included Matthews and Armstrong, but luckily the landlord had placed us in one of the cubicles near to the bar, where a large wooden partition shielded us from the view of all but a couple of our fellow diners. None of them noticed us take our seats, so we were left in peace to enjoy an intimate dinner. By tacit agreement we didn't discuss the murder or any of the surrounding mystery as we dined, but instead talked over our plans for the future, which at that stage seemed far more important.

It was only after we'd finished our main course, in which Eve demolished one of the steaks for which the pub was becoming well known, that she noticed those diners that were visible from her viewpoint. I saw her eyes widen with surprise. 'What's matter?' I asked.

'You know what Mr Calvert told us about that solicitor woman, Ursula Moore, and that man, Bartlett she's seeing?'

'Yes, what of it?'

'I took it with a pinch of salt at the time, but now I can see what she's doing to him under the table, I believe every word of it.'

'Why, what is she doing?'

Eve looked around, and saw that nobody could observe us in our sheltered nook. She gave me a mischievous grin and proceeded to demonstrate, under cover of the tablecloth, with her napkin draped over her hand for added privacy. I gasped with delight and astonishment, and have to confess I was more than a little disappointed when the demonstration was over. 'That's certainly convinced me,' I muttered, when I'd recovered my power of speech.

'That's nothing, wait until I get you home.'

I was still pondering Eve's implicit suggestion when we returned to the bar to settle up. Any plans she had to fulfil the promise were deferred as I was paying the landlord and expressing our thanks for the food. I looked up as the door opened, in time to see John Pickersgill enter the pub. He was out of uniform and clearly making a social visit, by the way he sauntered across to the bar, pausing for a friendly word with a couple of regulars on his way.

He greeted us, and I offered him a drink, suggesting to Eve that she might also like a nightcap. Pickersgill agreed, as did Eve, so I ordered a pint for him, a brandy for Eve, and a whisky for me. When he'd collected his beer and drank to our health, Pickersgill asked Eve what she thought of our local.

'It's a lovely pub,' she told him, 'and the food is excellent. Admittedly the company in the dining room wasn't exactly to my liking, but that's not the landlord's fault.'

Pickersgill raised an enquiring eyebrow.

'The shooting syndicate from Rowandale Hall,' I explained. 'Zeke Calvert made some cutting comments about a few of them earlier. That, added to our previous encounter with Matthews and Armstrong, is what Eve was hinting at.'

Pickersgill glanced towards the corner of the room, where Calvert was studying the dominoes on the table before him. 'Zeke is somewhat bitter, which is only to be expected, but he's also fairly accurate as a rule.'

'He reckons they let him go because he wasn't up to the

job.'

'Not Zeke, there's generations of keepers' blood in his veins. His father was head keeper before Zeke, and his grandfather came to Rowandale Hall from off one of the royal estates. What's far more likely is that his face didn't fit with the syndicate members. Not because they're nouveau riche as such, but because he doesn't rate their prowess with a shotgun. Unfortunately, Zeke is too blunt to suffer fools gladly, and sees no reason to hold back from expressing his opinion.'

I already suspected that, out of uniform and off duty, John Pickersgill was an inveterate gossip. All it took was a few direct questions from me and some discreet prompting from Eve for him to tell us all he knew or suspected about the members of the syndicate and all the others who were frequenting the Admiral Nelson that evening. From this we learned that Zeke Calvert's first wife had died in childbirth, leaving him to bring up their son alone. He had done this, and the two of them had been inseparable until the boy was nineteen.

'What happened then?' Eve enquired.

'Zeke got involved with a lass from the village. The inevitable happened and she fell pregnant. She moved in with Zeke and the following day Stan, the son, moved out. Zeke was very upset; he wanted Stan to follow him as keeper to the estate.'

'What happened to the son?'

'He went to live in America, or so I heard. Funnily enough, his son leaving brought Zeke and Rupert Latimer closer than they had been before. Both of them had fallen out with their sons, although in Rupert's case, the split was permanent, because young Brian Latimer died before they could make up their differences.'

'I heard something about that. In Mexico, wasn't it?' Eve asked.

'That's right,' Pickersgill agreed. 'He was shot to death

and his body buried in an abandoned mine. Apparently it was only by chance that it was discovered.'

'How very sad, and now it looks as if the Hall will pass to new owners. That man Matthews gave the impression that he'd already bought it.'

'I think he might be jumping the gun there,' Pickersgill said cautiously.

'I wondered if that was the case. He seems a bit of a dodgy character,' I suggested, 'what does he do for a living?'

'Matthews is head of a property company in West Yorkshire that specializes in buying up run-down property cheap, spending as little as they can tarting it up, and then renting it out for exorbitant sums to university students and the like. You're right though, he has an unsavoury reputation, but he's by no means the only one in that set. His big buddy Derek Bartlett is another. You've heard the expression "as thick as thieves"; well; it was never more appropriately used than to describe Matthews and Bartlett. I wouldn't trust either of them as far as I could throw them. Bartlett owns a company called DB Developments, which is a big civil engineering outfit. They're involved in everything from motorway construction to water and sewage systems. There's been some unpleasant rumours about them as well.'

'Whose idea was the syndicate?' I asked.

'I'm not sure. Matthews', I think. He certainly does all the organization, and presents himself at my house before the start of the season with all the syndicate members' licences for me to inspect. That's not strictly necessary, but I don't discourage it. Whether Matthews or Bartlett is the kingpin I couldn't say. Of course it could be neither of them. The rest of the guns are all well-heeled, and it might not even be a kingpin, it could be a queenpin, if you get my meaning.'

'You're talking about the lady solicitor?' Eve asked.

'Mr Calvert was gossiping about her and Bartlett earlier.'

Pickersgill gave a wry smile. 'The one word I wouldn't use to describe Ursula Moore is "lady", but I won't sully your ears with those I would use. She may be a good-looking woman, and she certainly gives the appearance of being sweet and gentle, but don't let that fool you. Underneath, she's as hard as nails and ruthless into the bargain. She specializes in criminal work, so teaming up with that lot is natural, I reckon.'

'She doesn't look the type,' Eve murmured.

'Appearances are deceptive. I've a pal in Leeds CID and when I mentioned her name I thought he was going to have a heart attack. Apparently she represents almost every villain in the West Riding, usually successfully. Last year, Leeds had a big fraud case coming to trial just before Christmas. On paper it looked to be open and shut, but when it came to court, several of the prosecution witnesses suddenly developed amnesia, and the case got thrown out. After that, one of the detectives nicknamed her "Satan's Little Helper" and it stuck. My pal commented that it was strange, because her partner, Rhodes I think his name is, specializes in civil law, and he's reckoned to be as straight as a die.'

Something Pickersgill had said rang a bell faintly in my mind, but it would be several days later that I remembered, and had chance to test my theory out. 'Are the rumours about her and Bartlett correct, do you think?' Eve asked.

'I can't say so for certain, but I think they must be, judging by the evidence. Not that I blame him. As I said, she's a good-looking woman, and if you'd seen Bartlett's wife, you'd understand why he would be tempted to stray.'

'What's wrong with his wife?' Eve's curiosity made me smile. Her obvious fascination with gossip meant she was sure to fit in well around Laithbrigg.

'It's difficult to know where to begin, to be honest. I only encountered the woman once. When the syndicate was being formed. Bartlett brought his missus here for a meal and the landlord had to very tactfully suggest that she shouldn't return.'

'Why was that?'

'Her behaviour was atrocious. I'd brought my wife here. It was our anniversary and we were in the dining room at the same time as them. I didn't see all of it, but my wife witnessed it, and got abused for the privilege.'

'What happened? What did the woman do?'

'First of all she ordered two starters and polished them off in record time. Prawn cocktails, as I remember; and she also ate almost a full loaf of bread. Watching her eat almost put me off my food, and that takes some doing. She was more like a pig at trough than a human being. Then she ordered a big T-bone steak, plus two helpings of chips and vegetables and cleaned them up in record time. Any normal person would have been struggling after that, but she then ate two huge slices of Black Forest Gateau to finish with.'

'Crikey, she must be built like a house side,' I murmured.

'You'd think so, wouldn't you, but she isn't, quite the opposite. She's like a stick insect. If she turned sideways you'd miss her. Added to that she has a face like one of Barbara Lewis's horses.'

'How on earth does she eat all that and still not put weight on?' I wondered.

'Ah, well, now we're coming to the point. My wife went to the ladies and Mrs Bartlett was in one of the cubicles. She was sticking her fingers down her throat to make herself sick. My wife asked if she was all right, or if she could help in any way, and all she got was a torrent of foul language. She was in tears when she came out, which was when I complained to the landlord. He had a word with Bartlett. Apparently it's some sort of disease she's suffering from.'

'It's a symptom of a condition they call anorexia nervosa,' Eve told us. 'I read an article about it recently. Apparently a lot of the top models suffer from it as a result of continuously dieting.'

'Anyway, her behaviour goes a long way to explaining why her husband has taken up with Ursula Moore.'

'What about Armstrong?' I asked. 'Zeke gave the impression he has no experience of keeping.'

'Zeke's a bit prejudiced, but to be fair he isn't too far wrong. Armstrong was under-keeper to an estate in Cumbria before he applied for this job. I understand he was fired because he was useless and lazy.' He paused for a moment, before adding, 'At least, that was the official reason given, but my sources tell me the true explanation is that he was caught having it off with the wife of one of the guns.'

'Not the most sensible of career moves. Just out of curiosity, how did you come by that information?'

John laughed; he obviously thought my question was naive. 'I told you, I make it my business to find out all I can about anyone who comes to live on my patch. It goes with the job.' He gave me a sly grin, 'That includes the two of you.'

'But I don't live here,' Eve objected, 'I'm only visiting.'

'Really? That's not how I read the situation.'

'What makes you think different?'

He looked at Eve for a moment before replying. 'For one thing, there's the fact that Adam drove you to catch the London train on Monday and you were back on Saturday along with a mound of luggage that suggested you were moving in. I was at Dene Cottage when Sherpa Bailey here was struggling with the load. Then you came for a romantic dinner here, and just watching the way you look at one another I can tell you're very much in love. And if that wasn't sufficient proof, there's that sizeable rock on the third finger of your left hand. I think it's so obvious that even a numbskull like Ogden could work it out, given time.'

'And what did you find out about me?' Eve demanded.

John smiled. He leaned forward and whispered something in Eve's ear. She burst out laughing. Maddeningly, neither of them would repeat the remark that had caused her amusement.

After a while, as I suppose was to be expected, the conversation turned to the murder. 'I've been given strict orders not to interfere,' Pickersgill told us. 'Ogden said in no uncertain terms that when he wanted my advice he'd ask for it, and unless and until he did, I wasn't to meddle in things I know nothing about. Technically, I'm off the case. Which means that it has little chance of being solved.'

'As you're no longer on Ogden's Christmas card list, I think I should tell you he came to search Dene Cottage.'

'Am I surprised? Did he think you were hiding Mrs Lewis under your bed?'

'Something like that.' I thought John was going to choke on his beer when I told him of Eve's assault, both verbal and with the dining room door.

'It's a shame it didn't hit him on the head,' John said, as he drained his glass. 'Might have knocked some sense into him.' He headed for the bar and refilled our glasses.

When he returned, I asked him, 'Do you remember you told me that Matthews and Armstrong had gone to the station and given statements about witnessing Lewis's encounter with Barbara and the tramp the previous Sunday?'

'I do; what of it?'

'That would be why Ogden searched my cottage, believing Barbara is a suspect.'

'Aye, you're probably right.'

'But how did they know he was dead? It hadn't been on

the news at that point and even when it was, the identity wasn't revealed. That means someone leaked the information. Either that, or they know far more about Lewis's murder than they've disclosed.'

'I knew Ogden would mess it up. Now you can see why I asked you to help.' He looked from me to Eve. 'What do you say? Will you look into it? Strictly off the record, of course.'

I waited for Eve to answer. 'I don't know,' she said after a long pause. 'Last time anything like this happened, Adam did his best to get us both killed. I don't want to push my luck.'

'Don't worry, I'll make sure you're safe,' Pickersgill reassured her.

We returned to Dene Cottage long after closing time; and much later than we'd intended. We were both a little bit tipsy and very amorous. At some point during the night, Eve whispered, 'I think we should get a puppy.'

'A puppy? Why on earth do you want a puppy?'

'It isn't for me really, although I would like one. I read somewhere that if you get a puppy and bring it up along with the children it is good for both of them.'

'Hang on, we haven't got any children.'

Eve put her arms around me, pulling me close. I didn't object. 'No, not yet, but the way things are going, it shouldn't be long.'

'Do you want children?'

Eve thought for a moment before replying. 'I never did. I used to watch Harriet's kids growing, and thought that was nice, but it didn't awaken any yearning for my own. Now, I can't think of anything more exciting than having our child growing inside my womb.'

It was then I put my idea of the extension to Dene Cottage to her. 'Oh, Adam, I've been meaning to mention it. I thought exactly the same. It would be ideal. A terrific place to raise a family.'

Anyone watching our antics next day might have had cause to doubt our sanity. To the casual observer, it must have seemed that Eve and I were taking it in turns to march around the garden of Dene Cottage attempting to emulate the exaggerated strides of some foreign army parading for the glorification of their dictator. In fact, what we were doing was trying to calculate how much space we had for the extension we'd agreed on, and to visualize what effect the proposed additional structure would have on the appearance of the building and how it sat in its surroundings. Fortunately, passers-by in that area were a rare event, especially in winter, so we were able to complete the exercise undisturbed.

By late afternoon we had even progressed far enough to have a rough sketch of how the property might look. This was purely down to Eve's artistic prowess, a talent I was unaware she possessed. Left to me, the drawing would have been a disaster, as I'm unable to draw a straight line without the aid of a ruler. Our preoccupation with our own plans for the future hadn't caused us to ignore our concerns over Barbara's prolonged absence, and our disquiet had only been marginally eased when we'd visited the stables again, earlier in the day.

The senior stable lad greeted us with the news. 'I had a note from the boss. It were stuck through our letterbox sometime during the night.' He scratched his head, no mean feat for someone wearing a flat cap. 'She must have sneaked up to the house right quiet, because my dog didn't make a sound and he usually kicks up a rumpus at the slightest noise. Anyroad, she said she'd be back here tomorrow.'

'Do you have the note with you? Can I see it?' Eve asked.

He fumbled in several pockets before producing a crumpled piece of paper. The jagged edge suggested the page had been torn from a book. Eve examined the note carefully before passing it to me. 'That's definitely Barbara's handwriting. There's no mistaking it. See that swirl round the letter B. She's been doing that ever since third form, despite the teacher telling her off about it.'

'At least we know she's all right.'

As I spoke, I turned the paper over. One glance at the back of the page caused alarm bells to ring in my mind, but I decided against voicing them. I didn't think it right in front of Barbara's employee, for one thing, and besides, I didn't want to worry Eve. I was happy to concede that Barbara had written the note of her own free will, but I couldn't for the life of me work out what she was playing at. Another concern that crossed my mind was that, although I had a shrewd idea who had provided the paper for her to write on, where was she? I opted to remain silent, in the hope that when Barbara returned the next day she would provide the answers to at least some of those questions. However, that hope went unsatisfied for a while longer.

Chapter Ten

Next morning we were at Linden House shortly after dawn. We walked down the yard in time to see Barbara's stable lads walking three of her horses along the track that bordered Rowandale Forest. I pointed towards them. 'Look, they're taking the short cut, despite what Armstrong warned about going that way.'

Before Eve had chance to reply, our attention was distracted by a sound we hadn't heard there before. It was someone whistling. At that moment Barbara Lewis emerged from one of the loose boxes. She stopped her recital and greeted us. 'Hello, you two lovebirds. Isn't it a lovely morning?'

We stared at her in surprise. Although we hadn't expected her to be grieving over her husband's death, her cheerful mood seemed out of place, given her present difficulties. I wondered what must have happened to enable her to forget the threat to her home and her livelihood. And was she sending the horses to the gallops via the shortcut as a last act of defiance? At the same time, I realized that she might not even be aware that Lewis had been murdered, or even that he was dead.

Eve must have reached the same conclusion, judging by her opening question. 'Babs, are you all right? Have you heard about Charles being killed? Where have you been for the past week?'

'Never better, Eve, never better. Yes, I knew about Charles. He's no loss, certainly not to me. He might be missed by that tart he's been shagging, but she'll soon get over it. As to where I've been, I've been sorting out my problems; that's all you need to know.'

I decided a change of subject was called for. 'Why are you sending the horses that way? Aren't you worried about what Armstrong said?'

'I don't give a monkey's toss what Armstrong says or does.'

If it hadn't been so early in the day I might have suspected that Barbara had been drinking, but her brightness and clear, alert tone of voice suggested she was stone cold sober.

'Why don't we go inside and have a coffee; then you can tell us what you've been up to,' Eve suggested.

'Coffee's a wonderful idea, Eve, but don't think you're going to wheedle information out of me that way. My lips are sealed.'

Although Eve tried every method of persuasion she could think of, Barbara refused to divulge even the most minute detail of where she'd been, or why, merely smiling benignly at us both throughout. I met with more success, even though I didn't realize it at the time, when I changed the subject and asked her about the Rowandale Hall estate and Rupert Latimer's will. 'Last week you mentioned the solicitor who was handling the probate, but you didn't tell me his name. Was it Rhodes, by any chance?'

'Yes, that's right, Norman Rhodes, his office is in Leeds.'

We were on the point of leaving when the stable lads returned from exercising the horses. The senior of them handed the reins of his charge to one of his colleagues and approached us. 'That Armstrong tried to block us from using the path alongside the woods like you said he might. I told him we were just obeying your orders and if he wasn't happy about it, he should take it up with you. He was still arguing the toss and then he saw somebody appear out of the forest and took off like a bat out of hell.'

'Who was it? Did you recognize them?' I intervened.

The stable lad looked from me to Barbara and back again before replying. 'The thing is, I did and I didn't. I thought it might have been that bloke who was here – you know, the tramp – but I can't be certain.'

'You must have recognized him if it was the tramp, surely. That beard is a dead giveaway. How many other men have you seen around here who look like a hippie or a young Santa Claus?'

'Aye, well, that's the problem, see. He was dressed like that tramp, but he didn't have a beard. So either there's two blokes dressed alike or he's found his lost razor.'

The knowledge that Barbara had returned safe and apparently unharmed from her mysterious absence gave Eve and me opportunity for some time to ourselves, and it was a couple of days later before either of us gave any further thought to the murder of Barbara's ex-husband. We might not have done so even then, had it not been for John Pickersgill calling in early one morning on the flimsy pretext of requiring a mug of tea. Not unnaturally, Eve asked about progress on the case.

'We're going nowhere fast,' Pickersgill told us. 'Of course, when I say "we," I mean Ogden and his sidekick in CID. They don't involve the likes of me in their deliberations. As I'm excluded from that club, I thought I'd come and see if you had any bright ideas to offer.'

'Not really,' I admitted, 'to be honest we've not paid much attention to it. One question I did mean to ask was if you knew when Lewis was murdered? Or is that part of the information Ogden is keeping to himself?'

'Actually, I do know that, but it's no thanks to Ogden. I saw a copy of the pathologist's report. I was handed the important task of delivering it to the coroner, and the envelope wasn't sealed. It wasn't *very well* sealed,' he added with a wicked grin. 'He put the approximate time of death at somewhere between late morning and evening of the day before his body was recovered from Thorsgill Beck. The report went on to state that he couldn't be more precise because he wasn't certain whether the body had been placed in the water immediately after death or at some later stage.'

We promised to give the case more thought, and with that Pickersgill left. I still thought he was being optimistic in the extreme hoping that amateurs such as us could succeed where CID couldn't. I was about to say as much to Eve, but then I remembered my two encounters with Ogden and revised my opinion.

Pickersgill had only been gone about half an hour when the phone rang. Eve answered it, and listened to the caller, her expression registering first shock; and then dismay. She put the phone down and turned to stare bleakly at me. 'That was John Pickersgill. He thought we should know that some public-spirited citizen has called Ogden to inform him that Barbara had returned. He's only gone and arrested her on suspicion of murder. What are we going to do, Adam?'

I thought about what we'd been told for a moment. 'First off, I want to go to the stables.' I glanced at the clock, 'If we're lucky, we might be able to catch the stable lads before they've finished for the day. Then I've got some questions I want to ask Mr Walter Armstrong. Come on, Evie, I'll explain as we go.'

We made it to Linden House just in time. As we pulled up, the stable lads were ambling up the yard, their work for the morning done. They would have finished much earlier, as one of them told us, had it not been for the incursion by the police. We offered the lads a lift to Rowandale village and on the way there, they told us about Barbara's arrest.

'The police arrived as we were returning from the gallops.'

'Did you have any problems with Armstrong?'

'No, never saw him. That was a surprise really, because his house overlooks the shortcut we take. Mrs Lewis came along with us in case he got stroppy, but he didn't appear.'

'Who was the man in charge of the police? Was it Inspector Ogden?'

'I don't know his name,' the senior of the lads told us. 'There was one older bloke in plain clothes who was ordering everyone else around and getting stressed up.'

'That sounds like Ogden,' Eve grimaced.

'There was another bloke in civvies, but he looked as if he should be in short pants. Added to them there was a van full of uniformed coppers and a policewoman, who all looked as if they wished they were somewhere else.'

'Ogden has that effect on people.'

'He was waving a search warrant in everyone's face. It didn't do him much good, because one of the horses snatched it out of his hand and tried to eat it. We only just rescued it in time, but it was ripped and a soggy mess when I gave it back to him.'

'Oh, I wish I'd seen that,' Eve muttered.

'You and me both,' I agreed. 'Did they find anything of interest?'

'I don't think so. Why would they? Anyone who knows the boss would have realized long ago she isn't capable of murder. They took a load of kitchen knives away, for forensic testing, they said.'

'And that was all they got from the house?'

'Yes, and when they turned their attention to the stables, the fun really started.'

'Why, what happened?' Eve beat me to the question by a split second.

'For a start they told us to stay clear whilst they went into the loose boxes. They were OK until they came up against The Boy.'

'Who?' I asked. 'What boy?' I thought for a moment this was a piece of racing slang for a stable lad.

'His full name is Blenheim Boy, but everyone refers to him as The Boy. He's Mrs Lewis's best hurdler. He's a five-year-old gelding with a nasty temper on him. The Boy doesn't like people much, certainly not strangers, especially when they go barging into his box whilst he's in the middle of eating his breakfast. He kicked one of the coppers on the shins and had another pinned up against the wall. By the time we got into the box, The Boy was on his hind legs and if that bloke hadn't put his arm up to defend himself he might have finished up with a fractured skull instead of a broken arm. We pulled The Boy off him before he could do any more damage, but it was a close-run thing.'

'Was either of them badly hurt?'

'The Boy only caught them glancing blows, but it might have been much more serious. I think the ambulance men were amused when they arrived.' The stable lad grinned. 'The bloke in charge got very stroppy about it, until Mrs Lewis pointed out how much Blenheim Boy and the other horses are worth; and that he'd be held responsible if any of them got injured. After that he agreed for us to lead each of them out of the box before they searched it.'

'Did they take anything away with them?'

One of the other lads burst out laughing. 'Two of them did, although they didn't realize it. It might be good for their roses, but it won't half make that van stink on the way back to the police station.'

We'd reached the house where two of the lads lodged before I had chance to ask them the question we'd gone there for. Their answer confirmed my suspicion, and the opinion expressed by Pickersgill, that Ogden was worse than useless. A few minutes spent checking his facts would have saved Ogden from making a fool of himself. As we dropped the third of the stable lads off, I asked him for directions to Armstrong's house. 'It's just outside the village,' he told us. There's a little terrace. Armstrong's is the end one. Funny, that,' he added, 'his house is right across from t' beck from where Lewis's car was found.' He lowered his voice. 'They reckon that's where he was killed.'

Something in his tone told me he wasn't too upset by Lewis's death. 'You didn't like Mrs Lewis's husband, did you?'

'No, he was a useless tosser. Cruel as well. The boss hid the bruises; she covered them up. Anyway, I saw him at it once. Some folk reckon she did him in. That's a load of rubbish, but I wouldn't have blamed her if she had taken a knife to him.'

Out of the corner of my eye, I saw Eve stir in the passenger seat. The topic of conversation was not to her liking. Given that she had attacked her abusive partner some years ago with a carving knife, I could understand why. I thanked the stable lad for his help and as we drove away, I apologized. 'I'm sorry, I had no idea he was going to say that.'

Eve patted my hand. 'It's not your fault, Adam. He wasn't to know, and it's all in the past now. Anyway, John Pickersgill thinks so.'

'Why, what's he been saying?'

'Remember last Saturday, in the pub, when he whispered in my ear. He told me he didn't think I'd need to look round Dene Cottage to locate a carving knife, because you would never harm me.'

Despite our wish to see Barbara released from custody, I thought it worthwhile making another call before heading to the police station. 'As we're in Rowandale,' I told Eve, 'why don't we go and see Armstrong and get him to tell us how he knew Lewis was dead before the news was released? It'll only take a few minutes.'

My final statement turned out to be wildly inaccurate.

We completed the half-mile journey to the far side of the village and pulled up outside the small row of terraced houses that marked the boundary of the Rowandale estate.

'How are you going to tackle him,' Eve asked as we got out of the car.

'I'm simply going to ask him the question outright and see how he reacts. If he's learned about it innocently, all well and good. It might be that someone from Laithbrigg who was around when we found the body told him. It's even possible that after he heard about it, Armstrong rang Matthews and told him. On the other hand, it could be that Armstrong and Matthews know far more about Lewis's murder than they're letting on, so the next few minutes should be extremely interesting.'

If my previous remark had been wildly inaccurate; this one would prove to be the understatement of the year.

The first sign of trouble came soon after we inched our way down the short gravel drive in front of Armstrong's house, where his Land Rover was parked in front of another, far more expensive vehicle. I looked at the Triumph Stag admiringly, wondering who the keeper's visitor was. I dismissed the idea of the car being his; even the most generous of employers doesn't pay their gamekeepers sufficient to afford such an expensive car. More probably one of the shoot members, who was there on syndicate business.

The building was at the end of a terrace of four small dwellings that I guessed had originally been tied cottages, from the days when the estate was far more labour-intensive, before the onset of mechanisation. The garden was overgrown; in urgent need of weeding, and the exterior of the cottage displayed similar signs of long-term neglect. The paint on the window frames and the front door was cracked and peeling. The window panes had obviously not been cleaned for many months.

However, it was the front door that commanded our immediate attention and set off the first alarm bells in my mind. It was a bitterly cold day, with a brisk north-easterly wind blowing, one that my father used to describe as a lazy wind. When I asked him what that meant, he explained that the wind cut straight through you because it was too lazy to go round.

I pointed towards the door, 'I don't like the look of that. Nobody in their right mind would leave their door open on a day like this.'

Even then, I don't think either of us really expected what we were to find inside. It isn't the sort of thing that would spring to mind, unless you had a really macabre thought pattern. There was no bell, so I knocked on the door panel. All this achieved was to move the door from ajar to wide open.

'Hello, Mr Armstrong, are you there?' My voice echoed down the hallway, but got no response from within the house. I tried again. 'Are you there, Mr Armstrong? Is everything all right?'

Still nothing but the reverberation of my voice. I looked at Eve. 'What do we do now?'

'It's obvious there's something wrong, don't you think?'

'Maybe, but I'm loath to go inside without being asked.' My reluctance had nothing to do with fear of what I might find, for at that stage I had no thought of trouble. However, as I explained to Eve, technically, once I stepped over the threshold I was committing an act of trespass. In the back of my mind, in addition to the minor misdemeanour; was the evidence I'd seen of Armstrong's temper. Eve, however, was made of sterner stuff.

'We can't simply ignore this door being left open. It's obvious that something's wrong. What if the poor man's ill and can't call for help? We'd feel terrible about it later if we find out we could have helped, but didn't. And, as well as Mr Armstrong, there's the house to consider. We can't just leave it with the door wide open like this. It isn't safe. Come on, Adam, follow me.'

I did as Eve instructed; feeling rather foolish and somewhat emasculated by her fearless approach. The cottage was typical of such buildings to be found throughout the county. To the side of the hallway was a small sitting room, behind which a flight of stairs led to the first floor. Beyond them was the dining room, which led to a galley kitchen. At the rear of the ground floor was a bathroom and toilet. Although we both called Armstrong's name several times during our inspection of the rooms, we evoked no response. If the gamekeeper was in residence, he must be on the first floor, but in such a small house, surely he must have heard us by now.

'This is weird,' Eve muttered. I looked at her and saw her shiver suddenly, 'I don't like this, Adam. I think something is wrong; seriously wrong.'

'Do you want to stay here whilst I check upstairs?' Curiosity had overcome my reluctance now.

'No, I'll come with you. Better if we stick together.'

There were two doors at the head of the stairs. I opened the one on the left, revealing what was obviously a guest bedroom, although I doubted whether anyone had slept there for a long time. Clothing was heaped in untidy piles on the bed, and by the faintly distasteful aroma of sweat and body odour; I guessed it had been dumped there unwashed.

As I looked across the room I saw two shotguns leaning up against the far wall. So much for gun safety, I thought. The regulations stated that they should be kept in a steel cabinet, bolted to the wall and secured by two five-lever locks. I pointed the weapons out to Eve. 'That's another reason why the front door shouldn't have been left open.'

Seeing the shotguns merely deepened my sense of unease; it hadn't at that stage reached full-blown panic. It didn't take long to get there. As I closed the spare room door, Eve turned the handle on the other door. She pushed it open; the first sign of alarm came via the stench. One of the effects of sudden death is the evacuation of the victim's bowels. Simultaneously, Eve screamed; turned and buried her head against my chest. Looking over her shoulder, I saw the reason for her terror.

Although my experience in war zones had hardened me to the results of extreme violence, the sight that confronted me made me feel sick. It was obvious that Walter Armstrong had not died easily. Evidence of the fight he had put up before being overwhelmed lay in the broken vase on the floor, the upturned chair and the expression of contorted rage and pain on his face. He had been caught unawares; that much was obvious. His nakedness proved that. In the few seconds that I looked directly at him, I counted at least half a dozen stab wounds to his chest and abdomen. There may have been more, but with so much blood it was difficult to say.

I was about to retreat; to take Eve away from this dreadful scene of carnage, when I noticed something even more chilling. Beyond the bloodstained double bed, just where the eiderdown hung close to the carpet, I saw a small, bright pink object, with two even smaller ones alongside it. I recognized them instantly. Only the previous night I had watched Eve varnishing her toenails. 'Eve,' I said gently. 'Look there, beyond the bed. Don't look at Armstrong. Concentrate on the foot of the bed. Am I seeing things, or is that a woman's foot sticking out from there?'

One glance was enough to convince Eve that I hadn't been imagining things. 'Oh, Adam, no. Oh, God, I'm going to be sick.'

'Turn away, take a deep breath, and then close the door.'

Eve did as I instructed and I helped her downstairs. We

hurriedly left the house and took in several deep gulps of fresh air. 'Take the car and go down the village and find a phone. Ring John Pickersgill and explain what's happened.'

'I don't know the number.'

'Get the operator to give you it.'

'Shouldn't it be Ogden I tell?' Eve saw the look on my face. 'No, I guess you're right.'

Chapter Eleven

Despite my revulsion, once Eve had left, I went back inside the house. I opened the bedroom door, taking care to use my handkerchief, and stepped cautiously past Armstrong's body. The second victim, a young woman who I guessed to be in either her late twenties or early thirties, was as naked as Armstrong. Her body was equally bloodstained and it was obvious that she was equally dead. I concentrated on her face, but didn't recognize her. I turned and glanced out of the window, across the broad shimmering water of Thorsgill Beck towards the narrow ribbon of tarmac beyond. As I looked, I remembered what the stable lad had told us. From this viewpoint I could clearly see the churned-up grass on the verge where the recovery vehicle had removed Lewis's Mercedes. I inched my way from the room, closing the door behind me. There was nothing more to be done for the victims. They were long past help.

Eve returned a few minutes later. She still looked extremely distressed. I was concerned, but when she asked me if I was all right, I realized I must also be showing signs of the terrible sight we had just seen. 'John said he was going to try to get hold of Ogden first. As soon as he's spoken to him, he'll set off for here. He said we hadn't to touch anything; or even go back inside the house.'

'I wasn't planning on it,' I said, the vision of those two bodies still far too fresh in my mind.

'What should we do now? I feel so helpless.'

'Apart from waiting around to ensure that nobody rushes in and disturbs vital evidence, there's absolutely nothing we can do until someone arrives to take charge.'

Eve looked around. The village street stretched for almost a mile towards the imposing entrance gates that marked the boundary of Rowandale Hall. There was absolutely no one in sight. 'I don't think we're going to get bowled over in the rush.'

I turned to face the cottage. 'I wonder if by any chance that Stag is unlocked. I don't suppose so; even out here nobody would be willing to take the chance with such an expensive piece of kit. I'll just go try the doors.'

Sure enough, the car was secure. 'Did you think there might be a clue as to the owner's identity inside?' Eve asked.

'Something of the sort, yes.'

'If the owner is security conscious enough to keep it locked even in such a safe place, I very much doubt whether they would leave personal details lying around inside for every potential car thief to find.'

'Was,' I corrected her.

'What?'

'You said, "if the owner is security conscious".'

'Oh, all right, but you're assuming the woman in the bedroom is the owner. Who do you think killed them? A jealous husband or lover, perhaps?'

'I might have gone along with that idea, but for seeing Charles Lewis's body last week. I'm by no means an expert, but I reckon the stab wounds on these bodies were made by the same knife that killed Barbara's ex-husband.'

There was a moment's silence before Eve spoke. 'Hang on, Adam, you said "the stab wounds on these bodies", but we could only see Armstrong. All that was visible of the other victim from the door was part of their foot.'

I realized suddenly how easy it is for someone to make an elementary mistake that could prove highly incriminating. I might as well own up. 'I went back inside and took a closer look. I thought I ought to, in case the second victim was only wounded. It would have been terrible to find out later that we could have helped them.'

'I actually knew you'd gone back into the cottage. Eve pointed down the street. ''You can see the front door from the phone box. I take it the woman was also dead?'

'Extremely dead; I think she'd been stabbed as many times as Armstrong, although I didn't stop to count the wounds.'

'Was she also naked?'

'Yes, her clothing was strewn on the carpet. At a guess I'd say it was a case of coitus *extremely* interruptus.'

'Did you recognize her face, or were you to preoccupied staring at her … wounds to look elsewhere.'

Eve's momentary hesitation and the slight extra emphasis on the word 'wounds', made me smile, in spite of the grim situation. 'What sort of pervert do you take me for?'

I saw Eve open her mouth to reply so I lifted a warning hand. 'No, don't bother to answer that, I can imagine. The woman was around thirty years of age, quite attractive, with long dark hair that appeared to be natural, and a decent enough figure, although some of the sand in the hourglass had trickled through to the bottom. I'm certain I've never seen her before, but then I don't mingle with the Stag-driving set.'

At that moment we saw Pickersgill's patrol car hurtling along the village street towards us at a pace far in excess of the speed limit. He brought it to a shuddering halt only inches from the back bumper of my car and leapt out. 'There's no rush, John, they aren't going anywhere,' I told him. 'Well, only to the mortuary, I guess.'

'Did anyone ever tell you what a sick sense of humour you have?' Eve enquired.

I ignored the snide remark. 'Did you manage to get hold of Ogden?'

'I did, eventually, but it took some doing. Inspector

High-and-Mighty was interviewing Mrs Lewis and gave strict instructions that he wasn't to be disturbed by anyone below the rank of chief constable.'

'How did you get round that?'

'I phoned the chief constable, of course, and asked him to intercede.' Pickersgill smiled wickedly. 'I'd have liked to have eavesdropped on the call he made to Ogden. The outcome is that Ogden will be here in about an hour, together with a full team of experts. I'm not going to vouch for what his temper will be like, though. In the meantime I have to secure the crime scene, keep you here, and ensure the onlookers don't disturb the area.'

I glanced down the village street, which was still empty. 'Another tough assignment for you.'

'Why does he want us to stay?' Eve asked. 'Is he frightened we might run away, or fly off to Brazil at a moment's notice?'

Pickersgill shook his head gravely, responding to Eve's sarcasm in like vein. 'It isn't for us lesser mortals to attempt to understand the workings of a fine mind like Ogden's. All we can do is stand by, proud to be onlookers witnessing such genius at close quarters.'

His expression changed. 'Are you both OK?' He looked from Eve to me and then back again. 'It must have been terrible for you, finding the bodies.'

'It wasn't pleasant,' Eve agreed. 'I was upset at the time, but I'm all right now. I think Adam was upset too. He didn't speak for almost five minutes, which shows he was in shock.'

'You said on the phone that Armstrong was one of the victims.' Pickersgill concentrated his attention on Eve. 'Have you any idea who the other one was?'

'I didn't actually see her body, only part of one foot. Adam went back into the room to make sure she was dead.' Eve paused, realizing at once what she'd said. 'I didn't mean that the way it came out. I meant that he went to check for any sign of life in case he could help.'

'I understand; very wise, too. I take it she was dead?' He looked at me.

'Well and truly. I didn't touch either of the corpses, but I'd guess they've been dead some time. I didn't count the wounds, but I reckon she was stabbed just as many times as he was.'

I described the woman, but Pickersgill couldn't place her from my brief account. 'There is one way we might be able to get her name. If I get the station to find out who the owner of the car is, that should do it.' He smiled. 'Promise you won't elope to Gretna Green whilst I'm on the radio.'

'Will it be OK to go sit in my car if I promise not to switch the engine on? It's a bit chilly out here.'

'I don't have a problem with that.'

It was almost half an hour later before Pickersgill returned with news of what his colleagues back at headquarters had discovered. During his absence, as much to take our minds off the tragic events nearby, we discussed our plans for Dene Cottage.

'I think we should change its name once we've added the extension,' Eve told me.

'What to?'

She grinned mischievously. 'I think Eden House would be appropriate, don't you? As long as we don't have a son and call him Cain, or Abel.'

I stared at her in surprise. 'That's spooky. I had the same idea the other day. Not only is it apt, but it has a real ring to it. I'm not sure if you're allowed to rename houses though, we'll have to check with the post office.'

Pickersgill knocked on the driver's window. I'd been looking at Eve at the time, admiring her beauty, and his tap startled me.

'The Triumph's registered keeper is a company in Leeds called MPD Ltd. That doesn't mean anything to me, how about you?'

I shook my head, but Eve said, 'How about that man from the shoot? Matthews, I mean. Isn't he something to do with property? I seem to remember you saying that at the Nelson. Couldn't MPD stand for Matthews Property Development?'

'Eve's right,' I told him. 'She's also something of a genius.'

'That makes sense, but who was the woman?'

'I don't know if Matthews was married or not, but if he was, perhaps Mrs Matthews decided she wanted someone else to make the earth move for her.' I grinned as I heard Eve groan. 'I can't see the attraction myself; I certainly wouldn't have Armstrong down as the Oliver Mellors type.'

Eve and Pickersgill both looked baffled. '*Lady Chatterley's Lover*,' I explained.

'You did tell us the reason he was sacked from his previous job was because he'd been having an affair with a married woman,' Eve pointed out. 'Maybe he prefers them with a wedding ring on.'

'You may be right, and if the dead woman is Mrs Matthews, it will give Ogden a ready-made suspect. It will be interesting to see if Matthews can account for his movements around the time of the deaths.'

Witnessing the arrival of Ogden, his CID officers, their uniformed colleagues, the pathologist, and sundry forensic scientists, was rather like watching a parade, or a royal procession. The long straight main street of Rowandale village was transformed momentarily in my imagination to Pall Mall, or Horse Guards Parade.

I watched with interest as Ogden emerged from the lead vehicle, to see if his attitude had been affected by the chief constable's intervention. I have to say I was unable to detect the slightest alteration. I wondered what it would take to dent the man's pompous arrogance. He scarcely acknowledged Pickersgill and paid little heed to Eve's presence. The focus of his attention was on me, although I couldn't for the life of me work out what I'd done to deserve it. However, Ogden soon put me right on that score.

'You seem to be making quite a habit of being first on the scene whenever a murder's been committed, Bailey. Some people would regard that as suspicious; highly suspicious.'

'By "some people" I take it you are referring to yourself, Ogden. Are you working on the principle that the person who finds the body must be the killer? It's an extremely interesting concept, and I can see that it would have several advantages. No murder would go unsolved; you'd have someone locked up for every crime, no matter whether they were guilty or innocent. Unfortunately for you, Ogden, that theory is about as flawed as the rest of your detective work. I ought to point out that it wasn't actually me who discovered Lewis's body. It was Mrs Price. I only became involved because I happened to be passing by when she needed to raise the alarm, but don't let that trivial detail spoil your reasoning.'

He turned to walk away, his whole demeanour one of anger, but I wasn't prepared to let him off the hook yet. 'I have two other matters to raise with you, Ogden.'

He whipped round and snarled, 'It's Inspector Ogden.'

'Yes, I know, so perhaps you will do me the courtesy of addressing me as *Mr* Bailey in future. That was one of the matters. The other was a request.'

'What request?'

'I wanted to ask you to contact your office and give them instructions to release Barbara Lewis immediately.'

'Are you mad? If it hadn't been for these killings, I'd have charged her with her husband's murder by now. I shall rectify that as soon as I've finished here.'

'OK, go ahead.' I paused, before adding, 'Go ahead and

make an even bigger fool of yourself than you already have done.'

'What do you mean?'

'I mean that if you charge Barbara you'll be the laughing stock of the county within days, hours even.'

'Oh yes, and why is that?' he sneered.

'Because Barbara couldn't have killed Charles Lewis. At the time he was murdered she was over thirty miles away.'

'How do you know what time Lewis was murdered?'

'One of your officers told me the pathologist had set the time of death as sometime between late morning and evening on Thursday of last week, and I happen to know Barbara was nowhere near Rowandale during that time.'

'Oh yes, and who is going to give her an alibi? You, I suppose. Do you honestly think I'm going to fall for such a lame story?'

'No, not me, but there must be quite a lot of people who will be able to confirm the facts.'

'What people? Give me names.'

'I can't possibly do that. What I can do, is tell you where Mrs Lewis was and what she was doing. According to her stable lad, she set off in the horsebox with him and Blenheim Boy to Wetherby racecourse around nine that morning. The horse won the most prestigious hurdle race of the day, and afterwards, Barbara was interviewed in the winner's enclosure for the benefit of several million people who were watching on television. Later, as they were driving back from Wetherby, the horsebox broke down. Because the horse is so valuable, they couldn't risk having the vehicle towed to a garage, so they had to wait until a mechanic completed the repair at the roadside. This resulted in them not returning to Linden House until just before midnight.'

Before I began my story, Ogden's face had been almost puce with anger, now it was ashen pale. 'All these facts will have to be checked before I can authorize Mrs Lewis's release. In the meantime, I've two other murders to investigate.'

As he walked away, Eve said, 'Oh dear, Adam, I think you've ruined the inspector's day. He looked quite upset.'

'Not likely, it would take a guided missile up his backside to upset him.'

'Now there's a sight we'd all like to see.'

'Unfortunately, there's a flaw in Adam's reasoning,' Pickersgill told her. 'Ogden is that thick-skinned the missile probably wouldn't penetrate his self-esteem. However, I definitely think you're off his Christmas card list, as well as me.'

'That won't cause me any lost sleep. He was never on mine.' I gestured to the milling throng of officialdom that was congregating by Armstrong's front door. 'Anyway, what's your contribution to this circus going to be?'

'Not so much a circus, more of a pantomime, or French farce, I'd say, considering Ogden's in charge of proceedings. I have no role, I'm not important enough, so I'll have to await instructions and hope against hope I get selected even for a walk-on part, or as an extra. Looking at that lot, it will probably entail crowd control or car parking, just like last time.'

'One good thing, though. It looks as if Zeke Calvert will be getting his job back.'

Eve shook her head despairingly. 'I suppose I'm going to have to get used to your sick sense of humour.'

Eventually, the young DC, whose name I still didn't know, came over to take our statements. We told him why we had come to see Armstrong, which seemed to go right over his head, and how we'd found the house door ajar on our arrival. In the middle of our explanation, I suddenly realized that I might have the answer to the question that had been troubling me for a week. And, if that was the case, I might also have a shrewd idea as to a possible motive for Armstrong's murder. In all this speculation, I couldn't be sure whether the gamekeeper's companion had been an intended victim, or whether she had merely been unlucky enough to be in the wrong place at the wrong time.

Once he'd reported back to Ogden, giving him chapter and verse on what we'd told him, the DC returned and confirmed that it would now be in order for us to leave. Although I realized there were procedures to be observed, I doubted whether what we had told the detectives would advance their search for the person responsible for the murders at all.

As we drove back to Laithbrigg, Eve noticed my silence, and remarked on it. 'What are you thinking about, Adam? You suddenly went quiet as we were telling that detective our story and I realized then your mind was elsewhere. Would you care to share your thoughts with your beloved?'

I smiled. 'You have no idea how great that sounds, Evie.' I told her the idea that had suddenly come to me. 'If I'm right, it goes some way to explaining why Armstrong was killed. However, that still doesn't provide us with a motive for Lewis's murder.' I paused; then changed the subject. 'Do you fancy dining out again tonight?'

'Where have you in mind?'

'The Admiral Nelson.'

'Have you a specific reason for wanting to go there? Not that I object. Quite the opposite, I'm starting to enjoy the lifestyle, although I'm not sure it's good for my waistline.'

'I simply wanted to ask one or two questions about local history; that was all.' I leered at her. 'And, if you're really concerned about your weight, I could suggest some intense physical activity for when we return from the pub, to burn some calories off.'

'You've got a point, Adam. The way you've been going on, I need have no fear of getting fat, so the Nelson it is then, and then back home for some aerobics.'

Chapter Twelve

I was surprised by how many people were in the bar of the Admiral Nelson when we walked in at around 7.30 that evening. At first, I thought there must be a darts or dominoes match scheduled to take place. I could think of no other reason for the pub being so busy on a cold midweek evening. 'Is it always this packed?' Eve asked the landlord as he served us. 'I don't remember there being this many people in here on Saturday night.'

'No, it wasn't. You two are the reason the place is packed, as I understand it.'

'Why might that be?'

'Everyone wants to know what happened today at Rowandale, and the local bush telegraph has reported that you two found the bodies.' He grinned. 'You might find it difficult to buy a round of drinks tonight. In fact, if trade continues to be this good for the rest of the evening, I might even buy you one myself.'

He was proved right within seconds. I was reaching for my wallet when Henry Price put a restraining hand on my arm. 'I'll get these,' he told the landlord, and placed a £5 note on the counter.

'That's very kind of you, Henry, thank you. I'm surprised to see you in here, though. I thought you'd be getting some kip before starting your milk round.'

'I had a few hours' sleep earlier. Besides which, the missus sent me to find out all I could about the latest murders. I heard that you found the bodies, is that right?'

'That's correct. Would you like to hear about it?'

Henry nodded. 'Yes, please.'

'I'll tell you everything I know.' I saw Eve's eyes widen with astonishment, 'But first, I'd like a bit of background from you. Call it recent local history, if you like. Shall we go over there, where it's a bit less crowded?'

I manoeuvred Henry to the end of the bar, and once we were safely out of earshot of even the most determined of eavesdroppers, asked him, 'Tell me what you can about Zeke Calvert's son, Stan, I think his name is.'

'That's correct.' As he pondered my request I could tell Price was wondering about my reasons for asking it. Defeated in this quest, he decided to open up. 'Stan is a true woodsman, which is hardly surprising given his ancestry. He has several generations of keepers' blood in his veins. Everyone felt convinced that Stan would take over from Zeke as gamekeeper to the Rowandale estate when his father retired. Zeke used to take him into Rowandale forest almost from the day he could walk. In the end, I reckon Stan knew those woods better than Zeke; better than anyone for that matter, apart from Brian, of course.'

'Brian?' Eve asked. 'You mean Brian Latimer?'

'That's right. Brian and Stan were inseparable as lads. They used to go off camping in the forest for days, sometimes weeks on end, during the school holidays. That was another reason everyone was convinced Stan would end up as the Rowandale keeper; his friendship with Brian. A lot of folk reckon the reason Stan left was all to do with Zeke getting remarried, but I think it had more to do with Brian's death. The news hit him hard, you could tell that. He'd been Brian's only champion when old Mr Rupert accused him of theft. Everyone else believed it, because the evidence was overwhelming, but Stan would have none of it. Even his father told him to listen to reason, but Stan was unshakeably loyal. I remember he got into a couple of fights with other youths hereabouts over the matter. They made the mistake of saying something derogatory about Brian, and Stan flared up. He was tough; far too strong for them, and they got the bruises to prove it. Eventually of course, the truth came out and Stan was proved right. That was all very well, but any pleasure he got from being vindicated was soon destroyed when the news came through that Brian had been murdered in Mexico. Myself, I think Stan was so upset he just had to leave the area because it held too many unhappy memories; he picked the fight with his father as an excuse.'

'I heard he went to live in America, is that right?'

'So I believe, but I can't be certain. Anyway, that's all I can tell you about Stan. Is there any reason for you asking?'

'Not really, merely curiosity.'

'OK, what about these murders? Is it true that they were killed in the same way as Lewis?'

I kept my end of the bargain, and with Eve's help, told Henry everything we'd witnessed earlier that day. Towards the end of our account, Eve said, 'All the houses in that terrace look a bit dilapidated, which is a real shame. They could look very pretty in that setting but they've been sadly neglected. Do they still belong to the estate? Is that the reason they've been left to deteriorate, because of old Mr Latimer's death?'

'They do belong to the estate, but Mr Rupert's death isn't the reason they've been allowed to get in such a sorry state. There's no point in spending a load of money on houses when there's every chance they might be demolished in the near future, is there?'

'Demolished?' Eve sounded horrified by the idea. 'Surely not! They can't be in such bad condition? They're stone-built and look really sturdy. Are they unsafe? If they're that bad, why are people still living in them?'

Price smiled, as much at Eve's vehemence as the questions themselves. 'No, there's nothing wrong with the houses. Structurally, they're as sound as the day they were built, or pretty near it. The rumour is that there's a new trunk road to be built and one of the routes under consideration will take it right across the corner of the Rowandale estate, past the end of the village, and right through that terrace. If that happens, the estate and those houses will be worth a heck of a sight more than their current value. That's always supposing the scheme comes off. If it does, the estate will benefit another way too.'

'How's that, Henry?' I asked.

'They'll need thousands upon thousands of tons of road-stone and aggregate; hardcore and the like. The top side of the estate is all limestone, but the lower end, beyond here, there's a lot of sandstone, shale, gravel, and so forth. It's ideal for the civil engineers, because extraction and transport costs will be minimal.'

'I hadn't heard anything about this road scheme,' I admitted.

Price chuckled. 'That's because you don't come in here often enough, Adam. It's been the major topic of conversation for weeks on end, before we had these murders to talk about.'

Shortly after, we were sitting at our table awaiting our meal. The dining room, in contrast to the bar, was almost deserted, so it was much later in the evening before I was able to obtain the other information I was seeking. I mentioned it to Eve as we were choosing from the menu. 'Did you notice whether Zeke Calvert was in the bar?'

'He wasn't; I looked for him specially, in view of your talk with Mr Price.'

'Never mind, I feel sure he'll make an appearance at some stage. Everyone else in the village seems to be in the bar, I can't think Zeke would miss out.'

Sure enough, Calvert was seated on a stool at the far end of the bar when we returned following another excellent meal. I bought him a pint and after chatting for a while, with no prizes for guessing the topic of conversation, I asked Zeke the question I'd had in mind all evening. I prefaced it by talking about Walter Armstrong. Calvert, who I knew had no time for his successor, was, unsurprisingly, somewhat less than sympathetic.

'Can't say I'm upset. Can't say I'm shocked. Bugger had it coming, I reckon.'

'Why do you say that?' Eve asked.

'He's only been here five minutes and already he's made enemies of everyone in t' villages. I reckon there's a mile long queue of suspects.'

'You might be included in that list,' I pointed out.

'Aye, well, I don't say I'd have done for him, but I wouldn't have rushed to give him t' kiss of life either.'

'You think he was murdered by someone he upset?'

'Isn't that allus the case? Anyroad, that's for t' police to find out. Not that I reckon they've much chance wi' yon Ogden running t' show.'

'What about the other victim?'

'I don't know owt about her. Maybe she just visited Armstrong once too often.'

'That wasn't the first time she'd been to his cottage, then?'

'Nah, she were there regular away. At least if that fancy Stag were hers.'

'Can you recall if you saw her at Armstrong's place on Thursday of last week?'

Calvert thought for a moment. 'Thursday, that'd be the day when Blenheim Boy won at Wetherby, wouldn't it?'

I nodded. 'That's right.'

'Aye, I thought so; I went into town specially to put a bet on. When I came back I saw that fancy car on his drive and thought to mesen he's at it again, the lucky bugger, that lass must need specs to take up wi' an ugly-looking sod like him.'

'What sort of time would that have been?'

'Early afternoon; around half past two, I reckon, near as owt. I got home just in time to put telly on and watch the race. Won a hundred quid on it, I did. Then I sat and watched Barbara being interviewed by that commentator; the one who talks like he's got a plum in his mouth.'

That was one more for Ogden's list of witnesses to Barbara's alibi, I thought.

We chatted as we walked back to Dene Cottage, but the subject of the murders was not mentioned until we got indoors, when Eve said, 'Your theory about Matthews and Armstrong is getting to sound more and more feasible, Adam. When you looked out of the bedroom window in Armstrong's cottage, did you get a clear view of the place where Lewis's car was found?'

'As clear as anything, Evie. I could even see the tyre marks on the grass verge where the recovery vehicle towed the Mercedes away. If Armstrong and his paramour were in that room last Thursday afternoon, and they weren't too busy playing hide the sausage, they couldn't help but witness everything that went on across the other side of Thorsgill Beck.'

'Don't be so coarse, Adam. The only flaw in your theory as far as I can tell is, how would the killer know they'd seen him? Even then, how could he be sure they could identify him? Unless he was known to them, of course, or one of them at least.'

'There's no easy answer to that. He might have seen that they were watching, but I doubt it. As I recall, last Thursday was quite a nice day, and the low afternoon sun at this time of year would have been right in his eyes as he looked across the beck.'

'If the killer didn't realize he'd been seen, then that rather destroys your theory, doesn't it?'

'It does,' I paused. 'Unless …'

'Unless what?'

'We don't know anything about the woman with Armstrong, but we do know a bit about him, and not much of it is good. Just suppose either Armstrong, or his mistress, or both of them decided this was too good an opportunity to miss, and decided to try and make a bit of profit out of what they'd seen?'

'Blackmail, you mean?' Eve looked dubious.

'That was the thought I had – but for that to work, as I said earlier, the killer would have to have been known to at least one of them.'

'There again, their deaths might be totally unconnected to that of Lewis. It could be that the killer was a jealous husband or lover after all; and that he thought this would be a good chance to take his revenge.'

'I think that might be stretching the long arm of coincidence a bit far, to have two such violent murders with no obvious connection taking place within two hundred yards of each other.'

'I suppose you're right. How do you think Ogden will view it? Do you think he'll look beyond jealousy as a motive?'

'At a guess, I think Ogden will opt for all the murders having been committed by a homicidal maniac; some sort of psychopath who chooses his victims at random. He'll probably issue a warning to the public which will have everyone too scared to leave their house for weeks to come.'

I had an uncomfortable feeling that if Ogden was seeking a deranged killer, who better to choose than a vagrant with no fixed abode, no visible means of support, and possible mental health issues. It was only later that I vowed to stop getting these notions, or at least to stop expressing them. They were being proved accurate far too often for my liking.

The following morning, I was less than surprised to see Pickersgill's car parked outside Dene Cottage as I walked back home with the morning paper and groceries I'd bought at the village shop.

Eve had already made Johnny a mug of tea. As I grew to know John better, I wondered how many of these he got through during his working day, and marvelled at his ability to consume that much liquid. It must put a severe strain on his constitution. However, given his in-depth knowledge of the area, no doubt he had plenty of secluded places where he could relieve the pressure, free from embarrassment.

The news he had come to impart merely confirmed what we already suspected. 'The woman whose body was found in Armstrong's bedroom was a Mrs Veronica Matthews. She's the estranged wife of Trevor Matthews; the property developer you met in that confrontation at the stables.'

'Did Matthews know that his wife was sleeping with Walter Armstrong?' Eve asked.

'Apparently he did, according to the garbled account Ogden gave me of his interview with him. The tale Matthews told our worthy inspector was that they parted amicably a couple of years back. Matthews had already taken up with a fitness instructor he met when he joined one of those new-fangled health clubs in Leeds and they're now living together. Mrs Matthews retained the marital home as part of the separation agreement, and by what he told Ogden; Matthews actually introduced Veronica to Armstrong after the split, and approved of the arrangement.'

'That's all very well, but it must have made the relationship between Armstrong and Matthews difficult.'

Eve disagreed with me. 'I'm not so sure about that, Adam. There was certainly no evidence of strain between them that Sunday at Linden House.'

'You could be right, and perhaps Matthews is telling the truth.' I turned to Pickersgill. 'Does the fact that Ogden repeated the details of his interview of Matthews in such detail mean you're back in his good books and in the loop once more?'

'I wouldn't go that far. He has to feed me a certain amount of information regarding any crimes he's investigating within my area. Besides which –' Pickersgill smiled cynically, '– he knows that if he pushes me too far I can always pick up the phone and have a quiet word in the chief's ear.'

'Do you have much influence with the chief constable?'

The smile broadened. 'You could say that – he's my cousin!'

'That must explain how you've kept your job for so long.'

Having made certain that Eve couldn't see what he was doing; Pickersgill gave me an extremely vulgar gesture. I ignored it, and told him, 'I'm glad you've come this morning, because I want to ask you about something I heard in the pub last night. I was talking to Henry Price and he mentioned something about a proposed new trunk road that would cross part of the Rowandale estate. Do you know if that scheme is going ahead? Henry was a bit vague about it.'

'That idea has been kicking about for the best part of twenty years to my knowledge, but either the government of the day or the county council never seem to get round to providing funding for it. They usually come up with an excuse along the lines of the country's economic situation, or other road schemes that are higher priority. Recently, though, there seems to have been a concerted move to apply pressure for the trunk road to go beyond the discussion stage. It's rather a novel situation, with everyone concerned suddenly taking it seriously. Is there any specific reason you wanted to know, or was the question merely down to idle curiosity?'

'No, it was a little more than that. I'll let Eve explain. It was an idea she had after she heard what Henry had to say.'

'I simply wondered if the motive for Lewis's murder might have something to do with this new road. I seem to remember Lewis worked in either the Planning or Highways Department of the county council, which would be closely involved in anything like a major trunk road construction. It just seemed to be a huge coincidence.'

'That's as maybe, and I take your point, but I fail to see what the motive would be.'

'Perhaps he was able to influence things such as the route the new road would take, or the awarding of contracts to the civil engineers who would build it. That may also explain how he was able to afford such an expensive car, which is something that Adam suggested needed investigation.'

'You could well be right, but it's a huge step from bribing a local government employee to murder, don't you agree?'

Pickersgill got to his feet as he spoke. Having thanked Eve for the tea, he said, 'None of that has any bearing on the reason for my visit. I'm on my way to the station to collect Barbara Lewis. Ogden has decided she's stayed at our hotel long enough. He checked out the details you gave him and is satisfied with her alibi. He now believes she had nothing to do with her husband's murder.' He paused, before adding, 'That's something that anyone who knows Barbara could have told him all along, had he asked.'

We set out for Linden House when we judged Barbara would be home. Our relief that she had been released was tempered by our curiosity over her refusal to explain what she had been doing or where she had been during her absence in the time leading up to her arrest. In respect of this, there was one question I particularly wanted to ask her. I was keen to hear her response and equally eager to see her reaction to my suggestion. In the event, I was both surprised and, to begin with, baffled by both.

It was Eve who provided me with the opening I needed to pose my question. Once Barbara had thanked us for providing the information that had persuaded Inspector Ogden to sanction her release, Eve returned to the subject of Barbara's missing week. The trainer's silence and the accompanying secretive smile only reinforced Eve's determination to prise the truth from her friend.

As much to distract Eve as anything, I suggested, 'I think you were in Rowandale Forest. Isn't that the case? And I guess you weren't alone. I think you were with the tramp.'

Barbara's smile faded to a mask of secrecy. Her reply, 'Rowandale Forest at this time of year?' failed to convince me, so I went one stage further.

'I think I might even be able to put a name to that mysterious stranger.'

'You do?' Barbara's response was a clear challenge.

'Yes, I believe that tramp isn't really a vagrant at all. I think it's someone you once knew extremely well; someone who has been at odds with his father, and has returned to the area after a long absence. I believe he is Stan Calvert.'

I watched Barbara very carefully as I spoke, noticing her expression become more guarded all the time, until at the end she smiled and shook her head, which in itself was more revealing than her words, which were directed at Eve. 'What was it you once told me about Adam? Something along the lines that he sometimes notices far too much for his own good, wasn't it? What you failed to tell me was that although his guesses are usually accurate, sometimes, he's wide of the mark.'

She smiled at me. 'Good try, Adam. Perhaps before long I'll be at liberty to tell you exactly what I have been doing and you'll realize just how wide of the mark you can be.'

We were seated at her kitchen table. As with many houses, her kitchen served as the focal point for activity. Having come to a mutual unspoken agreement not to discuss the matter further, we drank tea while Barbara tackled her pile of mail. It was noticeable that the junk mail was far more plentiful than the business post. Towards the end, however, she opened an envelope whose contents demanded far closer scrutiny than the casual glance she had given all the others.

As Barbara read the brief note we saw her expression change from one of mild irritation to outright anger. 'What a bloody nerve,' she muttered. She looked up and I could see she was close to tears, but whether these were of rage or sorrow, I couldn't judge, for the time being.

'Would you be available to come over here tomorrow afternoon? It appears I'm due to have a visit and I want someone here to witness that I didn't strangle him or give him a black eye?'

'Who is it?' we asked in unison.

'See for yourselves.' She flicked the letter across the table, the action one of disdain and resentment. One glance at the letterhead convinced me the visitor would be unlikely to be the bearer of good news.

Unaware that we already knew about the sender, courtesy of the local gossip factory, Barbara explained. 'Rhodes and Moore are the solicitors dealing with the estate of Rupert Latimer. Aside from Matthews challenging the validity of the bequest to me, which would entail me losing the house and stables, he's been a pain in the neck all the way through, demanding all sorts of information and asking stupid questions. That –' she pointed to the letter, '– is just the latest in a long line of pieces of unnecessary red tape.'

We read the letter, in which the writer, Norman Rhodes, stated that he intended to visit Linden House the following day, with a view to conducting an inventory of all property and assets that might or might not pertain to the estate, and requesting that Barbara make herself available to allow him access to all areas. Although the word used was 'request' the terminology made it sound more like a demand. There was, for example, no mention of whether the timing of the visit would be convenient to Barbara.

'Can he do that?' Eve asked. 'Is that normal practice, Adam?'

'I've absolutely no idea. None of my relatives had enough in their estate for anyone to worry about probate.'

'It's really quite immaterial,' Barbara said. 'That visit is an inconvenience, nothing more. Whatever he says or does won't make any difference. One way or the other, I'll either end up losing Linden House or gaining far more. That decision is out of my hands – and his, for that matter. However, I would be grateful if you were able to be here.'

Having promised to lend our moral support, we returned to Laithbrigg. We were both silent on the return journey, mulling over our conversation with Barbara. It was only when we were approaching the village that I realized what Barbara had meant by her final remark. The impact of that, taken together with her earlier cryptic comment hit me like a physical blow. I gasped aloud and out of pure reflex, slammed my foot on the brake. This caused the cyclist I'd just overtaken to wobble precariously as he swerved to avoid my stationary vehicle. A rich flow of invective drifted in through my open window and I raised one hand in apology.

'Adam, what on earth's the matter?' Eve demanded.

'I'll tell you after we get home. I need time to think this

out. If I'm right, it explains everything.' I started to laugh. 'And if I am right, a lot of people are in for one heck of a shock.'

Chapter Thirteen

The following day we arrived at Linden House long before the time specified by Rhodes for his tour of inspection. That gave us ample opportunity to brief Barbara on the plan we had formulated for dealing with the solicitor, although even then we fell some way short of explaining everything we had in mind. Despite this, I think Barbara might have suspected something of the strategy I was going to use, and that convinced me my theory might well be correct. If it was, as I had explained to Eve the previous night, we would have to handle matters with extreme caution.

'Why, Adam?'

'Because, like I said earlier, the news is bound to come as a shock, and will upset a lot of people. At least one of them has proved determined enough to resort to desperate measures. That could represent danger to Barbara and others.'

We discussed tactics with Barbara. One more item was needed in preparation for the impending visit. 'Do you have a copy of Rupert Latimer's will?' I asked. Barbara produced the document. I read the opening paragraph, which told me all I needed to know.

I had been prepared to take an instant dislike to Norman Rhodes before I met him, and he certainly lived down to my expectations. I'd even formed a mental image of the man as being small, tubby, and somewhat pompous. In fact, he turned out to be undersized, overweight, and *extremely* pompous; not to mention arrogant.

From the moment he opened the driver's door of his

Volvo estate and placed one highly polished shoe carefully on the concrete floor of the stable yard, I knew that Norman Rhodes and I were never destined to be friends. Nothing he said or did in the course of his visit caused me to alter my preconceived notion of him, except possibly to strengthen it.

I was aware that Eve shared my opinion of the solicitor purely by the expression on her face as she observed him enter the kitchen as if it was his own, and place his bulging briefcase on the table, before greeting Barbara with an excess of formality. Despite Barbara's introduction, he ignored us, turning his back as he faced Barbara and delved into the expanding pockets of the case to pull out a sheaf of documents which he shuffled into order. He examined the first of these, his lips pursed in concentration before he looked up. 'Right,' he said, 'Before I make a start on the inspection proper, I have received instructions from the prospective new owners of Rowandale Hall to establish precisely what items from the contents of Linden House belong to the estate, and which do not. Final evidence of anything you might claim to possess will rely on proof of purchase via receipts or invoices. I have made you aware that a challenge has been lodged to the validity of the bequest made to you in the will of the late Rupert Latimer, I believe?'

That gave me the cue I'd been waiting for to enter the fray. 'Isn't that rather jumping the gun?' I asked.

Rhodes was so fat he could not turn his neck easily. Instead, he swivelled his whole body in my direction. 'My instructions are to discuss this matter with Mrs Lewis. They certainly do not extend to persons who have no claim on the estate.'

It was intended to be dismissive, but things didn't turn out that way. 'Adam is here as my representative,' Barbara told him.

'I see; that rather changes things. I had hoped you

would be more cooperative. However, I am quite prepared to return when other people are not about. I am not prepared to discuss confidential matters in the presence of strangers and can always obtain sanction to examine the properties without interference from outside parties.'

He scooped up the paperwork and stuffed it into his case before turning to head for the exit, only to find that I was leaning against the door. 'Put your case on the table and sit down. You're going nowhere until we get some basic facts relating to the estate straightened out.'

For a moment I thought that Rhodes might be prepared to dispute my statement, but one look at my face seemed to decide him that discretion was the better part of valour. He turned back towards Barbara and sank heavily into one of the chairs. Fortunately, they were sturdily built. 'This isn't going to help, you know,' he told her.

Barbara ignored him. 'Carry on, Adam.'

'Right, I want to know what steps you've taken towards establishing certain basic facts before proceeding towards probate, because one thing you certainly cannot do is begin negotiating the sale of the estate or any part of it until that is granted.'

'What precisely do you mean by that?' There was just the vaguest hint of acquiescence in Rhodes's response.

'Well, to begin with, I'd like to see a copy of the death certificate.'

'Why do you want that? Are you suggesting there was something untoward in the manner of his death? Because I can assure you it was perfectly straightforward.'

'Nevertheless, I would still like to inspect a copy.'

I could tell that Barbara, as well as Rhodes, was puzzled by my insistence. Eve, who knew why I'd made the request, smiled at me encouragingly.

The solicitor delved into his case once more and after turning over what looked like a full ream of documents, managed to unearth the relevant sheet of paper which he passed to me.

I took a cursory glance before handing it back to him. 'That's no use. That isn't the document I was referring to. That is the death certificate for Rupert Latimer. I want to see the death certificate for Brian Latimer.'

Both Rhodes and Barbara stared at me in open-mouthed astonishment. 'Because,' I continued, 'if you are unable to produce conclusive evidence of the death of Brian Latimer, we have to assume that he is still alive, and as such, will inherit the Rowandale Hall estate in its entirety. The statement at the opening of Rupert Latimer's will makes it abundantly clear that the document was drawn up in the belief that there were no natural heirs to the estate. If Brian Latimer is alive, that will is invalid.'

'But Brian Latimer is dead. He died in Mexico years ago.'

'Prove it. Show me the death certificate.'

'I don't have one, not as such. What I do have is a statement from a captain of police in the area where the body was found. It was sworn before an attorney.'

'I'd like to see it, please. Do you have it with you?'

He nodded, and burrowed into the case again. It took over five minutes for him to find the document, which didn't surprise me, as I was beginning to suspect he'd emptied the contents of his filing cabinet into the case before coming to Linden House.

Eventually, he passed it to me. 'It won't do you any good,' he commented with a hint of malice, 'it's written in Spanish. The English translation is back at my office.'

'That's no problem, I read Spanish well enough.'

I scanned the document with interest. The body had been placed in the mine only a few weeks before it was found, which contradicted what I'd heard. Sometimes, it seemed, even the local gossip merchants got their facts wrong. Another point I hadn't known was that fingerprint identification had not been possible because both hands had been removed. I turned to the second page before finding the item I was looking for. I read it, before glancing across the room.

'Barbara, do you have a photocopier?'

'Yes, there's one in my office.'

'Would you be kind enough to take a copy of this document?' I looked at Rhodes, 'I take it you have no objection?'

He remained silent, which I took for consent.

Barbara was only out of the room for a couple of minutes, and on her return handed me both copies of the report. I passed the original to Rhodes. 'If I was you I wouldn't waste any more time or money applying for probate or even preparing the estate for such, and I'd tell those people who are so keen to buy the estate that it isn't for sale. Certainly not as things stand.'

'What are you talking about?' Rhodes regarded me with disdain.

I tapped the report I was holding. 'This isn't worth the paper it's written on, certainly as proof that Brian Latimer is dead. The only evidence linking him to that corpse is the driving licence found on the body.'

'That should be enough.'

'Hardly; not when you read the rest of the report.' I walked across the room and picked up a photo from the dresser, before setting it down in front of Rhodes. 'Mrs Lewis, this is a photo of you with Brian Latimer when you were kids, right?'

The photo was of two children, of about twelve years of age, I guessed. As they were both clad in swimming gear and were standing on a beach, I assumed it was a holiday snap. The girl was quite clearly Barbara and with her was a boy with his arm lovingly across her shoulders.

'That was taken on holiday in Scarborough when I was eleven. Mum and Dad took me, and Brian.'

'How tall were you at that age?'

'About four feet four, think.'

'By the look of this photo, I'd say Brian was a couple of inches taller than you. How tall was he when he was fully grown, can you remember?'

'He shot up when he was about thirteen, and by the time he left school he was a touch over six feet tall, I think.'

'That's interesting, because the Mexican police captain states that the corpse was only 1.7 metres tall, which is around five feet eight inches.'

'He could have made a mistake,' Rhodes said, a touch of desperation in his voice.

'He might have done, and it could also be that the medical examiner who conducted the autopsy, and who the police captain relied upon for much of his information, was colour-blind.'

'Colour-blind: what has that to do with it?'

I pointed to the photo. 'Because if the medical examiner got it right, I'd be very interested to know how Brian Latimer's eyes changed colour from blue to brown. If you can't explain that, I think it's safe to assume that the body found in Mexico was not that of Brian Latimer, and there is thus every reason to suppose that he is still alive.'

There was a long silence after Rhodes slunk out of the house. He had barely commented on the shock news, other than to say he would look into the matter. Eventually, Barbara said, 'Thank you, Adam, that was terrific. Do you really believe that Brian is still alive?' Her eyes were wide; innocence shone out of them. Which only proves how good women are at acting.

'Of course I do; in fact I'll go further. I know very well that he's alive, as you do. And the reason I know that is that you spent a week in Rowandale Forest taking care of him.'

Barbara gasped, but managed to ask, 'How did you know?'

I took that as an admission of defeat.

'You told us so yourself, although you didn't know it, and it took a while for the significance of what you said to sink in.'

'What did I say? What gave the game away?'

'When I said I thought you'd been in Rowandale Forest and that the tramp might have been Stan Calvert, you implied I was close to the truth but far from it. That suggested you had been there, but with someone else. The only other person who knows the forest that well is Brian Latimer. Then you said the future of Linden House was out of your hands and out of Rhodes'. Those two remarks convinced me, the evidence of the height and eye colour was merely confirmation that I was right.'

'How is he?' Eve asked. 'Adam and I were very concerned about him. When Adam saw those dreadful marks on his back he knew he must have been subjected to some terrible torture. We wondered how that treatment had affected him mentally. Adam thought he might have been held prisoner in North Vietnam.'

Barbara's face clouded over, her distress apparent. 'He spent three years in a prison camp there before he managed to escape. It's taken all this time for him to return to England. His memory was badly affected, to begin with, and he had no idea who he was, even when he reached the forest. He was in the American army and he doesn't think they even know he survived. For most of the time he was a prisoner they kept him in a cage that was no more than six feet high and four feet wide. They covered it with blankets so that he was in the dark for twenty-three hours a day. Once a week or so they took him out and beat him. Even now, after all this time, he can't bear to be in an enclosed space for any length of time.'

'How is his memory now?'

'Improving all the time. I didn't intend to stay away, but I found him in the forest. When I saw him at the stables that day when he saved me from Charles, I had my suspicions, I had to find out. I had an idea whereabouts he might be, if it were him.' She blushed. 'It's in the heart of the forest, a place we used to go to when we were young. He's built a little cabin there, it's really quite cosy, but when I found him he was suffering a bout of malaria, another souvenir of the war. I stayed and nursed him until the attack passed.'

'It must have been cold and miserable in the forest at this time of year,' Eve observed. Her face was expressionless; too much so, I thought.

Barbara smiled and with a touch of pride said, 'Not a bit of it. Brian has made the cabin really snug. With an open fire it's really comfortable.'

'But you must have been exhausted, nursing Brian, and with nowhere to sleep, to rest even.'

Barbara didn't reply, but her face was crimson with embarrassment.

'Eve,' I said sternly, 'stop tormenting Barbara. It isn't nice.'

As we returned to Laithbrigg, there was only one topic of conversation. I hesitated before tackling the subject; aware that Barbara and Eve had been friends for a long time. 'Judging by Barbara's reaction, I'd say there was more to her interest in Brian Latimer than merely concern for a friend. In fact, going from her expression when you were teasing her, I think that when she was caring for him, she also … er … they were … '

'Sleeping together? Of course they were, Adam. That much was blatantly obvious. I'd go further; I don't think it's the first time. Far from it.'

'How do you work that out? They haven't seen one another for years and years.'

'That only proves my point. Barbara isn't the type to jump into bed with someone unless there is far more to the relationship than sex. It would have to be someone she cares deeply about. I wouldn't be a bit surprised if she and Brian were lovers before he went away. Perhaps if he hadn't gone they would have been married long since. And perhaps she would never have got involved with a loser like Charles Lewis.'

'Those are fairly strong assumptions, Evie.'

'True, but if you think about it, she and Brian were more or less brought up together. Barbara was a very attractive girl; one any man would have wanted. Going from what we've been told about Brian Latimer I think he'd be just her type.'

'If you're right, let's hope it all works out for them. They've been through enough, so maybe they're due some happiness.'

'You know, Adam, sometimes you're quite romantic.'

'Ah, that's because I hoped to appeal to your sweet nature so that I could have my wicked way with you later.'

'I thought the fact that I am always tired was because I wasn't used to the country air. Now I reckon it's because I never seem to get a full night's sleep.'

'I haven't heard you object. Quite the opposite, wasn't it you who woke me up and seduced me two nights ago?'

'Did I? I thought I dreamed that.'

'Going back to the subject of Barbara and Brian, the only reservation I have about their relationship is what Ogden's reaction would be if he found out they were lovers. I doubt whether he would give it the same seal of approval that we have. In fact, I'd be prepared to bet he would see it as a prime motive for them to have murdered Barbara's ex-husband.'

I believe I've said before that I ought to stop making these prophecies. They're turning out to be far too accurate; far too often.

Chapter Fourteen

We'd arranged to go to Harrogate the following day; our prime objective being to discuss the design of an extension to Dene Cottage with an old schoolfriend of mine, who was beginning to gain an excellent reputation as an architect. The meeting was a success, to the extent that he was happy to take the project on. That was fine by us, and equally important, Eve was happy with the choice of someone she felt confident would do the project justice.

To make a day of it we went shopping. Eve, who had been used to the wide range of retail outlets in central London, was surprised and impressed by the scope and quality of the spa town's shops. To cap it off, I introduced Eve to the delights of Harrogate's famous Betty's Café, before we took a leisurely drive home.

On our return, we unloaded our purchases, which for the most part comprised Christmas presents for Eve's family, hopefully soon to be my in-laws. We were busy storing them in the spare bedroom when we were interrupted by the doorbell.

'It's far too late for visitors. Send them away; whoever it is,' Eve told me as I went downstairs, which promised well for an early night.

Unfortunately, that was far easier said than done. The caller was John Pickersgill, and the news he brought was alarming enough to drive all thoughts of a romantic interlude out of my mind. 'Ogden's made an arrest,' he greeted me.

I gestured for him to enter.

'He's gone one better this time; he's actually charged

someone with all three murders.'

'Who is it?'

Pickersgill shook his head. 'That's the problem; I don't know. None of us do, not even Ogden. The man he's charged refuses to give his name. In fact, from what I was told, he's refused to utter a single word since he was apprehended. All I know is what Ogden told me. Apparently the man is a tramp, who has been living rough in Rowandale Forest. You wouldn't happen to know anything about him, would you?'

'Me, why should I know anything?'

I don't think my air of innocence deceived Pickersgill for even a split second, for he eyed me with deep suspicion. 'What happened?' I asked, keen to change the subject. 'How did Ogden come to arrest him?'

'That's part of the reason I'm here; part of the reason I thought you might know something about this mystery man. Apparently, Ogden was far from convinced that Barbara Lewis had nothing to do with her husband's murder. He reasoned that she might well have arranged for someone else to kill her husband, ensuring that she had a cast-iron alibi for the time of the murder. With that in mind, he set up covert surveillance on Linden House and they apprehended the tramp first thing this morning as he was leaving the house. He managed to elude them, but in the process he caught his foot on a stone as he was vaulting the wall alongside the stable block. He wasn't injured, only winded, but it gave Ogden and Boy Blunder chance to put the handcuffs on him. Ogden's been questioning him all day, but so far he hasn't got a single word out of the man.'

Pickersgill paused, and then dealt the second of his hammer blows. 'He's also been trying to get something out of his other detainee, but Barbara Lewis isn't talking either.'

He saw my look of surprise. 'Oh yes, Ogden has

charged Barbara too. At the moment he's only got her as an accessory to three murders, but knowing Ogden, within twenty-four hours he'll probably have added treason and several other charges to his list. He's not very happy that they won't cooperate, even though Barbara did speak to confirm her name; and to ask that you and Miss Samuels be told of the arrests. That's why I'm here. Now why do you think she would do that, if you don't know what's going on?'

The question was unanswerable, so I did the only thing I could think of, which was to ignore it. 'Would you like a cup of tea? I'll put the kettle on and give Eve a shout.'

He nodded acceptance, and I went to the bottom of the stairs and called for Eve to join us. The problem I now faced was how to consult Eve on whether to reveal what we knew without giving the game away to Pickersgill. Amiable and friendly he might have been, but he was still a serving police officer with a job to do. As it transpired, thankfully, his opening remarks to Eve solved the problem for me.

'I'm sorry to disturb you, but this is urgent. Ogden has arrested the tramp and Barbara Lewis. The tramp won't give his name, and Barbara requested we inform you, so Ogden asked me to come and find out what you know about the man.'

'He thinks because Barbara mentioned us, we must be privy to all her secrets,' I added quickly. 'John doesn't believe me, so I thought you might be able to persuade him.'

I stressed the last few words slightly. I'm not sure whether Pickersgill caught the emphasis, but Eve certainly did. 'I'm sorry,' she told him with a sweet smile, 'I've no idea, but she might open up to me, if you want me to try? Are they being kept in custody or whatever you call it overnight?'

'That's right. They're being held in Thorsby police

station until tomorrow morning, when they'll be transferred to the cells at Dinsdale.'

'Then we ought to go to Thorsby first thing. Perhaps if you let me speak to her I might be able to help,' Eve said. 'What time will the transfer take place?'

'Not until after Ogden gets there, so we're talking about nine o'clock at the earliest. But you'll need me along to get you in.'

We arranged to collect Pickersgill early the next day, and when he'd left, we discussed tactics. 'Obviously, neither of them is ready to reveal Brian's identity yet, so perhaps we should keep quiet about it?' I suggested.

'I think we'll have to, at least for the time being.'

'But if they're held in custody for any length of time I think we'll have to speak out. I'm concerned for what Latimer might be going through. Barbara told us about how claustrophobic he is as a result of his Vietnam ordeal. I'm worried that being in a police cell for a few days and nights might do his mental state irreparable damage.'

By 7.30 the next morning we had collected Pickersgill and were on our way to the small market town of Thorsby, which housed the police station where Ogden and his team had set up their base for the murder enquiries. It was one of those units that didn't warrant opening twenty-four hours a day. Crime in the area was not exactly rife, and the expense wasn't considered justifiable. Out of office hours, the station was closed except when there were guests in their cells, when two uniformed officers would be in charge overnight. Pickersgill told us that the men liked the task as it meant valuable overtime, and in one case at least, got him away from his wife. Their usual duty was to supervise the board and lodging of any otherwise law-abiding citizens who had over-indulged their taste for alcoholic refreshment. Taking control of two people charged with murder was, he believed, a unique event in the station's history.

'This rural idyll isn't all it's cracked up to be,' Eve told us as I manoeuvred the car round the tight bends of Bleak Fell. 'I never used to get up this early in London.'

I swung the wheel to circumnavigate the final hairpin before reaching the summit. Ahead and to the west, the undulating hills and valleys of the Dales were visible in the early morning light. It was a clear morning, with a touch of frost in the air, and the view was staggeringly beautiful, stretching all the way to where the Pennines, the spine of northern England, ran north to south.

I gestured in front of me. 'On the other hand, you don't get views like that in London.'

'I suppose you're right, but the view would still be the same in a couple of hours' time, wouldn't it?'

'Some women are never satisfied. You have superb scenery, a quiet rural life – and me. What more could you want?'

'Hah! A quiet rural life? Is that what you call it? I like your terminology. I suppose you think it's quiet because there have only been three murders in the past fortnight? I'd hate to think how many there would be when it gets busy.'

'It *was* peaceful until you arrived. There hadn't been a murder for ages. You seem to attract them. Look what happened last Christmas. You arrived and dead bodies appeared all over the place.'

'It's lucky for you that you're driving this car otherwise I might be tempted to add to the body count.'

I glanced in the rear-view mirror in time to see the grin on Pickersgill's face. 'I don't know what you're laughing at. I hope you've taken note of what she said, Officer. That was a clear and unmistakeable threat from a woman with a history of violence. Did you know that within a couple of hours of meeting her, she'd given me a black eye? Totally unprovoked, it was.'

Eve interrupted, 'Unprovoked? I like that. A total distortion of the truth. Ignore him, John. I'll have you know it was Adam that assaulted me.'

'I didn't assault you; all I did was kiss you.'

'Yes, and look where that landed you.'

I gave her a sideways glance and Eve suddenly realized I'd put a totally different interpretation on her words to the one she'd intended. 'I meant in that dungeon,' she hissed.

'Oh, I thought it meant when you seduced me. I tell you, she's a very wicked woman, John.'

'Don't bring me into your squabbles. I was just thinking that you sound like an old married couple. It's as if I never left home this morning.'

It was still well before the normal opening time for the station when we pulled up outside. Thorsby's streets were still deserted, and the few pedestrians and cars that were about all seemed to be heading for the nearby marketplace.

'We'll have time for a cuppa, and I should be able to persuade the duty officers to allow you to have a word with Barbara Lewis before Ogden gets here,' Pickersgill told us as he opened the rear door of the car.

He stopped in the process of getting out and muttered, 'That's strange.'

'What is?' Eve and I asked in unison.

'The front door of the station; it's wide open. It shouldn't be. They never leave it open out of office hours.'

'Maybe one of them stepped outside for a fag, or went to collect bacon butties for their breakfast,' Eve suggested. 'Come to think of it, I could murder one myself.'

'Perhaps you're right.' Pickersgill didn't sound convinced, but I don't think any of us was prepared for what we found after Eve and I followed him into the station.

The tiny reception area and the small office, which was little more than a cubicle, to the left of it were both deserted. The only sign of life was the music, which we could hear coming from a transistor radio in the office.

'They usually sit in there,' John told us, pointing to the room. 'They listen to the radio, or read, or do crosswords. Most of the time I think they try to sleep. One of them at least ought to be in there. I'd better go check the cells.'

As he opened the door leading to the corridor containing the cells we could see that it too was deserted. I was beginning to feel as those who had first boarded the *Marie Celeste* must have, finding the ship abandoned. Eve and I waited, but not for long. After a few seconds Pickersgill returned, his pace little short of a headlong stampede.

'Prisoners all present and correct?' I asked, but then stopped short as I noticed the expression on his face.

'There are prisoners in the cells, right enough.' As he spoke, Pickersgill went through into the office. 'They may be present, but they're certainly not correct.'

'What do you mean?'

'I mean that the prisoners in the cells aren't the ones who were supposed to be there.'

He snatched a bunch of keys from the top of the desk and Eve and I followed him into the corridor. We watched as he tried several keys from the bunch before he succeeded in opening the first of the cell doors, and we were able to see the man sitting uncomfortably on the narrow, hard bunk on one side of the small room.

His discomfort didn't stem from the bed, but from his wrists, which were secured behind his back with handcuffs; and the handkerchief which had been converted into a makeshift gag. Only the stripes on the sleeves of his tunic showed he was a sergeant. Eve and I exchanged glances of astonishment as we watched Pickersgill remove the gag and as he tried to find a key to fit the handcuffs, the sergeant began his explanation. It was one he'd had plenty of time to rehearse, we learned as he told his tale.

'It was about nine o'clock last night when it happened.

I know that because I was listening to the news on the radio. We heard the woman shouting; screaming for help, she was. She said the man in the cell next to her was having some sort of a fit. We opened the door and it looked like she was right. He was lying on the floor, writhing and thrashing about, his face all contorted and twitching, and foaming at the mouth. He was muttering something, but we couldn't make sense of what he was saying. I told Joe to go phone for an ambulance whilst I went to put the prisoner in the recovery position, like we're taught on the first aid courses. That was when he moved. I tell you; he was like greased lightning. One second he was on the floor, to all intents and purposes completely out of it; the next he was on his feet and he'd got me in some sort of fancy wrestling hold. Then I felt his fingers pressing on my neck and I passed out. When I came round I was handcuffed and gagged. What happened to Joe? Is he all right?'

'He's in the next cell,' Pickersgill told him. 'Looks as if he's had the same treatment as you. I'll go release him and we'll find out. I'm still amazed that this man, whoever he is, managed to subdue the pair of you without you putting up a struggle.' He shook his head. 'There's going to be a stewards' enquiry about it when Ogden gets here, that's for sure.'

'Thanks for reminding me,' the sergeant snapped. He massaged his wrist where the handcuff had chafed. 'I was feeling bad enough already, John, without your help.'

Once we had watched the release of the constable, whose story matched that of his superior more or less word for word; Eve suggested we should leave before Ogden arrived.

'No fear,' I told her. 'I wouldn't miss this for all the tea in China. If I'd known beforehand I could have sold tickets for it. We're not in London now; we have to make our own entertainment around here.'

Eve gave me a long, thoughtful stare. 'I never realized it, but there's a streak of sadism in you, Adam Bailey.'

'Adam's right,' Pickersgill interrupted. 'You ought to stay. Not for the amusement part, although that will be worth witnessing. However, if you're here it just might rein in Ogden from calling down the wrath of the Almighty on those two. Either that, or blowing a gasket,' he added with a grin.

As we waited for the inspector to arrive, most of the time was spent fending off or ignoring John's questions regarding the identity of the tramp, as he referred to Barbara's companion. 'You do realize this will merely reinforce Ogden's opinion that the pair of them must be guilty, don't you?'

I acknowledged the truth of this. To anyone who didn't know Latimer's background and his dreadful claustrophobia, their actions in going on the run from police custody could only be construed as having sinister implications. 'That may be so, but there could be other reasons for them to have run away.'

'Such as? I can't think of one offhand.'

Neither could I. Not one I could reveal without risking exposing Brian Latimer's identity and alluding to the nature of his relationship with Barbara, which is exactly what Eve and I were trying to avoid. I chose my words very carefully as I replied. 'If I was you, I would attempt to discourage Ogden from that line of thinking. Believe me, it wouldn't do him or his career any good whatsoever. That might sound like an idle threat at present, but I feel sure eventually you will recognize the soundness of my advice.'

'What I do recognize is that the pair of you are withholding information in a big way. You're lucky we're not having this conversation in front of Ogden, or he'd have you thrown in the cells for obstruction.'

That, as it turned out, was what Ogden threatened. His

initial reaction to the news of the jailbreak was predictably explosive. After some minutes, he calmed down, which I guessed was because shock, disbelief, and fear of the consequences had begun to take over. Having listened to the sergeant's tale twice, he searched for a scapegoat other than the two hapless uniformed officers. He didn't have to look far. His opening words made it clear we had been selected for that dubious distinction. 'You're in league with them, I'm certain of it. Can you vouch for your whereabouts last night?'

'I take it you're referring to the time the prison breakout occurred?'

My flippant description of the escape enraged Ogden even more. 'Nine o'clock it happened. Where were you then?'

'At home.'

'At home? Oh, how very convenient.' I have to admit that Ogden did a very good sneer when he put his mind to it. 'And I suppose you have only each other to witness your alibi.'

'Er ... no, as a matter of fact there was someone else.'

'Oh yes, another close friend, I suppose. Someone you can rely on to cover for you.'

'Not exactly a close friend; and I don't think you should make slanderous suggestions about people until you know the full circumstances.'

I have to admit I was drawing it out, tormenting Ogden. But then, I reckoned he'd earned it.

'Very well,' he breathed heavily, 'Who is this *reliable* witness?'

I gestured to my left, where John was talking to the other officers. 'PC Pickersgill. He came to our house to relay a message from you. I know he'll confirm the time, because he checked his watch when our lounge clock struck the hour.'

Ogden seethed in silence for a few minutes, then;

thwarted in his attempt to prove our direct involvement in the truancy, changed his point of attack. 'You may not have been involved personally, but I'm sure you know far more about it than you've told us. I would be well within my rights to have you locked up for obstruction.'

'I wouldn't risk it,' I told him. 'Remember, I have a lot of friends and former colleagues in the national and international media. One or two phonecalls and they'd be here like a shot. If I was you, I'd be tempted to remain a local laughing stock rather than ruin your reputation worldwide. Added to which, you've not exactly got a good record when it comes to keeping hold of prisoners, have you? I mean, locked up two, mislaid two isn't much of a recommendation for your security measures, is it?'

For a moment, I wondered if I'd pushed Ogden too far. He looked as if he was about to explode. I was concerned that his blood pressure might be reaching dangerously high levels, so attempted to calm him down. My efforts met with mixed success.

'Look, Inspector, let's be straight about this. We know very little more than you do. What we are sure of is that Barbara Lewis could not have committed these crimes, either herself or by proxy. I also think you could be treading on dangerous ground if you continue to pursue the stranger everyone refers to as a tramp. I've only seen him a couple of times, but anyone less like a tramp you could not imagine. It would be dangerously foolish to underestimate someone simply because they prefer the simple outdoor life. It does not necessarily mean that they're impoverished, or dishonest – or,' I added with great emphasis, 'that they lack powerful and influential friends who could have a detrimental influence on your career.'

At the time I was speaking the veiled threat in my final statement was little more than guesswork. It was a week or so later before another of my prophecies was fulfilled, and the extent of Latimer's influence became apparent.

Ogden waved my warning aside and told us to get out of his sight. I signalled to Pickersgill, who strolled across to our car. 'Where do you think you're going?' Ogden roared after him.

'Back to Laithbrigg with them. I could wait and get a lift with you, but I thought you'd be too busy. I feel sure the chief constable will be keen to hear your account of what happened to the prisoners.'

At John's insistence, the return journey involved a detour via Rowandale. There was no sign of life at Linden House. The building was securely locked, so Pickersgill announced that he intended to go interview the stable lads.

'I've a key if you want to look inside,' Eve said. 'Barbara gave me it while I was staying with her.'

'I can't do that,' Pickersgill told us. 'Ogden's already executed the search warrant for this property. However,' he looked at Eve, 'there's nothing to stop you going inside. Especially if you're concerned about your friend. For all you know she might be helplessly in the grip of a homicidal maniac. I'd say it was your duty to check.'

The house felt cold and I was certain the absconding prisoners weren't in residence. Eve went to check upstairs whilst I had a look round in the kitchen. The first thing I noticed was two used mugs in the sink. That was an indication that the couple might have been here, but were no more. However, when I opened the refrigerator, I knew that my guess had been accurate. The main compartment was all but empty, as was the ice box above it. I turned my attention to the freezer, and found this to be no more than half full. I had no idea if anything had been taken out of it or not.

Eve had returned to the ground floor and was opening and closing doors. I tracked her down to the hallway, where she was peering into the clothes cupboard. 'What are you looking for?'

She closed the door and turned round. 'Something that isn't there. Barbara has been here, that's for certain. She's taken a lot of warm clothing, jumpers, thermal underwear, thick cords, and so forth. I looked in here,' she gestured behind her, 'and her wellingtons, hiking boots, scarves, gloves, and Barbour coat are all missing.'

'It looks as if they're planning a prolonged stay in the forest,' I agreed. 'The fridge is empty, so is the ice box, and the freezer is only half full. It looks to me as if they've taken all the food they can carry.'

'You're joking! The freezer was full to the brim. When I went shopping with Babs we bought half a dozen large pizzas. We had to put them in the fridge ice box because there was no room for them in the freezer.'

'What do we tell John?'

'I don't like deceiving him.'

'We're already doing that by not telling him who Brian is.'

'Perhaps we'd be better off simply saying we can't be certain.'

Minutes later, in answer to Pickersgill's question, I said, 'They're not in the house. Nobody is. They might have been here, but we can't be sure. What did the stable lads have to say?'

'Barbara left a note for them pinned to the door of one of the loose boxes. She told them she would be away for a few days, but that they should carry on as normal. That's all.'

'What do you plan to do now?'

'Go home, if you'd be so kind as to drop me off. I'm going to see how Ogden reacts before I decide my next move.'

It was over a week before we learned what Pickersgill's next move was, by which time the hue and cry was in full swing, and had taken on similar dimensions to the TV series, *The Fugitive*. So much so that one of the more enterprising reporters had compared Barbara's companion to the lead character portrayed by David Janssen.

In retrospect, although he has never confirmed or denied it since, I think Pickersgill had guessed the tramp's identity. I believe that Pickersgill opted to wait in order to give Ogden chance to change his mind and redeem himself, or to continue on his reckless self-destructive path.

Ogden, naturally, did the latter.

Chapter Fifteen

Although we were both concerned by the problems besetting Barbara and Latimer, we were comforted by the knowledge that if Latimer had survived undetected in Rowandale Forest for that length of time, the efforts of Ogden to capture or dislodge them were scarcely likely to cause them much concern. Nor, as I pointed out to Eve, could Barbara be in safer hands, especially if our suspicions as to the true nature of their relationship were accurate.

Over the ensuing days, Rowandale became the focus for the attention of most of the local population; certainly almost everyone who was sufficiently mobile to get within range of the manhunt. It had to be one of the most exciting events in the area for many a long year, competing with the recent murders for that dubious honour.

The locals were joined by a considerable and growing contingent of media representatives. To begin with these were from the regional networks and newspapers, but they were soon augmented by national press, radio, and television reporters, together with their entourages.

It was towards the end of the first week that one of them hit on the eye-catching headline 'Bonnie and Clyde on the run – Again!' Quite where he got the resemblance between Barbara and Latimer and those murderous bank robbers from, I'm not sure. I could see no similarity in their characters to Warren Beatty or Faye Dunaway.

Not to be outdone, another continued with *The Fugitive* theme and came up with 'Eat your heart out, Dr Richard Kimble'. The effect of these two headlines was to escalate the media interest from national to worldwide status. Rowandale was all but impassable, the narrow streets being choked with vehicles belonging to the media.

As far as the search itself was concerned, Ogden, who had become something of a minor television personality, was fortunate enough to have the assistance of a regiment from the nearby garrison at Catterick, whose commanding officer volunteered them in order to give his men some rough terrain and jungle experience by helping search for the fugitives in Rowandale Forest.

Along with many others we watched in bemused wonder at this circus. I suspect that many of the other onlookers shared our disbelief at this reckless expenditure of resources. The whole thing was conducted like a military operation, with military precision, and military predictability. As I observed the long line of soldiers and police officers marching in single file towards the outskirts of the forest, I gave an appalling imitation of Winston Churchill.

'Never,' I told Eve, 'in the history of Rowandale, have so many spent so much time searching for so few.'

'I get your point,' Eve agreed. 'But you'll never make it as an impressionist.'

'It's ludicrous; they end the search when the light fails each evening, and then start again at dawn the next day, looking in a different area. All Brian and Barbara have to do is move to the area that was searched the previous day and as long as they don't build a fire and start cooking bacon, they'll be perfectly safe. As long as they stick to that method of searching, they're wasting their time. For all the good they're doing, Brian and Barbara might as well be miles away from Rowandale Forest.'

I stopped speaking suddenly; my brain whirling with the crazy idea that had just occurred to me. I was aware that Eve was speaking, but I failed to take on board what she said.

I looked round; we were standing on the hillside above and slightly to the east of Linden House. Our vantage point was shared with several dozen reporters and local inhabitants, all of whom were experts in the art of eavesdropping. I took Eve's hand and squeezed it gently. 'Let's get out of here. I need to talk to you without anyone else to overhear the question I'm going to ask.'

Once we were safely in the shelter of the car, with the engine running, I asked, 'Remember you said Barbara's freezer was full? What was in the top half, can you recall?'

'There was a lot of meat. Steaks and chops, joints and mince, bacon and sausages. Quite a few packets of frozen vegetables too. Oh, and some cartons of milk and sliced loaves. Why do you ask?'

'If you add that to what was in the refrigerator ice box, how long do you think it would last if only two people were eating it.'

'Weeks and weeks, I reckon.' As she answered my questions, Eve was looking at me with a curious expression on her face. I was convinced she thought I'd taken leave of my senses. Especially when I started laughing. I put the car into gear and took the handbrake off.

'Where are we going?'

'Back home; we're wasting our time here.'

'Adam, are you all right?'

'I'm fine, Evie, but I reckon I know where Brian and Barbara are hiding, and that lot –' I gestured towards the forest, '– haven't a cat in hell's chance of finding them.'

'Why not? Where do you think they are?'

'Bearing in mind that Ogden has no idea of the tramp's identity, where do you think is the last place he'd look for them.'

'Of course: Rowandale Hall!'

'It was the sheer volume of frozen food they took from Linden House that gave me the idea. If they'd taken all that into the forest most of it would have gone off before they got round to eating it. Added to which, they'd risk discovery by lighting a fire to cook with. Whereas in Rowandale Hall there would be fridges, freezers, ovens, all they'd need. All the home comforts.'

I heard a rich gurgle of laughter as Eve was overcome by the absurdity of the situation. 'You're dead right, Adam. I'm absolutely sure of it. How very clever of them.'

'That would explain why Brian refused to give his name or reveal anything about himself when Ogden tried to question him. Without any clues to suggest otherwise, Ogden would assume he would return to the forest where he'd been living all these months. All that warm clothing Barbara took from Linden House was part of the smokescreen. They knew we'd be the most likely ones to look, and they wanted us to be deceived along with everyone else.'

'Why? Why try to fool us? We wouldn't have given the game away. Surely Barbara would know that.'

'They might have been worried that we'd do it accidentally, or go racing across to Rowandale Hall. For all they knew Ogden might have put a tail on us. Besides which, if we behaved exactly as we did, by watching what was happening in the forest, it would help their deception strategy.'

'How? In what way would it help?'

'Remember Ogden's immediate reaction on learning they'd escaped? He rounded on us; convinced we had to have been involved. With that as his mindset, what more natural than to keep an eye on us, to see if we could point him to where the fugitives were. The longer we watched the forest, the more convinced he would become that they were inside it.'

'That's extremely deep thinking, Adam.'

'Yes, and I'd say it shows that Brian Latimer is no mean tactician.'

Next morning, we had barely finished breakfast and cleared the dining table when we received a visit from the local police. John Pickersgill's car pulled up outside, and was quickly joined by two more. Both of these were far more luxurious than the local officer's. I watched the trio of men walking down our short drive, reflecting that we might need to incorporate a car park into our plans to revamp Dene Cottage. As they approached, I recognized one of them, but only vaguely.

'We've got visitors, Eve.'

She peered out of the window. 'That's Detective Inspector Hardy, isn't it? One of the officers who came to Mulgrave Castle; he was leading the inquiry.'

'Yes, I think you're right. I thought I knew the face, but couldn't put a name to it.'

'Hardly surprising; you were badly concussed when you met him.'

It was Hardy who greeted me as I opened the door, and introduced his colleague. I glanced at the chief constable, and was immediately struck by the family likeness to his cousin John. I suppose this appeared to be more pronounced because they were standing close together.

'We need to talk to you and Miss Samuels as a matter of some urgency,' the chief constable told me.

I invited them inside and offered them a cup of tea. All three accepted, and having ascertained how they took their drinks, I told the chief constable, 'I ought to warn you that if you're to become regular visitors, I might have to invoice you for refreshments. Your cousin already costs me a small fortune in tea bags.'

The chief constable gave me a piercing stare, one which would have nervous recruits trembling at the knees. I guessed this to be habitual, for his face soon relaxed into a smile. 'So John told you we're related, did he? That's good, because he doesn't mention it to many people. Shows he trusts you, which is good enough for me.'

When we were settled with our drinks, he continued. 'I'm taking you into my confidence on John's assurance; backed up by Detective Inspector Hardy. I was a little reluctant, given your previous career in the media, but both of them seemed convinced it was the right thing to do. Will you both give me your word that what I am about to tell you will remain completely confidential?'

Having received our promise, he went on. 'Tomorrow, Detective Inspector Hardy will be taking over responsibility for the investigation of all three murders. Inspector Ogden will be re-assigned to other duties. I'd like Hardy to start with all the facts at his disposal, and John told me he was under the impression that there might be some information that you possessed which hadn't been given to Ogden. In particular, he told me he believes you might know more than Ogden about this mysterious tramp he believes committed the crimes. Is that so?'

I looked at Eve for guidance, and saw that like me, she was undecided. 'That's not easy to answer,' I told them. 'Yes, we may know or suspect something, but we have other confidences to keep, not just the one we've given you.'

'I'm not sure if this helps,' Hardy interrupted, 'but I can assure you I'll start the inquiry with a completely open mind. I won't rule anything out, but on the other hand I won't take anything for granted.'

I looked at Eve again, and by way of answer, she told the detective. 'The tramp didn't commit the murder. I don't know who did, neither does Adam, but I can safely say that any time you spend investigating him will be wasted. Apart from anything else, the man isn't a tramp at all. If you listen to Adam, he'll tell you the man's identity and then you can judge for yourself.'

Rather than going straight ahead with the identification, I led them to it by a circuitous route. I was pleased I had, because in the course of it, the chief constable strengthened my case by contributing some useful background.

'How well do you know the recent history of Rowandale Hall and the estate?' I asked.

'Very well,' the chief constable replied. 'I was a regular guest on the estate when Rupert Latimer was fit enough to organize and hold his own shooting parties. We also played golf together regularly, and when his wife was alive we dined with them quite frequently.'

I seized on this information, drawing him closer into the tale. 'You'll have met the tramp quite often, then,' I told him.

'Why, did he work for Rupert?'

'No, but he would be there most of the time, when he was younger, certainly.'

He sighed. 'You'd better tell me his name, if you know it.'

'I do. His name is Brian Latimer.'

I believe I could have exploded a grenade in the room at that point and neither man would have noticed. They stared at me with utter disbelief written clearly in their expressions.

The chief constable was the first to recover. 'That's impossible; Brian Latimer is dead. He died a long time ago.'

I held up my hand. 'Please, don't give me that Mexico story again. That body wasn't Brian Latimer. I saw the pathologist's report and checked certain facts with Barbara Lewis. The report states that the dead man's eyes were brown, and Barbara confirmed verbally and with photographic evidence that Brian Latimer has blue eyes. She should know, she's stared into them often enough; both recently and when they were youngsters.'

'I never saw that report.' The chief constable's face was sad. 'If I had, I would have known that the body couldn't have been Brian's. You're right, he did ... er ... does have blue eyes. Poor Rupert; he died without knowing Brian was still alive. That knowledge might have helped him get over the guilt he felt because of what happened years ago. If the man Ogden has down as a tramp is Brian Latimer, I think we'll have to look elsewhere for the killer.' He smiled ruefully, before adding, 'The reason I know so much about Brian is that I'm his godfather.'

If I thought I was good at delivering conversation-stopping speeches, the chief constable was even better. Eventually, Hardy leaned forward and asked, 'Can you tell us the whole story; or as much of it as you can?'

We began to relate what we could, starting with Eve's encounter with the tramp at the stables. I explained what we'd discovered about Brian's past, including the imprisonment and torture, which shocked all three men immeasurably. The effect on his memory and his severe claustrophobia merely added to their horror at what Latimer had suffered.

After we finished giving the facts as we knew them, there was a silence as all three reflected on the shocks they'd received. Hardy cleared his throat. 'I think the chief constable's opinion has to be taken into account, as well as your knowledge of Latimer, and with that in mind I shall rule him out as a possible suspect for the murders. I will issue orders that the arrest warrants for him and Mrs Lewis are to be cancelled, and we'll make a fresh start.'

He smiled at Eve and me. 'As it appears you're the best detectives in the area; can you tell us if you've any idea who committed the murders, and what the motive might have been?'

'I wouldn't go that far, but we we've been lucky enough to view the case from the inside, so perhaps we've been able to pick up things that Ogden missed. One of them in particular we found interesting.'

'And that was?'

'Several members of the shooting syndicate that now holds the rights at the Rowandale estate are involved in the construction and civil engineering industry. That in itself isn't sinister, but when you add in the proposed new trunk road which will cut across the estate, and which will entail the use of a lot of sand, gravel, aggregate, and road-stone, all of which is contained within the estate, then you get a very interesting possible scenario. Especially as they seem desperate to get their hands on the estate. Even then I have a feeling there might be still more to it than just the trunk road, but as to what the full motive might be, I don't know.'

Hardy accepted that, and made a couple of notes in a small Filofax he had pulled from his coat pocket. After a few seconds he looked up. 'Strictly off the record; do you know where Brian Latimer and Barbara Lewis are?'

'No, we don't,' Eve spoke before I had chance. 'Not for certain, although Adam has a theory. In fact,' she added, 'I've never known Adam not to have a theory.'

'I'm not suggesting you tell us, but if you can get word to them, please inform them that they are no longer being sought, and that it's quite safe for them to come out of hiding.'

The chief constable turned to Hardy. 'We must also remember to notify the Mexican authorities that their victim isn't Latimer.'

They thanked us and with Pickersgill in tow, headed for the door. 'This has been very interesting,' I told the chief constable. 'It's the first time I've seen John sitting for so long without speaking.'

The chief grinned. 'Me too; and I've known him far longer than you.' He stopped with one hand on the doorknob and handed me a fifty-pence piece. 'For the tea bags.'

I think I may have mentioned before that I ought to stop making prophecies, because of the regularity with which they come true. My comment to Hardy that there may be more to the motive for the murders than the trunk road scheme was another example. However, this one would bring danger to Brian and Barbara; a danger they shared with Eve and me.

Chapter Sixteen

'How are we going to set about getting the news to Brian and Barbara?' Eve asked.

'What do you mean?'

'If we simply walk up to the door of the Hall and knock, I doubt they would answer. They won't know it isn't a trap. For all they know, we might have been persuaded or bullied into cooperating with the police. Remember, their only experience of the local force is with Ogden.'

'You have a point.' I thought over the problem for a minute. Eve had thrown up a snag I hadn't foreseen. 'Why don't you write a note to Barbara, explaining why we're there and we can take it with us, knock on the door, and push the note through the letterbox. If you phrase it right, once they've read it, they should realize that we're there to help, and hopefully they'll know that we haven't been put up to it.'

Between us we concocted the note and later that afternoon, as the light was beginning to fade, we set off. Shortly before we left, I had an idea. I nipped into the study and collected the gold coin I'd secreted in my desk drawer and put it in my coat pocket.

The weather had turned appreciably colder during the day, and there was a feeling of snow in the air. As I drove, I glanced around; the sky was uniformly leaden-grey, another indicator of what we might be in for. I mentioned the possibility to Eve, who groaned. 'Not again; I thought we'd had enough of travelling in snow last winter.'

Our first problem came when we reached the entrance

to Rowandale Hall. The lodge was empty. I remembered hearing gossip in the village pub. 'The caretaker who lives there is away visiting his daughter and her family in California. I recall overhearing someone talking about it in the Admiral Nelson last week,' I told Eve.

His absence didn't create the problem in itself, but the ten-feet-high wrought iron gates were secured with three chains, each bearing a sturdy padlock, set at varying heights. 'He obviously wasn't leaving anything to chance,' Eve commented, pointing at the chains. 'What do we do now?'

'One thing's for sure, it's scuppered any plans I had for driving up to the front door.'

'There must be another entrance if Babs and Brian have got in.'

Eve was right; the problem was in finding it. We were already in semi-darkness, and missing a narrow lane, or choosing the wrong one, would be easy to do.

During the next thirty minutes, I began to appreciate just how numerous were the cart tracks, unmade roads, and dead ends in the vicinity of the Hall. This snag was compounded by the many promising-looking entrances that led to us staring at a five-barred gate, being eyed with mild curiosity by the sheep or cattle in the field beyond.

As I reversed with considerable difficulty for the fourth or fifth time, my language was less than polite, although deep down I knew the problem was of our own making. We had deliberately delayed setting off for the Hall until dusk, to avoid attracting the attention of the police or media. The amnesty on the runaway couple would not come into force until after Hardy took over the investigation the following day and it was beginning to look as if our haste to inform Brian and Barbara that they were no longer fugitives had backfired on us badly.

Eve put her hand on my arm. 'Hang on, Adam. Why don't we go back to the main gate? The stone wall surrounding the Hall grounds is only about eight or nine feet high. I'm sure we could climb over it and then walk up the drive. It'll be much easier than struggling to find another way in, and you won't swear half as much.'

'Brilliant, Evie. Why didn't I think of that?'

'You don't have a monopoly on good ideas, Adam.'

We parked across the end of the drive, secure in the knowledge that nobody would be using that entrance – unless they had a bulldozer. I took a torch from out of the glove compartment and checked that the batteries weren't dead before we set off for the nearest section of wall.

From a distance, the stonework looked rough, and there appeared to be places where the mortar was missing; giving us good points to establish finger and toeholds. However, it was obvious that the shadows cast by shrubs and bushes surrounding the wall had deceived us. On closer inspection, the surface was smooth, the stones lined up perfectly, and the mortar was intact. 'Let's try further along.'

I followed Eve, knowing there was little alternative. Eventually, the torch beam picked out a promising spot. The mortar had crumbled in places and the long-deceased stonemason had been less than accurate in aligning the stones. Or possibly this was where his apprentice had been doing his training.

Eve scaled the wall first, with my help – or hindrance. As she started her climb, I put my hands out to support her and prevent her from falling. Seconds later, she was astride the top of it.

Now it was my turn. I made it, having acquired several painful bruises to my shins on the way, which provoked a further outburst of Anglo-Saxon. I joined Eve and shone the torch onto the far side to inspect our landing area.

'What are those?' Eve gestured towards the bushes below us. 'Are they what I think?'

In amongst the foliage I could just see one or two dark,

shrivelled fruits that the birds had missed. 'They are – if you think they're brambles. Lots of them by the look of it. Better let me go first and I can clear a space for you.'

Chivalry is all right, but it can have its drawbacks. The descent was far more difficult than the climb had been. Luckily, the bushes, which were capable of delivering countless scratches, did not quite extend to the wall side.

Having reached ground level, I helped Eve down, seizing the chance to hug her as she landed. She didn't seem to object. 'Now all we have to do is battle our way through this lot.' I indicated the wilderness of foliage, which appeared far denser at ground level than it had from above. 'I suppose we could try and force our way straight through. The only problem is we don't know how far they stretch.'

'Why don't we follow the wall back towards the gates? You said yourself that the bushes are thinner close to the wall, and they're bound to have been cut back near the drive.'

We adopted Eve's suggestion, which on reflection was a sound one. I say 'on reflection' because it certainly didn't seem so at the time. It was with considerable relief that we emerged onto the grass that ran alongside the drive. 'Now all we have to do is walk up to the front door, pop the note through the letterbox, and attract their attention.'

My confident statement was greeted by silence. A long silence, which Eve broke eventually. Her voice was soft and apologetic as she said, 'Adam, there's a bit of a problem.'

'What is it?' I went for a little humour. 'Don't tell me – you left the note in the car.'

The silence was even longer. 'You didn't – did you?'

'Yes, Adam. I'm sorry.'

'We'll have to manage without it. One thing's for certain; no way am I going to attempt to fight my way through that Amazonian jungle again unless I have to.'

The drive was protected by trees which gave an eerie backdrop to our path. It seemed to go on for miles, but was probably less than half a mile. During our walk, the only sound was that of Eve's footsteps, and even those seemed curiously muffled. We were no more than half way I guess, when Eve stopped walking. 'Adam, switch your torch on for a second. I think the snow has started. I felt something cold and wet on my hand just now.'

Sure enough, the torch beam picked out occasional snowflakes that drifted lazily across the path of light. Great fun! At least the wind wasn't blowing strongly. I'd forgotten that we were protected by the trees there. When we emerged from the avenue, and the tarmac gave way to gravel that crunched underfoot, I felt the wind sharp and cold on my cheeks. Ahead and to our left I could just make out the massive, dark brooding shape of the mansion.

We walked for a minute longer and then climbed the wide stone steps leading to the front of the building. I switched the torch on; intent on examining the huge oak double doors for a knocker or doorbell, and then started to laugh.

'What's so funny?'

'If I was you, I wouldn't get too upset about that note you left in the car. It wouldn't have done any good even if you had remembered it.' I gestured to the doors. 'There's no letter box.'

'Of course! The mail would be left at the lodge, wouldn't it?'

'Naturally; they wouldn't want the postman trudging all the way up the drive when they had their own man to do it for them.'

'That doesn't help us, though. Got any bright ideas as to what we do next?'

I had a couple of ideas, but neither of them seemed particularly bright. 'I reckon all we can do is hammer on the door, and if you call out for Barbara, we'll just have to hope they hear us. And if they do hear us, we'll have to hope they trust us enough to let us in. One thing for sure, having come so far and gone through all that morass of undergrowth, I'm not about to give up now.'

Ten minutes later my knuckles were getting sore. Added to which, Eve said she was starting to get a sore throat from yelling Barbara's name. 'Wait there a minute,' I told her.

I went back down the steps, which were just beginning to be coated with snow. I found what I was looking for. I returned to Eve and handed her a stone that was about the size of my fist. 'Use that and keep hammering on the door. My hand isn't making enough noise.'

'What are you going to do?'

'I'm going to try round the back. There has to be more than one entrance.'

Like much of what we'd attempted that afternoon, going round to the back of the house was easier said than done. I trudged down the path that ran along the facade of the building for what seemed an age. As I walked, I wondered why people needed to build such enormous houses. When I eventually reached the far end I found my route was blocked by an immense stone wall. No way was I going to even attempt to climb another one that day. As it turned out, climbing that wall would not have done me any good, as it formed the back of the old stable block, converted since mechanisation into a series of garages.

Having reached this impasse, I took the only option open to me and retraced my steps to the front door. I paused for a word with Eve, whose assault on the oak was as yet yielding no results, before continuing my trek. 'Keep it up, Evie, I'm off to try the other end. There has to be a way to get round to the back of this blasted mausoleum somewhere.'

It was as I heard Eve resume her attack on the door that

I was struck by a terrible thought. What if I was wrong? What if Brian and Barbara hadn't taken shelter in the Hall? The idea was only speculation, based on the amount of food they'd taken from Linden House. I didn't think this was worth mentioning to Eve. Certainly not when she had a sizeable rock in her hand.

I reached the right hand side of the mansion and glimpsed what looked like an opening beyond the cornerstones. I was right; it was an arched wrought-iron gate that fronted a path along the side of the building. 'They certainly like their wrought iron around here,' I muttered. 'Probably had their own blacksmith.'

Fortunately, this gate wasn't padlocked, or indeed secured in any way. I touched it and it swung open. I shone my torch, aware that the snow was falling more heavily. I wondered briefly how Eve might feel about spending our winters abroad in future. The path was screened on one side by the building; on the other by some sort of evergreen hedge. Far from keeping the snow off me, this acted as a sort of wind tunnel, channelling the snow that was being driven by a strengthening wind straight into my face. The route to the back of the house was much shorter than the front of the building, and I soon emerged into a large courtyard. I reflected that Rowandale Hall was much like Mulgrave Castle in its layout. That was hardly surprising. There can't have been that many architects working in the area during the Middle Ages.

I walked across the open space to the rear of the building; my efforts were rewarded when I noticed a narrow strip of light at about waist level. This proved to be from the bottom of a window, where the blind failed to reach right to the sill. My mood was lifted immediately, and I felt certain my theory was about to be proved correct. Alongside the window where the light was showing I could just make out the dark oblong of a door. I switched the torch on and stepped forward. As I reached for the doorknob, I stopped abruptly.

There's nothing guaranteed to stop a man in his tracks quite as effectively as having an exceedingly sharp knife pressed none too gently against his windpipe. My assailant had appeared from the shadows silently and swiftly, and I knew at once who he was.

'Brian, it's me. Adam Bailey. Adam and Eve, remember. Barbara's friends. We're here to help. Eve's banging on your front door.' I was desperate to get my message across; not knowing what state of mind Latimer might be in, or how he'd been affected by the recent turmoil in his life.

My attacker didn't reply, but a second later I felt the pressure on my throat ease as he reached past me and opened the door. I was thrust unceremoniously inside and the door was slammed shut. I blinked, accustoming my eyes to the bright light and heard the sound of bolts being drawn across. I was trapped inside the building with someone whose mental state I could not be sure was friendly.

'Go down there; along that passage to your left.'

I obeyed – who wouldn't? I walked along a short corridor, conscious that my knife-wielding assailant was shadowing me closely. A hand on my shoulder stopped me a couple of yards before the end of the passage. 'Open that door; the one on your right.'

I did so and was pushed into the kitchen of Rowandale Hall. The room was massive; big enough to take the whole of the ground floor of Dene Cottage, I guessed. The kitchen contained only one occupant. Barbara Lewis was seated at the table; her expression anxious.

She relaxed slightly when she recognized the intruder. 'Adam! What are you doing here?'

'I've come to bring you some good news.'

I risked a glance over my shoulder and all but failed to recognize Brian Latimer. With the exception of the knife he was carrying, any resemblance to the wild man of the woods had gone. 'Would one of you mind letting Eve in? Your front door might be able to withstand being battered by a rock, but her arm must be getting tired. Added to which it's snowing heavily and she must be getting very cold. She can be very grumpy at times.'

'We can't open the front door, Adam. The police might be watching the house,' Barbara said.

'They're not. We didn't see anyone. That was part of the news I came to give you. You're no longer on the wanted list. The manhunt will be officially called off tomorrow. Ogden has been removed from the investigation and assigned to other duties. I know all this because we had a visit from Brian's godfather this morning.' I noticed Barbara's puzzled frown and added, 'He's the chief constable.'

Five minutes later, Eve and I were reunited, and whilst we drank the tea Barbara provided, we filled them in with all we knew. I let Eve do the talking; she's even better than me at it. Besides which, it gave me chance to study Brian Latimer.

It wasn't only physically that his resemblance to the vagrant had gone. I could see that much of the stress and tension that had been all too apparent on our previous meetings was no longer there. His facial expression; even his posture were much more relaxed. I wasn't sure to begin with if that was due to having the burden of suspicion lifted from him; or whether it was the fact that he was now back in the family home, or a combination of the two.

Then I saw him look at Barbara and realized that it had little to do with either his surroundings or innocence. I suppose my ability to recognize and identify the loving glance they shared might have been heightened by my own situation. I rejoiced quietly at what seemed to be their contentedness.

After a while Brian got up and walked over to one of

the windows facing the courtyard. All the others had shutters in place, which was why they had not shed any light when I had passed them. He twitched open the curtains and stared out. 'There's a blizzard raging out there,' he told us cheerfully. The snow is already settling and it doesn't look like stopping.' He turned to face us. 'Why don't you stay the night? Adam and I can go retrieve his car from the main gate and bring it round the back whilst you girls start preparing dinner.' He smiled ironically and added, 'It's nothing fancy, I'm afraid, only Beef Wellington.'

Faced with the prospect of driving home in a blizzard or staying the night in a country mansion where the offering was my favourite gourmet dish was really no contest. Apart from that, I was pleased to note the humour in Brian's remark and the smile that accompanied almost everything he said; proof to my mind that he was back to normal.

As in many large houses, one of the corridors that ran here and there like the strands of a maze contained a long line of pegs on which were sundry items of clothing to keep out the worst of the British weather. Below them, in neat order of size, was an equally varied selection of footwear for almost all occasions. Once we were suitably attired, Brian collected a key ring containing somewhere in excess of two dozen keys. Half an hour later, with the gate once more secure and the car safely transferred to as close to the back door as I could get, we were back indoors. 'I have to say I'm glad I don't have to drive in those conditions; even the short journey to Laithbrigg would have been a nightmare,' I told our host.

'It seemed pointless,' Brian replied, 'unless you had some urgent reason to be back home. It's not as if we're short of room, and Barbara could do with some company. She's had to put up with me and my problems on her own and that can't have been easy.'

I was surprised that Brian was so open, but then I guessed that Barbara might have told him about Eve and me. 'You seem fine now,' I said, not wishing to push him in any direction he might not wish to go.

'That's all Barbara's doing,' he told me, 'she's helping erase a lot of the bad memories, or at least putting them in their place.'

A couple of hours later we sat down to our evening meal in the splendour of a dining hall that would have seated fifty or more guests with great ease. I remarked on this. Brian chuckled, 'It has done, Adam, many times. It has even been graced by royalty on at least a couple of occasions. The bed you and Eve are sleeping in tonight has been occupied in the past by Henry VIII and George III.' He smiled slightly before adding, 'But don't worry, we've changed the sheets.'

Chapter Seventeen

We must have presented a strange sight, had there been anyone present to observe us. We had all put on whatever clothing we could find that would fit us and help keep us warm. There was a log fire blazing in the hearth, but in spite of this the temperature in the dining hall was on the cold side of frigid. Barbara had utilised a device I'd never seen before to keep the food warm. It was a water-heated serving dresser, like a forerunner of the Hostess cabinet. Brian had produced a couple of bottles of claret which he placed on the hearth close to the fire to keep at drinkable temperature. 'We dare not light the fire in here during daylight hours,' Barbara explained, 'the smoke from the chimney would have been a dead giveaway. We were lucky that Brian's father had the Aga converted to run on oil, otherwise we'd have had to survive on cold rations. Only the reception rooms and the bedrooms have central heating, and it's temperamental at the best. Don't worry, there's an open fire in your room. I lit it an hour ago.'

'If that's not sufficient,' Brian added, 'I'm sure you can find some way to keep each other warm.'

'Brian, don't be vulgar,' Barbara scolded him. He grinned sheepishly, but winked at me. I was still marvelling at the extent of his recovery, when Barbara asked, 'Anyway, how did you find us? How did you know we were here?'

'Adam worked it out from the amount of food you took from Linden House. He realized you would have needed access to fridges and freezers otherwise a lot of it would have gone off before you could eat it.'

'We had this long discussion about whether or not to tell you where we were hiding. In the end we decided it was safer for us; and fairer for you. That way you couldn't be dragged into the case as accessories, or tricked or bullied into giving away our location.'

'I'm glad we didn't know; it made it far easier to deny any knowledge of you when Ogden pressed us.'

'In the end, it was academic anyway.' Brian grinned as he explained, 'The phone lines to the Hall have all been disconnected. That's hardly surprising, as the house has been empty for the past twelve months.'

'I'm surprised the electricity was still on.'

Brian smiled. 'It wasn't. They switched it off at the main, but luckily they didn't disconnect the supply, so all I had to do was locate the switches and turn it back on. It only took a few seconds.'

'Yes, it took far longer to go round every room in the house,' Barbara interrupted, 'to ensure that no lights had been left on. A task I was given, for some reason that I haven't yet fathomed.'

'It's called the art of delegation, I believe.'

The derisive snort Barbara gave expressed her opinion of the art of delegation better than words.

'We had to make certain that there was no risk of anyone passing by seeing lights on in a house that was supposedly unoccupied,' Brian explained. 'We were restricted to four rooms at the back of the house where we knew we wouldn't be overlooked.'

'Plus the bedroom,' Barbara added; then blushed.

Brian changed the subject quickly. 'So you worked out where we were simply by taking note of the food we'd got from Barbara's fridge and freezer?'

I nodded. 'Of course it was easier for me because I knew your identity, which Ogden didn't.'

'Nevertheless, it was a bit of clever detective work.' Brian paused, before changing the subject. 'I owe you both an apology. The time I met you, after Eve hit me on the head, I was confused, but nowhere near as badly as I made out. I put on a bit of an act because I wasn't sure who you were, or what your intentions might have been. Seeing you there in the place where Babs should have been, almost immediately after I'd seen the children really threw me. When anything happens to upset me, I tend to regress, so the safest thing to do was to retreat back into the forest. If Babs hadn't come looking for me, I might not have ventured out again for weeks, months perhaps.'

'I suspected it was Brian who'd been at Linden House but I couldn't be sure. Even when he rescued me from Charles I had my doubts; his voice was wrong.'

'What made you suspect?' Eve asked.

'It was the skipping rhyme. Brian always got the words wrong. I used to tease him about it when we were children. He said "covered with blood" instead of "covered in blood". So when Adam repeated that verse and told me exactly what the tramp had said, I thought the coincidence too strong. So I went to find out.'

'Queen's English,' Brian added by way of explanation. He got to his feet. 'We could have eaten in the kitchen, but we thought it worth celebrating tonight. Hence the posh nosh and the claret.'

He walked over to the hearth and retrieved one of the bottles to top up our glasses. He raised his to Barbara's. 'Here's to the future; and to the future mistress of Rowandale Hall.'

Congratulations followed, and when the meal was over, we pulled our chairs around the fireplace, which enabled us to peel off at least one layer of clothing as we chatted about their plans and so much more.

Although Brian Latimer appeared much improved, I was concerned that bringing up the subject of his past, and in particular stirring up memories of his imprisonment and torture could have damaged his fragile recovery. In retrospect, however, I think being able to tell his story to comparative strangers proved far more therapeutic than harmful. The other, unforeseeable result of where the conversation led us was without doubt the most astonishing outcome of the evening.

It was Eve who touched on the subject first. 'How does it feel to be back here in the Hall?' she asked, 'It must be a bit strange, given the circumstances surrounding your departure. We were told about the row with your father,' she added.

'I had to bully and cajole him to get him inside,' Barbara explained.

'I thought the place would have been locked, barred, and bolted to prevent burglary, or squatters and the like. How did you get in?' I asked.

Brian chuckled. 'The same way I used to sneak in when I'd been out late as a teenager. I devised a foolproof way of getting inside without anyone knowing. It still works, even after all these years.'

'Go on, tell us.'

'I turned myself into a sack of coal.' Latimer's smile widened at our puzzled expressions. 'There's a chute where they used to tip coal into the cellar. Although there's a cover over the entrance, there's no lock on it, simply a bolt. If the insurance company knew how vulnerable the Hall was, they'd probably have cancelled the contents policy immediately. That method of entry isn't available any longer. I secured it once we were safely inside.'

'And you've no regrets about being here, now you've spent time in the Hall?'

Brian stared into the fire, seemingly lost in watching the flames that danced and curled round the bark of the logs he'd just placed there. Eventually, he cleared his throat and spoke, his voice quiet and reflective. 'My father wasn't an easy man. Not someone you could warm to, or get to know easily. He was unapproachable; people thought him arrogant, which wasn't really true. They didn't appreciate the problems he had to contend with. To be fair, neither did I, and I was far closer to him than most. Outsiders only saw the estate and believed there must be a fortune to go with it. That certainly wasn't so when I was growing up.

'It didn't help that my mother died when I was born. That left Father to bring me up with only his mother to help. Not that Grandma was much help. She had her own problems.' He touched his forehead with one finger. 'The estate was all but bankrupt. Father managed to rescue it but I think the strain took its toll. He was remote sometimes, at other times he'd rant and rave; then again you'd find him in a jovial mood, the best of company.

'At the time he accused me of theft he was – let's be charitable and call him unpredictable – whereas I was young, impetuous, hot-headed, and with a violent temper.'

'You still are,' Barbara interrupted, 'except you're no longer young.'

Brian grinned at the insult. 'True enough, I reckon.'

The fact that he responded well to the ribbing was another sign of how far he'd come along the road to recovery.

'I was so furious and sad that he should even begin to believe that I would steal from him. So I told him that if he thought so little about me, could suspect me of such dishonesty, then I wanted nothing more to do with the Hall, the estate, and in particular I never wanted to speak to him or see him ever again.'

He smiled with bitter irony. 'Well, I got my wish there. I left here determined never to set foot in the place again. I was determined that the Latimer dynasty had run its course here. Future generations would have to live elsewhere.'

'If you and Babs were so close, then why didn't you

leave together?' Eve asked.

'Barbara was away when I walked out. Not having Barbara to share my troubles with was the darkest moment of my life. I wrote her a letter, including the address and phone number of friends in York. I asked her to call me. I said I'd be there until my visa was sorted out and begged her to come to America with me. When she didn't reply, I assumed it was over between us. I even wondered if she believed the stories about me. If she, like everyone else, thought I was a thief, then that explained her failure to call.'

'Not everyone believed the tale,' I corrected him. 'Stan Calvert didn't, for one. Neither did his father. Stan got into several fights because of it.'

'Really? Good for Stan. As it turned out, Babs didn't believe the lies either.'

'I never got that letter,' Barbara explained. 'When Brian told me what he'd done with it, I knew why. He left it with the butler to deliver; the man who was sacked and went to jail for the theft Brian had been accused of. He hadn't even the decency to pass the letter on.'

'How mean and spiteful,' Eve said, her tone furious. She looked at Brian. 'So you didn't know that your father had become aware of your innocence?'

'No; by the time the truth came out I was busy dodging Viet Cong bullets.'

'And when I believed Brian left without a word I could only think that he didn't want me. I thought he meant more to me than I did to him. I'd have gone anywhere with him; all he had to do was ask. But I waited for word from him and when nothing came. I got angry. Finally, we heard that he'd been killed in Mexico. I believed it, like everyone else. In desperation, I married Charles Lewis.'

'Why did you return here, Brian? Why hide in the forest?' I asked.

'That's not easy to explain, because my mind was still

mixed up.'

'It still is,' Barbara interposed.

'Maybe you're right,' Brian smiled briefly, then his face changed as he related some of what he had undergone at the hands of the North Vietnamese. How he had been detained for three years, brainwashed, kept in solitary confinement, and beaten on a regular basis. 'The American prisoners were kept together, so that they could be paraded in order to prove how brilliant the Viet Cong were. By contrast, I was kept hidden, as I believe other non-US personnel were. This was because they were afraid their people might wonder how just the cause they were fighting for was if people from different nationalities were contesting it.

'They never referred to me by anything other than "*English*". "Now you eat, *English*. Now you talk, *English*. Now we punish you, *English*". That last one was their favourite.

'By the time I managed to escape the war was as good as over. It took me ages to get back to Europe. I was stateless, homeless, rootless, and pretty much mindless. Eventually, I managed to make my way to Yorkshire.'

He stopped speaking and sipped his wine. 'The answer to your other question, why live in the forest? That's simple. After I escaped in Vietnam, the only way I managed to avoid being recaptured was to stay in the forest; in deep cover, living off the land. The Vietnamese think they're pretty good in the forest, but I was better, thanks to the military and all the training I got in my youth with Zeke and Stan. When I got back here, the forest seemed the most natural place to be. It was only when I saw Barbara again that I realized I'd been fooling myself. She was the real reason I'd returned.'

'When was that?'

'I'd seen her out with the horses several times but was unsure of my reception. I certainly didn't know I was supposed to be dead! Goodness knows who that poor devil was,' he added. 'Once I'd been inside Linden House with you that awoke a lot of sleeping memories; ones I'd suppressed, but these were happy ones.'

Brian's mention of the racing stables prompted my next question. I had no idea that his answer would provide the key to the riddle surrounding the murders and everything connected with them.

'What were you doing in that loose box when Eve disturbed you?'

'I went inside to look for something I hid there just before I left for America.'

'But there wasn't anything in the loose box. The room was completely empty.' Barbara said.

Brian looked at her, seemingly reluctant to explain. 'It wasn't quite empty. I found what I was looking for. Unfortunately I seem to have lost it again.'

I fumbled in my jacket pocket, produced the gold coin and passed it to Brian. 'Was this is it? Was this what you were looking for?'

'Where did you find it?'

'It was on the loose box floor. You must have dropped it when Eve clouted you. But why did you hide it in the first place? I mean, what made you choose that place?'

As I spoke, I glanced at Barbara, who had gone red in the face. Brian too appeared embarrassed. He looked at her, saw her nod of approval. 'It was in that loose box that we first made love.'

Tactfully, I changed the subject. 'Where did you get the coin from?'

'My father gave me it on my twenty-first birthday.'

'That was an unusual coming-of-age present. Did he explain why he chose that?'

Brian smiled. 'Don't get me wrong, that wasn't the only present he gave me. He told me his mother had given him it when he was twenty-one, and he decided to do the same for me. Then he told me a very strange tale. Even now I don't know how much, if any of it is true; and how much came from either his imagination or my grandmother's ramblings.'

It had been clear from Barbara's response that this was the first time she'd heard of the coin's history. She hadn't recognized it when I'd shown her it at Linden House, now it was obvious she didn't know it belonged to Brian, which I found rather surprising, until I realized that this must have been only weeks before he'd left Rowandale.

Barbara's question confirmed my thoughts, and her slight pique at not having been taken into Brian's confidence earlier. 'Why didn't you tell me about it, Brian? I liked your grandmother, even though she was dotty. I'd have loved to have heard one of her weird stories.'

'You were away when Father gave me the coin. He told me it was the Latimer family legacy, and then laughed. I can understand now why he thought it was comical. For years the estate had been run down, the Hall had been mortgaged to the hilt, and there had been times when there was barely enough money to pay the wages. He'd spent most of his waking hours with his nose buried in the *Financial Times*, trying to find a way to dig us out of the hole we were in. To his eternal credit and a huge slice of luck he managed it, and secured the estate for the future.'

'How did he do that?'

'He invested every penny he could spare in the chemical and pharmaceutical industries just as they were beginning to make huge leaps and bounds via technological advances. The shares he'd bought rocketed in value, and he was lucky enough or astute enough to sell out when they were at their peak. That's how I came to have money of my own; the other part of my twenty-first present.

'As for the coin, you have to take everything with a

pinch of salt. As Barbara said, my grandmother was far from normal. I think they call it senile dementia. Amongst her strange behaviour she'd taken to wandering around the Hall and the estate clad only in her nightgown. That wasn't the worst part of it. If anyone tried to stop her, she'd get extremely angry and accuse them of trying to steal her fortune. Her language was appalling, using words we didn't even think she knew. Given our circumstances, I suppose the idea that we had a fortune or anything worth stealing had its comical side. Father said she was beginning to act and talk strangely even before he was given the coin. He blamed the fact that Grandfather had died young and she'd been on her own for so long with the whole burden of managing the estate on her shoulders.

'The gist of her tale was that the coin came from Africa, Cameroon to be exact. I do know that Grandfather had been posted there as a young infantry captain at the outbreak of the First World War, so at least that part has an element of truth to it. Apparently he returned to Africa once the war was over, and that was when he contracted the tropical disease which killed him. In her lucid moments she used to talk about him. It was all rather sad. He used to lock himself away in the study for hours on end; only emerging when it was time for dinner. Towards the end, he even stopped doing that, and eventually, he died in there. I think that is possibly why my father never used the study much.'

'What possessed your grandfather to go back to Africa?' Barbara asked.

'That's exactly what I asked Father; and that's where the fantastical part of the story comes in. According to Grandma, he went to recover some treasure he and another soldier had looted from a dead German. If you believe Grandma, it was worth a fortune, even at the values current all those years ago.'

'Surely he would have cashed the treasure in long ago,

especially if the estate needed money so badly,' Eve objected.

'He might have been tempted to, if it existed at all, but that might not have been possible. The coins would have been seen as stolen property in the eyes of the authorities. It's regarded as theft if it's carried out by private individuals, but it's the spoils of war if the government does it. Grandma reckoned he knew he was dying; knew he would never be able to profit from it personally, and decided to secrete the treasure somewhere around the house or the estate. He told her there was a document hidden somewhere that would provide a clue to whoever went looking for the gold once the heat died down. As I recall, she said something along the lines of, "Your grandfather told me the clues he had left would shed light on the whereabouts of a hidden fortune to anyone who knew how to interpret his message. I hope they'll find it when the time is right". Whatever she thought he meant by that, I really don't know.'

'That last bit seems to bear out the theory that he dare not cash them in for fear of being arrested,' Barbara pointed out. 'If we're to believe any of it, that is.'

Brian smiled a trifle sadly. 'That's it; now you have one small example of why we thought Grandma was loopy, God bless her.'

Chapter Eighteen

I sat staring into the fire for a while. Eve must have read more into my silence than the others, for she asked, 'What do you think of all this, Adam?'

I took my time before replying. 'It's just possible that everyone has done Brian's grandmother a grave injustice. Yes, I agree it might all be nonsense, but she is by no means the only one to tell tales of fabulous treasure that had its roots in or around the Great War. I spent some time in Africa when I was a foreign correspondent and there were rumours circulating then about stashes of treasure hidden by the Germans as they retreated. It's the sort of story tribesmen love to tell at night as they're sitting by the fire –' I smiled, '– much as we are now, I suppose, but without the claret. The type of treasure and its location vary with every telling, and the amount almost always increases each time they recount it. One thing that is constant, though, is the area where they reckon the treasure might be, and that area does include Cameroon.'

It was late when we retired. The snow was still falling heavily as I looked out from the bedroom window. Eve and I slept in a four-poster bed, which was a novel experience, far grander than our separate rooms at Mulgrave Castle. My sleep was punctuated by dreams of a treasure hunt, during which I was pursued by nameless, faceless individuals bent on stealing it from us. As things turned out, it seems I can prophesise equally well when I'm asleep.

Light was beginning to show around the edges of the curtains when I woke up. At first I thought I'd slept in, and it was only when I looked at the luminous dial of my watch that I realized how early it was. That could only mean the light was being reflected from lying snow outside.

I tried to settle, but sleep evaded me and as I was lying there, warm and drowsy, I had a random thought which I could only assume had been prompted by my recent dreams. The idea was startling enough to make me sit up in bed, a reflex action that disturbed Eve.

What is it they say about buses? You wait ages for one to arrive, and then three turn up one after the other. It was a little like that with me; one idea prompted another and that in turn provoked a third.

'What's wrong?' Eve's voice was heavy with sleep.

'Nothing, I had an idea that's all. Go back to sleep.'

I was beginning to think she'd done so, but a few minutes later she asked, 'What time is it?'

I told her. After a pause she replied, 'Your watch must have stopped. It's daylight outside.'

'I think that must be because of the snow.'

'Oh yes, I'd forgotten about that. What was it then?'

'What was what?'

'This strange phenomenon; you having an idea.'

I explained as well as I could what was little more than a series of guesses I'd strung together, with no proof that a connection existed beyond the assumptions I'd made to get from one stage to the next. 'Do you remember when Brian was talking about his grandmother's story, he used the words "my grandfather and another soldier" when he described the alleged discovery of the treasure in Africa?'

'If they did find treasure, you mean. Yes, I remember that. What of it?'

'Isn't it natural to assume that the other soldier also kept one of the coins?'

'That sounds logical, even for you.'

I smiled in the semi-darkness. 'If that's the case, and

the story is true, how come all the treasure ended up here? Why not only half of it?'

'Perhaps that's what did happen; you've no proof otherwise.'

'True, but if that were so, why did Brian's grandfather think it necessary to hide the stash of gold? If the authorities weren't aware of their existence, who else could he be concealing them from but his partner in crime? Think about the sequence of events that we know for a fact actually took place. Grandpa Latimer served in Africa. When the war was over, he returned there. Why? What possible reason could he have for returning other than to recover the loot? And why did he return alone? Why not take his companion along? Remember, they were in the middle of one of the bloodiest wars of all time. Isn't it possible that the other soldier might have been killed in battle? That would explain Grandpa returning alone.'

'I'm with you so far; even though I've no idea where you're taking me. However, there is one snag. If Grandpa knew his companion had been killed, why the need to hide the treasure?'

'I think he would have to have worked on the assumption that the other soldier would also have told his family about the treasure, and in doing so would have given them details of who his companion had been, in case he didn't return. Going on from there, if the story got passed down his family as well as Grandpa's; there could also be someone else around nowadays who knows all about the gold. The family members who passed the story on might not have been seen as crazy like Brian's grandmother was, and so the story would have been taken far more seriously.'

'Surely they would assume that the coins had been sold and the money used by now.'

'Not necessarily. If the two men talked and planned their course of action, they might have agreed to hold tight until it was safe to dispose of the coins without risking exposure as thieves. If that was so, and that part of the story also got retold over the years, the present generation might assume that the treasure is still here, somewhere within Rowandale Hall or the estate. When Brian's father died, seemingly without an heir, they might have seen it as their best chance to acquire the estate and the treasure within it. Especially as there were other benefits to be gained.'

'What other benefits?'

'The chance to make another fortune out of a large civil engineering project is what I mean. They would benefit via the sale of the land, through the quarrying operation, and the sale of materials to the road makers. What do you think?'

'I think you should see your doctor about prescribing some sleeping tablets. That way you might not get such wild ideas at such unearthly hours and I might get a decent night's sleep. Do you realize it's at least two hours before we need to get up and I'm wide awake? What are we supposed to do until then?'

'I could make love to you if you like?'

'That sounds nice, but what about the other one hour fifty-five minutes?'

Half an hour later, Eve said sleepily, 'OK, so I was wrong.'

'How do you mean?'

'One hour, thirty-five minutes.'

It seemed little brighter when we went downstairs. Despite Eve's forebodings we had both fallen asleep again, and it was nearer three hours later when I awoke for the second time. I might not have done, even then, had I not been tickled awake. Eve has a wicked sense of humour, and the place she chose to attract my attention proved that. 'I thought I was on a promise,' I grumbled.

'You've already had an early morning dip, don't be

greedy.'

We ambled down the broad staircase, hand in hand, and made our way towards the kitchen via the large dining hall, where I noticed that Brian had acted on the knowledge that they were no longer wanted by the police by placing half a dozen logs and some small pieces of coal on the grate to revive the fire. It was blazing cheerfully as we passed and there was a faint, deliciously aromatic scent in the air.

'Adam, whatever we do when we're talking to the architect about the extension to Dene Cottage, we must insist on open fires. Ones that will burn logs like this one.'

'That's quite spooky.'

'Why?'

'Because I was thinking exactly the same.'

Eve groaned. 'If we're starting to think alike, does that mean I shall also start to get really wild ideas?' She paused, then added, 'Come to think of I already have done, when I agreed to marry you.'

When we reached the kitchen, we were treated to a view of the rear ends of our host and hostess protruding from the front of a chest freezer that I thought would comfortably have housed a small flock of sheep. 'Are we interrupting an intimate moment?' I asked; only to get a savage dig in my ribs from Eve for my trouble.

Brian straightened up and looked round at us. 'Good morning, lazybones. We were trying to find some bacon for breakfast, but I think Barbara might have scoffed it all.'

'No, I haven't.' Barbara emerged, brandishing a large freezer bag triumphantly. 'I knew there was more, lots of it. There's plenty in this freezer, unless we're marooned for over a fortnight.'

'I hope you're not too hungry. Rowandale Hall doesn't run to a microwave oven to defrost things.'

'Not yet,' Barbara told him. 'That will be the first thing

to go on the wedding present list.'

'I thought that was the way things were headed when you toasted the future mistress of Rowandale Hall last night,' I told Brian.

'Yes, I thought it best to make an honest woman of her. We could have simply lived together, but what would the neighbours think?'

'You don't have any neighbours,' I pointed out.

'That's true.' He turned to Barbara. 'How do you fancy being my mistress instead of my wife?'

'I already am your mistress.'

'That settles it, I suppose. I have one condition, though.'

'And what might that be?'

'No bloody Mendelssohn when you walk down the aisle. Or Lohengrin for that matter.'

'What do you suggest? And if you say "Oh God Our Help in Ages Past" I swear I'll strangle you.'

I thought it high time to change the subject. 'Did someone mention coffee a while back?'

They hadn't, but the prompt reminded the happy couple of their duty as hosts. Once we were seated with our drinks, Brian said, 'I hope you've nothing urgent planned for today. The forecast isn't brilliant and the roads could be quite tricky, even for that beast of a car of yours. You might be better staying a bit longer.'

'Does that mean we're stuck with them for another night? It's starting to feel very crowded.' Barbara's voice echoed in the enormous kitchen, emphasizing the irony in her words.

'Adam had an idea halfway through the night,' Eve told them. 'He woke me up especially so he could share it with me.'

'What was it about, or shouldn't we ask?'

'It was all to do with what you told us last night, Brian.' I explained my theory, and awaited their reaction.

Barbara was the first to respond. 'What is it you write, Adam? I thought it was crime novels, not fantasy.'

'Hang on, sweetheart, maybe he has a point. There was something else; something my grandma told me several times, but I can't quite remember what it was. All I can think of at this stage is that it had something to do with treasure. Maybe we could do worse than look around for some clue, if we've nothing better to do.

'Brian, think about the size of this place. It's huge. Searching Rowandale Hall would take an army of men with years at their disposal.'

'It would if they had to search the whole of the building, but I think there are a lot of areas we could discount before we start. I'm thinking of the servants' quarters, the public rooms, working areas such as this.' He gestured round the kitchen. 'There's no way the clues could have been hidden anywhere they could have been discovered by accident; or by the wrong person.'

'I suppose we could have a look, but no way am I going to start on an empty stomach,' Barbara said and headed for the stove.

During breakfast, I asked Barbara if the eggs we were eating had been brought from Linden House.

'No fear, we used those in the first couple of days we were here. Brian got these, but don't ask me how, or from where. I happened to mention we were out of eggs and next morning there was a tray with two dozen on it sitting over there on the worktop.'

'I nicked them out of Zeke Calvert's barn,' Brian explained. 'I'll settle up with him later.'

'You took a bit of a risk, didn't you? What if you'd been seen, or arrested?'

'There was no danger of that. I passed within twenty yards of the village bobby and he didn't even notice me. It's the sort of thing I was trained for, and avoiding recapture in the jungle made me even better at it.'

Chapter Nineteen

Once we'd finished eating we set about our self-imposed task of searching the Hall, and even Barbara, who was a devout non-believer in the legend of the treasure, admitted to a sense of excitement. The first room Brian took us into was the library. 'I thought this might be the likeliest place to start,' he suggested.

I heard a muttered, 'Oh no, not again,' from alongside me and Eve gave me a look of mock horror and despair. We had spent countless hours the previous Christmas searching through nearly every book in the library at Mulgrave Castle; a task neither of us was keen to repeat. Before we plunged ourselves into a search of the room, I asked Brian, 'What sort of person was your grandfather? I appreciate that you didn't know him, but your father and grandmother must have told you something about him.'

'To be fair, my father would have been too young to form much of an opinion of him, or his character, or how he thought. All I can remember him saying was that the old man, as he referred to him, used to shut himself away in his study with the door locked.

'When I asked Grandma about that she said it was because he was far too proud to let anyone, even the servants, and especially his son, see how frail and ill he had become.'

'Maybe that was the case. But it might also have been the excuse he came up with to mislead people, and to disguise what he was really up to behind that locked door. Perhaps he was busy hiding the clue that he hoped would lead Rupert to where he'd stashed the treasure.'

'You could be onto something, Adam.' Brian looked at Eve. 'He's quite intelligent at times, isn't he?'

'He does have his moments. Not many, I grant you, but one or two.'

'OK, the study it is.' I smiled as Brian spoke, not at his words, but at the audible sigh of relief from Eve.

In the study, my immediate thought was that if this was the lesser of two evils, the margin between them wasn't that great. The room was impressive, with one wall being given over to four long French windows that reached from the floor almost to the high ceiling, flooding the interior with light. The other three walls were panelled with oak that had darkened with age. The only breaks were where the door was, and on the opposite wall, where a beautifully patterned marble fireplace had been set in to provide warmth and comfort for the occupants. 'I think it would be a good idea to light that before we start,' Brian suggested.

I helped him by carrying a hod full of coal and arms full of logs from the bowels of the cellar where he had made his burglarious entry to his own home. By this time the girls had made paper firelighters and Brian set about getting the blaze started. As he worked, I examined the wall panelling, and noticed a small mouse carved discreetly in one corner, the trademark of the famous manufacturer.

'Wow, I bet this wasn't cheap,' I exclaimed. I told the others about the significance of the mouse.

'It's been here a long time,' Brian said as he straightened up from his task. 'Way before I was born, I think. It's always been that colour. Isn't oak usually lighter than that?'

'Yes, which is why I think you're right. This must be getting on for a hundred years old, I'd say. Anyway, I think we can rule out looking for a hiding place behind here,' I tapped one of the panels. 'You'd have to cut through them to make room, and that would be sacrilege.'

Even discounting the walls, our task was a mammoth one. Given that the item we were looking for, even if it existed, which was still very much in doubt would likely be very small, there was a multitude of potential hiding places within the room. The study contained no less than three desks. Two were of the roll-top variety popular throughout Victorian times and into the early part of the twentieth century. The third, which occupied pride of place in front of the French windows, was a magnificent flat-topped piece of furniture with an oblong inlay of leather on the writing surface. Seated behind this, I could imagine the owner staring out across the grounds towards the forest beyond. Not the worst view in the world, I reflected wryly.

In addition, there were two long, low storage cupboards, positioned to one side of the other desks. All three desks had chairs in front of them. As we were likely to be spending a fair amount of time in the room, these would come in very handy. If we tired of our work, there were also two comfortable-looking armchairs and what looked like a folding card table stacked behind one of the cupboards.

Eve followed up on my earlier question by asking Brian, 'Your grandmother must have talked about her husband, surely, even to a small boy? Especially if she wanted her grandson to be proud of his ancestors. Did she give you any indication as to his nature, perhaps?'

'The problem was that by the time I was old enough to take heed, she wasn't actually saying anything that made much sense, to be honest. That's probably why I can't recall it all that accurately. I know it's frustrating, but all I can remember is one instance when she told me something about a woman and a bell. It didn't make sense because she wouldn't explain why she was telling me, but now I come to think about it she got quite agitated when she realized I wasn't paying attention. She told me it was very important, but I have no idea why.'

Although I was listening to the conversation, my attention had been drawn to a portrait hanging on one of the side walls. The subject was a man I guessed to be in his mid to late twenties. He was dressed in military uniform and the insignia on it denoted his rank to be that of major. The abundant moustache and mutton-chop sideburns suggested that the portrait had been painted during the early part of the century.

Brian noticed my interest in the portrait and confirmed that my suspicion as to the subject's identity was correct. That's my grandfather; Major Everett Latimer. Grandma had the painting commissioned immediately after the war ended to celebrate his safe return from France. That is one thing I do remember her telling me.' Brian grinned. 'In fact, sometimes she'd tell me it twice or three times during the same conversation.'

'I don't suppose the clue could be hidden behind the painting; or inside it even?' Barbara suggested.

'It's as good a place to start as any, I suppose,' he agreed. 'Adam, will you help me lift it down?'

What was immediately obvious was that the painting hadn't received the attention of a duster for a very long time. This in itself was no bad thing, as it was a minor indication that nobody else had been looking at the portrait as a potential place of concealment for a treasure map.

Although we inspected it closely, we could see no evidence that the back of the painting had been tampered with to allow for the clue to be secreted within. 'I suppose it was too much to hope for that we would strike lucky with our first guess,' Eve said. 'Perhaps the painting was a little too obvious.'

She was right, and with little or no knowledge of Everett Latimer's character, or how his mind worked, we were ignorant of the extent of his deviousness or the lengths he had gone to in order to protect his secret.

Brian and I carefully replaced his grandfather on the

wall and we turned our attention to the rest of the room. We divided the search up, with Brian assuming responsibility for the desk in front of the window. Eve and I took a roll-top desk apiece, whilst Barbara searched the store cupboards.

Brian finished well before the rest of us, even though his search had been just as thorough as ours. He had even removed each of the drawers and inspected the underside of them and crawled into the kneehole space to inspect the skeleton of the desk. 'That was easy,' he remarked as he replaced the last of the drawers. 'It's strange, though, having said I don't remember anything my grandmother said to me, as I was going through the desk, something else came to mind.'

'What was that?' Barbara asked.

'The first thing I noticed was how neatly everything had been stored inside. Nothing had been put away in a hurry, or carelessly. That brought to mind a telling-off Grandma gave me when I left my bedroom in a mess. "You must learn to be more like your father and your grandfather. They would never leave their bedroom in such a state." Then she made me repeat ten times, "A place for everything and everything in its place" whatever that means.'

'It certainly rubbed off,' Barbara told him, 'I've never met anyone as obsessively neat as you.'

'I know this is probably going to get me lynched,' Eve said after we'd all finished, with no success to report, 'but I think it would be sensible if we swapped places and that way, we might pick up on something the other person missed.'

Her suggestion was greeted with dismayed silence. It made perfect sense; but it meant a lot more work. 'We need coffee before we start again,' Barbara insisted.

Before we adjourned to the kitchen, Brian placed four more logs on the fire. 'At least we'll be warm as we search.' He repeated the operation in the dining hall. Slowly, it seemed, he was coming to terms with living in Rowandale Hall, the place he had sworn never to return to, and slowly, almost literally, the house was warming to him. That may seem a little fanciful, but that's the way it felt at the time.

In the kitchen, Brian said, 'Although coffee is a good idea, I think we also need sandwiches – lots and lots of sandwiches.'

'You always need sandwiches, except when you need a full meal. I've never met anyone with an appetite like yours,' Barbara told him. 'It's a wonder you're not built like a house side. I don't know where you put it, the amount of food you eat. I'll tell you something, I'm going to need a huge housekeeping allowance simply to pay for your food.'

An hour later, suitably refreshed, we resumed our search of the study, but by mid-afternoon we had met with no success. Having changed places twice, we were confident if the clue did exist, it was not hidden in that room, unless it had been stashed under the carpet, and I wasn't about to suggest taking that up.

'What time is it?' Brian asked.

I saw Eve and Barbara look around the room before I glanced at my watch. I told him the time but something in what had just occurred niggled at the back of my mind. I struggled with the errant memory, but the harder I tried, the more elusive it became.

'I vote we adjourn,' Barbara told us. 'I'm sick of the sight of this room. I want to take a shower before I start preparing food. What time do you want dinner this evening?'

There it was again, something about the mention of time, but still the penny refused to drop.

Later, we foregathered in the kitchen, where Barbara had

already begun preparing the meal. 'Do you need any help?' Eve asked.

'No thanks, everything's sorted.'

Brian had just entered the room from the steps leading down to the cellar. He was carrying two more bottles of claret. 'What time will the meal be ready, Babs? I need to let these stand.'

He didn't get a reply, because everyone was staring at me. I'd gasped aloud as he spoke, not at his words, but at the interpretation I'd put on them. The penny had finally dropped.

'Something wrong, Adam?' he asked.

'How did your grandfather know when it was time for dinner?'

They all stared at me as if I'd taken leave of my senses. 'Sorry, I'm not with you.'

'You said last night that your father told you your grandfather locked himself away in the study and only came out when it was time for dinner, right?'

Brian nodded; still puzzled as to where this was leading.

'How would he know when it was time for dinner? I suppose he might have had a wrist watch, or even a pocket watch, or possibly someone called him, but from what little I've been able to gather, he wasn't the sort of man you'd want to disturb if he'd said he wanted to be left alone. Assuming all that, how would he tell the time? There is no clock in the study.'

One idea was rapidly superseded by another. 'You also told us your grandmother said the clue would be found "when the time is right", and perhaps that phrase was a clue in itself. Can you remember there ever having been a clock inside that room?'

Brian didn't need time to consider the question; his answer was immediate. 'Yes, there was. The grandfather clock that is now in the dining hall used to be in the study.

My father shifted it years ago. It had stopped working and he intended to get someone in to fix it, but when he moved it, the clock somehow started working again, so he didn't bother. I remember him saying how lucky it was because that meant he didn't have to spend money we could ill afford.'

'I think the clue might have been hidden inside that clock, don't you?'

Dinner preparations were temporarily suspended as we went to check. We watched with increasing tension as Brian opened the door to the long case and felt cautiously inside; taking care to avoid the pendulum which was swinging to and fro with metronomic precision. He struck a match and peered into the most remote recesses before turning to deliver the bad news. 'There's nothing in there, except what the clockmaker intended there to be. If this was where the clue was hidden, it's already been removed.'

I suppose I felt the disappointment more keenly than the others. It had been my idea, and I'd been so certain that the hint in Brian's grandmother's words would lead us first to the missing clue, and then to the location of the treasure itself. My enthusiasm was such that it had infected the others, and they too now believed in the existence of a stash of gold coins somewhere within the Rowandale estate. Our sense of deflation lasted until dinner was almost over.

The conversation during the meal had been low-key; now it was flagging, reflecting our lowered spirits. I think tiredness had combined with disappointment to leave us all at a low ebb. Brian lowered his cutlery and broke one of the long silences by telling me, 'I think I owe you an apology, Adam. I misled you last night. Not intentionally, but I suppose when we were talking I wasn't taking the business of the coins seriously. I didn't get Grandma's word right. When I quoted her, I told you she'd said

"When the time is right" but that wasn't correct. Blame my bad memory if you want. I've only just remembered her actual words. She told me I'd find the truth out "if I have a little time, a lot of patience, and some piety". Perhaps I dismissed it as her eccentricity, or perhaps I thought it was too bizarre to have any real meaning.'

'I don't see it making a lot of difference, Brian.'

'It could do,' Eve interrupted. 'Going back to the way you worked out the grandfather clock idea, what if "a little time" refers to a small clock, not a large one?'

'Eve's right,' Barbara added, 'And what if "patience" also had some significance; and "piety" too?'

'I suppose "patience" could refer to a game of cards,' Brian suggested. 'Isn't there a card table behind one of the cupboards?'

'We could take a look, I suppose.' I still wasn't sure.

'After we finish dinner.' Brian wasn't going to be rushed.

Barbara shook her head sadly. 'See what I mean, Eve? Always thinking of his stomach first.'

At the risk of getting indigestion, we went through to the study immediately we'd finished eating and removed the card table from its resting place to examine it. There was nothing unusual to be seen on the top. We even examined the area where the green baize was secured to the wooden frame but there was no sign that anything had been secreted below the material. However, when we turned the table over to inspect the underside we immediately noticed a set of grooves that had been made in the wood, marking all four sides. We stood in a group, each of us standing in front of one of the sides, and read out the letters that had been carved on the mahogany.

'I've got K–I–N,' Brian told us.

'Mine says T–H–E–C,' Barbara added.

It was Eve's turn next, 'H–U–R–C,' were her letters.

I completed the message with, 'H–L–O–O.'

The anagram didn't take much solving. 'What does, "Look in the church", mean? I know it tallies with the piety bit your Grandma mentioned, Brian,' Barbara frowned. 'But what church was he referring to? The nearest church is St Mary's at Elmfield. I should know, I had to walk there every Sunday morning. I hated that walk.'

'Why?' Eve asked.

'It was all right until I got to the graveyard. We'd have to walk the full length of it to get to the church, past all the graves. That used to frighten the life out of me. All those tombstones with dead people underneath them. I used to think that at any moment they would appear out of the ground, grab me, and carry me off to a horrid place where small children were eaten alive.'

'Phew!' Brian exclaimed. 'I never realized what a weird and vivid imagination you had. You never told me any of this.'

'No, I thought you'd laugh at me and call me a sissy.'

'Good point, I probably would have done. Was that why you used to hold my hand?'

'Yes, I knew I was safe because I was sure you would never let anything bad happen to me.'

He smiled at her, a warm, glowing expression. The discovery, and the confirmation it gave of the possible existence of the treasure had fired his enthusiasm – and, it seemed, stimulated his recalcitrant memory. 'St Mary's isn't the nearest church, though. Not if I've got Grandpa's meaning right. There's one no more than twenty yards away.'

He saw our puzzled expressions and added, 'I'm assuming I've got the meaning correct. If so, it means the old man was far more cunning and devious than we anticipated. Follow me.'

He led us out of the study and into the spacious

entrance hall where visitors to Rowandale would be greeted by the butler and then presented to the house-owner and his lady. Brian directed us towards the broad staircase leading to the first floor and gestured to the wall. 'There it is.' He indicated the beautifully veneered mahogany wall clock alongside the staircase. 'There's your church.'

We walked up to it and inspected the face. The maker's name was clearly visible in bold characters, "Church, Norfolk" it read.

Brian opened the door and felt inside the body of the clock. After what seemed an age, with tension mounting, he eventually pulled out a small envelope. The single word "Rupert" was just legible on the front of it, the ink faded by time. 'This was obviously intended for my father. Grandfather couldn't have anticipated that he would have dismissed the tale of the treasure as a fairy story dreamed up by a lonely widow who had lost her marbles.'

'Open it up, please, Brian?' Barbara pleaded. 'Put us out of our misery.'

He did as she instructed and drew out a scrap of paper. I saw him frown as he deciphered the handwriting. 'I don't understand,' he muttered. 'All it says here is, "Ask the Fair Maid of Perth", whatever that means.'

Barbara and Eve looked equally mystified. 'Another bloody cryptic clue,' Eve said despairingly.

I shook my head in mock sorrow. 'And I thought you lot were well educated. Didn't they teach you anything at school or did you sleep through all the lessons? Have none of you any idea what he meant by that? Don't you know who the Fair Maid of Perth is?'

'Adam, stop showing off and tell us,' Eve demanded.

'*The Fair Maid of Perth* is one of the Waverley novels, written by Sir Walter Scott. I suggest we adjourn to the library and search for the book. It's one of a set of twenty-five tomes, it shouldn't be difficult to spot. Eve can lead the way; she's used to hunting through libraries.'

Eve poked her tongue out at me, and to emphasize her message, gave me a two-fingered salute into the bargain. Although the library at Rowandale Hall was by no means as large as the one at Mulgrave Castle, in this instance we knew exactly what we were looking for. When we located it, we opened the book carefully and found a sheaf of notepaper that had been secreted at the end of the text; the pages secured with red ribbon threaded through the pre-punched holes and tied in a bow.

I held it out. 'Brian, this belongs to you. I think you should be the one to read it.'

'I agree, but not here,' Barbara said. 'Can we go somewhere a bit warmer, please?'

We settled by the fireplace in the dining hall. Brian added several more logs to the fire and placed coal around them to get the blaze going faster. We sat back to listen as Brian read aloud his grandfather's memoir, confident that the location of the hoard of purloined gold was about to be revealed. However, we had reckoned without the devious and security-conscious mind of Everett Latimer.

Chapter Twenty

'Kamerun, 1915

Our patrol had run into trouble. I and my companion were the only two survivors of the ambush. We had been walking for several hours, stalking our prey. Although we had killed our attackers, an hour later we had seen the lone figure of a German officer. Revenge for the deaths of our four comrades burned as fiercely as the African sun.

At first, when I spotted the man on the horizon I'd assumed him to be a local tribesman. We had been warned to stay clear of them. Most were friendly, but some were hostile. It was only when I brought my field glasses to bear on the figure that I realized my assumption to be incorrect.

I passed the binoculars to my colleague and he agreed we should follow him and see what he was up to in case he was spying on our positions.

We tracked our quarry through the heat of the day. The plain was covered in scrub and undergrowth, sufficiently thick to provide cover. Towards the end of the afternoon, when the power of the sun was beginning to diminish, we reached the foothills of the first of a chain of mountains. The cover was less plentiful here and concealment thus more difficult. Fortunately, the German had paused and appeared to be scrutinising a sheet of paper he had removed from his knapsack.

As we were looking for a place to hide, my companion moved, dislodging a stone that rolled down the slope, clattering loudly against several more before coming to rest. The German turned in our direction, snatching up his rifle as he did so. My colleague and I split up to attack him from both sides.

He died bravely; that German whose name I never discovered. Had I been alone, I am by no means confident that it would be me writing this memoir, nor that the language would be English. As it was, he almost did for my companion before a round from my Martini-Enfield carbine proved decisive.

Having first made sure the German was dead I attended to my colleague's wound, which fortunately was only to the fleshy part of his upper arm. Painful, but not immediately life-threatening. That done, we examined the contents of the German's knapsack. I was particularly intrigued by the paper he'd been studying. It turned out to be a hand-drawn map which seemed to be of the immediate vicinity and indicated he was heading for the top of the hill.

In that searing heat the corpse was soon covered with insects; big, fat, obscene, disease-bearing insects. We knew we needed to get away from the scene and began the climb. I looked deeper into the bag which we had brought along with us. The German had also been carrying a small brass plaque, some screws, a screwdriver, and a hand-operated drill. For the life of me I couldn't work out why he was taking these into the wilderness.

Climbing the hill was far from easy. The surface was littered with scree, small rocks that threatened our footing at almost every stride. The map had a circle drawn on it, which corresponded with the summit we were heading for. Had it not been for that, and my overweening curiosity, we would have abandoned the expedition earlier.

Our slow progress was compounded by the equipment we were carrying. Or, to be more accurate, that I was carrying. We had augmented our own rations of food and water with those of our dead comrades and the German troops. We would not starve or die of thirst as long as I was able to bear the load, for my colleague declared himself unfit to share the burden because of his wound.

It was true that when I changed his dressing, the wound did look very inflamed, but I suspected he was making more of it than necessary. At the time, I dismissed the idea as unworthy. I left him to rest and determined to see if I could find what the German was aiming for.

I was in luck almost immediately. The setting sun was at such an angle that it reflected from a piece of metal. Seeing the glint I looked closer and discovered it to be the blade of a trenching tool, the sort used for digging ditches. The reason for it being discarded was obvious. It had been snapped in two, the jagged edge of the handle lying alongside the broken blade.

I stepped beyond it into a small cluster of bushes. I noticed that several branches had been broken, further evidence of some activity here. Almost at once I saw a flat boulder, about three feet square. Along the edges the earth had been disturbed and there was a small pile of dirt, soil, and rocks to one side. The unmistakeable furrows left by the diggers' tools were the last piece of evidence showing that I had discovered the German officer's target. But what lay beneath? There was only one way to find out. I retraced my steps to bring my colleague up to date with my discovery.

He examined the rock, but with his injured arm there was nothing he could do to help. I might not have managed it but for the broken tool. I manoeuvred the blade under the lip of the boulder, and supporting my weight on my companion's good shoulder, brought my full weight onto the handle. The boulder lifted, then, to my relief, moved sideways several inches. By moving the spade and repeating the process, three more attempts and I had cleared enough space for us to see what was beneath.

There were four wooden boxes. Although they measured no more than about ten inches square and eight inches in height, when I bent to pick one up I could scarcely move it.

The British bayonet has many uses. One of the more obscure ones is to prise the lid off a small crate. However, I soon removed enough of the nails to reveal the contents. By that point, I had a fair idea of what these would be. I was not disappointed. The crate was crammed full of coins.

We each snatched one up and examined it. I turned mine over and saw the image of Kaiser Wilhelm II. The coin I was holding was a twenty mark gold piece. I knew we ought to report this and told him so. Even as I spoke, I did not believe in what I was saying. Nor did my words deceive him.

He thought I was mad to make such a suggestion. We knew we could not take them back with us. They would be far too heavy to carry, even if we were both fit.

When he asked me what I suggested, I thought there was just the faint suggestion of a sneer in his voice.

We retained one coin each and I decided to think about it whilst I put the box back under the stone. I was weary by the time I completed the task, and as we dined on our cold rations, I explained my idea to him. We knew the war would not last for ever. I suggested we wait until it was over, return, and recover the treasure. It might be many years before it was safe to dispose of the coins without too many questions being asked, but once we did so, we would be set for life.

My colleague was concerned that others may know of the site but we agreed that with luck, we might have already killed the only ones who knew of this location; the troops who ambushed us and the officer we had killed. Why else would they be out here in this wilderness?

Still, he argued with me. Citing that the war was not yet over and we may also be killed. As he spoke, I noticed him staring at me, an odd expression on his face. It was then I realized he had used his right hand, the injured one, to pick up the coin. I was beginning to entertain some very unpleasant suspicions about my companion.

It was decided we should each have a copy of the map and when we returned home we should write an account of what happened. Then, even if we were unable to return, our children might retrieve it. We should be careful with names, having already committed one crime. Petty theft is a minor offence but what we were planning was altogether different. If we left a statement that was in effect a confession it could be highly incriminating.

Although I cannot pretend to great insight into the way men's minds work, that night, once I was sure he was asleep, my suspicion of his intentions led me to take some basic precautions. We had been thrown together not by any great affection, or the desire for each other's company, but by the ambush and the adventure that followed it. The next morning we set off back to our encampment on the other side of the plain.

We were somewhere close to halfway across the plain and I was about to call a halt when I hear an unmistakeable sound behind me. I turned to see my companion staring in dismay at the rifle he was pointing in my direction. I smiled, but I felt less than humorously inclined. I was right; the lure of the gold had proved too much for him. I had mentioned serious crimes to him last night. There is none more serious than murder. That was why I had taken his bayonet and removed the rounds from his rifle and his revolver whilst he slept.

He thought I was going to kill him but from thereon, I made him walk in front. We made it back safely to the camp and soon afterwards we were posted to different theatres of war.

Given what had happened, I have decided to revoke my earlier plan not to name my companion. I will inform him of my decision before we set out to retrieve the treasure.

That is the only way I can ensure my survival. If he knows his name is in my journal he will think twice before acting rashly.

His name is Harold Matthews.'

As he'd read the name aloud, Brian looked up and saw the astonishment on the faces of his listeners. 'What is it?' he asked. 'Does that name mean something?'

I was struck by the irony that the person most affected by the scheme to buy and exploit the estate was the only one to be ignorant of the man potentially behind the plot.

'Matthews is the name of the detestable creep who threatened Babs that day you showed up at Linden House,' Eve explained. 'He was the one driving the BMW.'

'I didn't take much notice of him,' Brian admitted, 'I was too busy sorting out the other two.'

Any doubts we had regarding the perpetrator of the crimes and the attempt to wrest the estate from its rightful owner were resolved when he showed us a cutting from the obituary column of an old newspaper, the *Halifax Courier*, dated Wednesday, September 28th 1921 which he continued to read aloud.

'Matthews, Harold, MC.

The death has been announced of Capt. Harold Matthews, late of the King's Own Yorkshire Light Infantry. Having served with distinction during his secondment to the Royal West African Frontier Force, during which he saw action against the enemy in Kamerun, Captain Matthews rejoined his regiment in France, where he effected the rescue of three of his men who were trapped in no-man's-land, pinned down by artillery and sniper fire. It was for this act of unselfish bravery that he was awarded the Military Cross. Although he received no direct wounds during the action, he was exposed to a large quantity of poison gas which contributed to his untimely death.

Mr Matthews was born in Halifax on February 4th

1882, and prior to the war worked as a trainee yarn salesman. He married Frances Allen, of Slaithwaite in 1913. The couple had one child. Captain Matthews volunteered as an enlisted man at the outbreak of hostilities, rising through the ranks until he was commissioned.

He died at his home in Luddendenfoot on 24th September 1921. The funeral will be held at St Mary's Church on Monday 3rd October at 2.30 p.m., followed by interment at the Luddenden Public Cemetery.'

Beneath this Everett Latimer had written:

'Post Scriptum. 1921.

After reading about the fate of Matthews, any qualms I had about revealing his name are eased. It can bring little comfort to his widow and child to know that he became a hero, but perhaps in time it will dull the pain of his passing.

His death, like mine, will take us beyond the scope of human censure, and we need only fear divine retribution. For I too am dying. My return to retrieve the treasure, using my status as an officer in the British Army, enabled me to travel with my precious cargo, unchallenged, but there my luck ran out. The expedition caused me to contract the tropical disease that will bring about my demise. There is no cure for what ails me. I have composed a riddle for those who follow me. My wife has been entrusted with the conundrum, and a hint as to what it refers, which she will repeat to my son when he is old enough to understand its significance. I do so in the hope that he will solve it and retrieve the treasure. If he does so, he must also judge whether in so doing it will be safe to dispose of what I must suppose the authorities will consider as stolen goods. I will leave it for the finder to decide whether to share the good fortune with the family of

Matthews. If my son, or whoever searches for the treasure, hopes for reward, they should remember these words before they begin their quest. Without first solving this riddle, they will stand little chance of success.
  Look for the bell that never rings,
  Close by the maiden who seldom sings.
  Search for the wealth that lies within
  Resting with those who are free from sin.'

If our first evening at Rowandale Hall had resulted in a late night; our second was even later. The memoir and the revelation that the gold existed beyond the realms of family legend would have ensured that. However, even the excitement generated by that knowledge was all but surpassed by the sobering knowledge of the identity and fate of Everett Latimer's companion in their adventure.

Brian continued to study the obituary. 'Where is this place, Luddendenfoot? I've never heard of it.'

'Somewhere west of Halifax, I believe, but I wouldn't swear to it.'

'I have to say I'm rather surprised,' Eve looked across at me as she spoke. 'What do you think, Adam? I didn't have Trevor Matthews down as a cold-blooded killer. I certainly wouldn't trust him further than I could throw him where business is concerned, but I wouldn't have thought using a knife to achieve his purpose was his style.'

'Perhaps we were too keen to view the murders of Armstrong and Veronica Matthews as part of a bigger plot rather than what they actually were. Maybe Matthews was more upset by his wife's infidelity than he admitted, and the motive for the murders was the oldest one of all – jealousy.'

'That doesn't explain Lewis's murder,' Eve pointed out.

'That's true, but perhaps they were unconnected, except that it gave Matthews the idea, and the chance to throw suspicion on someone else.'

Brian saw that I was looking at him, and misread my thoughts. 'Hey, don't you start, Adam. I've had enough with that Ogden character accusing me of everything since the Jack the Ripper killings. I'll have you know that I haven't killed anyone for years and years, and that was several thousand miles away.'

Listening to Brian, I remembered a question that had been puzzling me for a long time. 'That reminds me: if you were held prisoner for all that time, how come you got your Ka-Bar back?'

Brian grimaced. 'The one you saw wasn't mine. I suppose it is now, but it wasn't the one I was issued with, if you follow me. You could say I inherited it, but in not very pleasant circumstances.' He hesitated, as if the memory was too uncomfortable to recount, but then continued, 'During the time I was on the run, after my escape, I had to move by night and hide during the day. That made progress extremely slow, especially as I had to scavenge for food along the way. One of the places where I hid was a burned-out village. At first I thought the Yanks had done it with napalm. I later found out that the VC had torched it, killing all the inhabitants as a reprisal because they'd given food and shelter to some American soldiers. I discovered the bodies of two of the Americans in the shell of one of the huts. They had both been machine-gunned. I removed the knives from their bodies, but the guns they were carrying were useless. The heat had caused the round in the breach to explode.'

We returned to the main topic of interest; the new puzzle that Everett Latimer had set for us. 'Read that rhyme again, Brian,' Barbara urged. 'Let's see if it makes any more sense.'

'Look for the bell that never rings,
Close by the maiden who seldom sings.
Search for the wealth that lies within

Resting with those who are free from sin.'

There was a long silence as we struggled to find the meaning behind the cryptic rhyme. Barbara was the first to admit defeat. 'The problem I have with that –' she waved her hand at the paper Brian was still clutching, '– is that although I recognize all the words, when they're put together and read out I can't make head nor tail of them. He might as well have written them in Mandarin or Ancient Greek.'

We continued to try for the meaning, but without making any progress whatsoever. In retrospect, Eve or I should have stood a better chance of recognizing one of the pieces of the puzzle than the others, but when we gave up for the night we were no closer to deciphering the rhyme than when we first heard it.

Meanwhile, we were confronted with another problem, the question of Everett Latimer's companion in that long-forgotten adventure and the consequences at the present time. It was Eve who brought the subject up again. 'Before we go to Inspector Hardy with accusations left, right, and centre, shouldn't we make certain we've got our facts straight?'

'I'm not with you,' Brian admitted.

'Well, for one thing, Matthews is a fairly common name. Who's to say that the man who tried to acquire the estate is related to the soldier your grandfather mentioned? I read something last summer about a village cricket team where all eleven players had the same surname, even though only three of them were related to one another. I know it might seem to be a huge coincidence, but such things do happen, and I think we'd be sensible to make sure first.'

'You've got a point, Evie, a very good point. The only snag I see is how to find out if Matthews is descended from the man who served with Brian's grandfather. Normally we'd be able to ask Hardy or someone like him to use their official capacity to enquire for us, but we can't do that in these circumstances. The first question they'd ask is why we wanted to know, and that could take a bit of explaining. I'm not certain how the law stands with regard to a theft that took place sixty years ago, but I think it's better not to take the risk.'

The glum silence that followed my words of caution signalled the end of the evening. I'm not certain whether that was due to the fact that we had no idea how to get round the problem, or simply because the wine bottles were empty.

I lay in bed listening to Eve breathing gently as she slept, I was unable to settle; the revelations from the memoir turning over restlessly in my brain. Even with the passage of time, the most poignant image that remained with me is one that I formed of the ex-soldier, his own body racked by a disease for which there was no cure, reading that obituary of his former colleague. How bitterly ironic he must have considered it that both of them should have been so close to untold wealth, only to have it snatched from them.

How cruel was the fate that delivered this obituary to Brian's grandfather when he was himself so close to death. I wondered if he had been seated at the desk in the room where he composed the clues to the treasure, when he read of the death of his companion in that great adventure. Even as he hid those clues, did he wonder if their secret would ever be revealed, or if it would die with him and the treasure lie undiscovered for all eternity.

An even darker thought also came to mind as I thought of that long-dead soldier. As his time approached, did he or any of those close to him glimpse the dread vision of those blood-bespattered children of ill-omen? Would they know what the sight of those children foretold? Did they perhaps hurry home to check that their nearest and dearest had not suffered some tragic misfortune?

As chance would have it, almost sixty years had passed before some at least of those mysteries would be revealed. For the other part, I can offer no logical explanations for those apparitions. And perhaps it is better so. Only those who claim to have seen them can vouch for their existence. As at last I drifted off to sleep I decided it was certainly a subject I preferred not to dwell too long on.

Chapter Twenty-one

Getting inspiration during the early hours was beginning to become a habit, but certainly not one I was keen to encourage. My sleep had been fitful, wracked by a strange dream. It was inspired by Barbara's tale of walking to church and her admission that, as a small child, she found the experience terrifying. Quite how this reminiscence of her childhood translated itself into the nightmare I suffered, I'm not sure. Barbara certainly hadn't mentioned anything about huge, misshapen, and revolting-looking ogres haunting the graveyard, flitting in and out of their places of concealment; the one purpose behind their presence being to mock my ignorance and stupidity.

Once again I awoke far too soon, this time with one word racing around in my brain. I tried not to disturb Eve, but that was difficult, as her arm was across my chest and she was lying so close to me that her hair was tickling my cheek. She sensed that I was awake, and asked with a sort of long-suffering drowsiness, 'What is it this time?'

'Gravestones,' I told her. 'Captain Matthews' gravestone, to be precise.'

I didn't need to explain further. 'Of course! The inscription will tell us what we need to know, along the lines of "Harold, beloved husband of Ermyntrude and dear father of Peregrine".'

'His wife's name was Frances.'

'Don't be so pedantic, you know what I mean. If we have that information it would give us a starting point, certainly, but depending on when the child was born we might still have to trace another two generations to bring us up to date.'

'We'll cross that bridge when we come to it. At least we have something to work on, which is more than we did a few hours ago.'

I began to caress her, and Eve turned towards me. Later, as we snuggled down to sleep, Eve murmured, 'Your sense of timing is lousy, Adam, and your idea of foreplay is the weirdest I've ever heard of.'

Breakfast that morning turned out to be less of a meal, more of a business meeting. Naturally, we were keen to share our idea of the gravestone with the others. Although they were clearly interested by it and prepared to join in the discussion over the mysterious rhyme left by Everett Latimer, it was clear that Brian had something else occupying his mind.

Eventually, I asked what was troubling him. 'Nothing,' he replied, 'not troubling me, at any rate. I'm still getting accustomed to sleeping in a bed again; last night I was wide awake by three o'clock. I went for a walk round the house to try and settle myself and visited parts of the building I haven't been in for close on twenty years. I even went into my old bedroom. I haven't felt much like going in there since I returned, but when I did, I found this.'

He held up a piece of paper, which I could see contained names and numbers. 'Do you remember when I told you my father had given me that gold coin as a twenty-first present? You said it was an odd sort of gift, as I recall. Well, that wasn't the only strange present he gave me. This was the other one. Or rather,' he corrected himself, 'these are the details of it. This is a list of companies. My father bought shares in each of them, putting them in my name. He told me he'd chosen companies that he thought would provide good long-term investments. I'd forgotten all about them until I saw this. Now, I'm wondering if they're valuable or worthless.'

'Do you still have the share certificates?'

'I certainly hope so. I used some to raise the funds I needed when I left for America but I lodged the rest with my bank in Thorsby. Here, take a look.'

He passed me the sheet of paper. I glanced at it; my interest sharpening with each name I recognized. One thing was certain, I thought, the money Rupert Latimer had made on the stock market had owed little to chance. The investment portfolio he had bought for his son read like a roll of honour of British industry and the overseas companies were equally illustrious. Granted, the shareholding in each of those companies was not huge, but even without precise details to hand I could tell the value was substantial.

'Are you still keen to find that gold?'

Brian frowned. 'I suppose so. Why do you ask?'

'Because I don't think you need the money. I'd say these shares will make you extremely well off, should you decide to sell them. I wouldn't like to guess how much they're worth, but I think you can look at somewhere close to seven figures. And that's without the money your father might have left you. At a guess I'd say he might have had at least the same amount of shares in his own name.'

'Good Lord, I never thought of that.'

'How does Rupert Latimer's will affect Brian's claim?' Eve asked.

'If I remember the wording correctly from when Barbara showed us her copy, the opening clause read something on the lines of, "In the absence of a next of kin" and ends up with, "The claim of a living relative would take precedence over and nullify all other claims on my estate". It was dressed up in legalese, but that's what it meant.' I looked across at Barbara. 'I'm afraid Brian's reappearance will result in you losing the bequest of Linden House.'

'I already guessed that. Why do you think I agreed to

marry him? And that was before I knew he was worth a fortune. Now he's got no chance of getting away.'

To be fair, the way Brian was looking at Barbara, I think escaping the bonds of matrimony was the last thing on his mind.

The plan was for us to return to Linden House, where Brian would contact the solicitor handling the estate as well as attempting to get the phones to the Hall reconnected. I agreed to speak to Detective Inspector Hardy, who, I warned them both, would doubtless need to take their statements with regard to the murders as soon as possible. 'Not as suspects,' I reassured them, 'he's already made it clear he doesn't regard you in that light. More for background, I reckon.'

'I need to see to my horses,' Barbara added. 'I've a runner at Catterick in a couple of days, and although my lads are capable enough, the owners would be far from happy if they got to know that I've been neglecting their valuable investment.'

The roads had cleared of snow, so the short journey presented no problems. On our arrival, Barbara found the phone number for Norman Rhodes, the solicitor, and handed it to Brian before she and Eve departed for the stables. He dialled the number, and after a brief verbal tussle with the receptionist, who seemed to believe her job was that of a goalkeeper rather than a facilitator, he got through to the partner.

I listened to Brian's half of the conversation as I made coffee. He didn't seem to be making much headway in his attempt to persuade Rhodes that he was the rightful heir to Rupert Latimer's estate. From what I could hear, or guess, it seemed as if the solicitor was being deliberately obstructive. Perhaps that was my hyperactive imagination, I thought. Possibly he was treating Brian's miraculous and timely reappearance from the dead with understandable suspicion.

When Brian put the phone down, it was clear that he too was less than happy with the solicitor's attitude. 'He doesn't believe me. He's demanding all sorts of documentary evidence to confirm I am who I claim to be. He cited a birth certificate, my passport, and a driving licence. I had to point out that the driving licence had been stolen in America years ago and that I had never got round to replacing it.'

'Have you got the other stuff?'

'Oh yes; I'll even show him my discharge papers from the US Army.'

I blinked in surprise, almost spilling the coffee I was passing him. 'I didn't know about that. How did you get them? I thought you came home without contacting them.'

'No, that was the story I was asked to tell anyone who asked. The truth is that I got fed up of roaming around and surrendered myself to their embassy in Rome. They flew me back to the States where they interrogated me for ages. It took a long time for me to convince them I was who I claimed to be. I believe they thought I was some sort of secret agent bent on infiltrating them. In the end, it was my fingerprints plus the physical evidence of the torture that convinced them I was telling the truth.'

'How did you manage to get to Rome? It's a long way to swim.'

'Eventually, I managed to scrape enough money together to bribe the captain of a cargo vessel, bound for Italy, to let me stow away.'

'Why the need for secrecy over the way you returned then?'

'They asked me to keep quiet about what had happened to me. Their reasoning was that it wouldn't have been good for relatives of other US personnel who had been listed as MIA, sorry, missing in action. If they believed there was a chance that their nearest and dearest was still alive it would give them false hope.'

'I can see that. So what actually happened?'

'They let their shrinks loose on me for ages, and in the end the doctors reported that they believed the best thing for me would be to return home to England. Their opinion was that I stood a better chance of recovering from the nightmare of my ordeal at the hands of the Viet Cong within my own environment rather than thousands of miles from home, amongst strangers.'

Brian smiled. 'For a long time it had the opposite effect and I was beginning to doubt the wisdom of agreeing to return here, but then I saw Babs and everything started to come right from that moment on. I knew my feelings for her were as strong as ever, and I couldn't leave even if I wanted to. Then I found out she felt exactly the same about me.'

'Better not tell Hardy that. He's not a bit like Ogden, but even he'd be bound to see that as a reason to get rid of Lewis. Does Barbara know the truth about how you got back home?'

'Of course she does. I would never hide anything from her. I asked her to tell the other story because of the promise I'd made to the Yanks.'

Getting the telephone line to Rowandale Hall reconnected was easier than proving Brian's identity. Or at least it would have been, had it not been for the trifling detail of payment. Eventually, he promised to send them a cheque to enable reconnection. Having got that sorted out, which would involve using Barbara's cheque book, he passed the phone to me so that I could inform Inspector Hardy of the fugitives' whereabouts.

Hardy's first question was, 'Have you found Latimer?'

'Of course I have, Inspector, as you expected me to.'

'Where was he?'

'At Rowandale Hall, where you expected him to be.'

I could hear the laughter in Hardy's voice as he asked,

'And was Mrs Lewis with him?'

'Naturally, as you expected her to be.'

'When can I interview him?'

'Why don't you ask him yourself? He's standing only a couple of feet from me. I'll pass the phone to him, if you want.'

Brian explained that the meeting would have to take place at Linden House. 'I'm staying here for the time being. It's more convenient until I can take formal possession of the Hall and get things like the phones back on.'

The meeting was scheduled for later that afternoon. I was on the point of telling him I was going to do some shopping, when Barbara and Eve returned with bad news.

'Two of my lads are down with flu,' Barbara told us as they entered the kitchen. 'That's bad enough, but to add to it, I've had to send the other one home. He's coughing and sneezing all over the place and he'll end up infecting us.'

'I can help you with the work,' Brian offered, 'but what about riding out?'

'You might have to do that as well. It won't be ideal, you're a bit on the heavy side for a jockey. Eve and I can ride two of them, but it would be better if we can take three at a time up to the gallops, which only leaves either you or Adam.'

'Count me out,' I responded. 'I know which end of a horse is which, but I've never been on one in my life. I wouldn't know where to start.'

'You could be useful in other ways,' Barbara told me. 'In the stables, for example. As I remember it, the last time my father tried to get Brian involved in working there he spent most of the time trying to grope me.'

'I don't recall you objecting too strenuously, and it's obviously stuck in your mind.'

'That's beside the point; it didn't get the work done.'

Brian told them about his phone call to the solicitor,

and how difficult he had been. He also explained that DI Hardy would be visiting.

Later, as we awaited Hardy's arrival, Rhodes phoned back. He informed Brian that if he was in a position to present the necessary documentary evidence, the solicitor would be prepared to grant him an interview in a couple of days' time at his office in Leeds, during which he would assess the validity of Brian's claim. 'Those were his words, not mine,' Brian explained, 'he made it sound as if he was doing me a great favour.'

'When is that meeting exactly?' Barbara asked. 'I mean, what time of day?'

'Three o'clock in the afternoon.'

'Damn, that's the day I'm at Catterick races. Blenheim Boy's running and he stands a really good chance in the big hurdle race of the day. I can't miss out. I was hoping Eve would come with me to help get the horse ready. He's a bit of a handful at the best of times, but he seems to respond better to women than men.'

'I'm sure Adam could take Brian through to Leeds; then I can come to Catterick with you,' Eve said.

I picked up on Eve's point. 'That's a good idea. We could set off early and go through to Halifax first. Brian and I could inspect that gravestone and that way we get everything sorted out in one trip. It isn't as if you and Eve will need us at Catterick, by the sound of things.'

The interview with DI Hardy, although to all intents and purposes purely routine, proved more difficult than anticipated in certain parts. Our problem lay in trying to explain Matthews' interest in trying to acquire the Rowandale estate, without revealing the existence of the gold.

It was helpful that Hardy didn't object to Eve and me being present when he spoke to Brian and Barbara, and this gave me a chance to lead him to the belief that the reason was purely to do with the proposed trunk road and the chance for profit the scheme would provide to the estate owner. Hardy seemed to accept this at face value, and also appeared to go along with the couple's version of events surrounding Barbara's absence and Brian's reappearance. The gist of his questions and the relaxed nature of the interview confirmed my earlier statement that they were no longer being treated as suspects.

Once he declared himself satisfied, Hardy asked me to walk out to the car with him, as he needed a little extra information from me. I walked alongside him, with the young DC, who had apparently survived the reallocation of duties, trotting along behind us.

I asked Hardy what had happened to his predecessor. 'Transferred to traffic division,' he told me succinctly, 'which isn't good news for motorists. I wanted a word because I'm by no means sure I've heard all there is to hear about Latimer. That's why I wanted to get you on your own. I can see how the land lies between him and Mrs Lewis and that would have got Ogden all hot under the collar. However, it's clear you don't believe either of them has done anything wrong, so what's the story? I got the impression that Latimer was only telling me as much as was strictly necessary. I know I ought to question him in greater depth, but for some reason you, Mrs Lewis, and Miss Samuels seem keen to protect him. What do you make of him? Is he sound in body and mind, or should I revert to treating him as a suspect?'

'I suppose we have been a little protective. Not in the physical sense. Brian Latimer is more than capable of taking care of himself there, but his state of mind is fragile. Hence his need to escape the confines of a prison cell. To understand that without becoming suspicious of him, you have to know the circumstances. It's a long story, and I think it would be better if I was the one to tell you it. What's more, I think I should do so away from here, where there's no chance of us being interrupted.'

Before he left, we'd arranged to meet at Thorsby police station the following morning, when I would be in town on the pretext of shopping for food.

My decision to fill Hardy in with the details of Brian's past all but caused a row with Eve. Luckily, I was able to convince her that it made sense for us to cooperate with the police. 'At the moment, Hardy doesn't suspect either Brian or Barbara. However, if we don't explain the background and he works out that Walter Armstrong and Mrs Matthews were probably killed because they witnessed Lewis's murder; that might change. Telling him everything we know maintains our credibility, which might be extremely handy. For example, if at some point we need information that would be much easier for the police to obtain than us, it would be useful to have them on our side. Above all, if we are lucky enough to be able to identify the killer, we'll need Hardy around to make the arrest.'

Eve accepted my reasoning, having thought it through, but with one reservation. 'Do you intend to tell Hardy about the gold?'

'Not in so many words. All I was planning to say was that Brian found some papers of his grandfather's that mention the name Matthews and it seems a curious coincidence that Trevor Matthews is so desperate to get his hands on the estate. Hopefully, that will plant the seed of suspicion without giving too much away.'

Even as I spoke there was a niggling doubt at the back of my mind. Something I'd just said didn't quite tally with my memory of events. I was unable to identify the discrepancy, so I dismissed the idea. Which was a huge mistake.

Not surprisingly, Hardy was both fascinated and appalled by the story of what Brian had endured before his return to England. At the end, he looked at me, assessing my capability to answer his question, I think.

'What do you make of his state of mind now? Having been brainwashed and tortured that way has to have a lasting effect, I'd have thought.'

'I think he's far more resilient than anyone could possibly have guessed. I'd say his fragility lies in anything that might remind him of those days in captivity, but he's coming to terms with everyday things such as being indoors. From what he said, a few months ago that wouldn't have been possible. Being reunited with Barbara has been very good for him, too.'

'You realize I'm having to rely on your word for almost anything to do with Latimer.' He jerked one thumb towards the ceiling. 'Orders from above,' he explained. 'The chief constable won't hear a word against his godson. Latimer certainly won't be facing any charges. The chief doesn't want the media latching on to the *Great Escape* story. He more or less told me I'd to handle Latimer with kid gloves and at the same time look elsewhere for the killer, because there's no way he could have been responsible. Is he right, or is he being too trusting because he's too close?'

'I think the chief constable's got it right. If you were to ask me if Brian Latimer was capable of killing someone, I'd say yes, in certain circumstances. If he felt his life, or that of Barbara, was in danger, he would act in self-defence. And if he was in action, faced with an enemy, in a kill-or-be-killed situation, then he would certainly be capable of that. But if you were to change that question, and ask instead if I thought he was capable of cold-blooded murder, I would say absolutely and categorically not.'

'Yes, that more or less bears out my own impression, but you've seen far more of him than I have. OK, so if we believe Latimer wasn't the killer, have you any idea who might be? And what the motive for the murders might be? Given that we're not dealing with a complete psychopath, of course, which is always a detective's worst fear.'

'Why is it your worst fear?' I asked, momentarily sidetracked by Hardy's comment.

'Because they're far more difficult to catch. With most crimes, there's a motive, which leads to a suspect. Random killings are another matter entirely.'

'I have the germ of an idea as to what the motive is and that leads me to a possible suspect, but none of what I believe can be proved. One thing's for certain: I think you can safely discount the idea of a random killer.'

'You've already mentioned the man Matthews, but I still don't see the profit motive as sufficiently strong enough a reason for three murders.'

'There is more that I could tell you, but it isn't my story. However, one thing I can say. Have you thought that the two later murders might be the consequence of the first one?'

'In what way?'

'Go back to Armstrong's cottage and look out of the bedroom window. You will be able to see the point where Lewis's car was found, which I presume is where he was killed. What if Armstrong was in his bedroom at the time of the murder and witnessed it? What if he then tried to blackmail the killer?'

'That would take some proving. The murder happened during the daytime. Why would Armstrong be in his bedroom, unless he was ill?'

'Or unless he was indulging in a little extra-marital encounter with Veronica Matthews.'

'What makes you think that happened? Granted, they were obviously lovers, but there's no proof she was there that afternoon.'

'Oh yes there is.' I told him what Zeke Calvert had said about seeing the car on the day of the race.

'That's all very well, but we still have to find the person who killed Lewis. Matthews might have had a motive for killing his wife and her lover, but where's the motive for the first murder?'

'I'll leave you to work that out, Inspector. I have shopping to do.'

'That won't be easy. If the killer *is* Matthews, proceeding against him won't be by any means straightforward. I can't simply arrest a respected law-abiding citizen on suspicion of three murders without a shred of concrete evidence.'

'I'm afraid I can't help you there. Not as things stand, anyway.'

Nor, at that point in time, could I see any way of proving guilt even if we did have a definite suspect. What we needed was some way of getting the guilty party to show their hand. As I pondered how that might be achieved, the saying, 'be careful what you wish for' never entered my mind. It should have done.

Chapter Twenty-two

When I collected Eve from Linden House I took the opportunity to tell Brian about my conversation with DI Hardy. I was a little apprehensive as to how he would react to having his most private and personal history exposed to a complete stranger, but fortunately he was more relieved than upset.

'I suppose one good thing is that it saves me having to go through it all over again. I knew I should have told him it myself yesterday, but somehow I couldn't face it. The shrinks seemed to believe that talking about my ordeal would help in some way but it doesn't work that way, at least not for me. Whenever I have, something inside me seems to curl up with shame and embarrassment. The only time it was easy was with Babs. That was another reason I knew everything was right between us.'

Before Eve and I left, we promised to return the following morning to help out in the stables. 'Not that I'll be of much use,' I told Barbara, 'except perhaps to make coffee. Like I said, I know very little about horses.'

'Don't worry about that, Adam, Eve's got the ideal job lined up for you,' Barbara told me with a wicked smile. 'She said you'll be absolutely perfect for it, given your long career as a reporter.'

I looked at the woman who had promised to marry me; the woman who was wearing my ring. Her expression was one of total innocence. A little too much innocence for my liking. 'Oh yes, and what might that be?'

'The loose boxes will need cleaning out. Basically, that means shovelling manure.'

'Oh, how lovely.'

Any doubt I had about how serious Eve had been was settled the following morning on our arrival. She handed me a shovel and pointed to a large wheelbarrow that was leant up against a wall. 'Once we have the horses saddled up and out of their boxes you set to work. When you've cleaned one of the boxes, swill the floor down and sweep the excess water into the yard. There's a hosepipe connected to the outside tap over there. Enjoy yourself,' she added, a trifle spitefully, I thought.

Barbara had taken the opportunity provided by our assistance to exercise all the horses in her care, so it looked like a full morning's work for me. Once they all disappeared in the direction of the gallops, each riding one of the expensive thoroughbreds, I set to work in my role as equine chambermaid.

I had just finished the last of the empty boxes when the clatter of hooves warned me that my clients had returned. This gave me chance to relax as I watched the riders grooming their mounts before returning them to their en-suite facilities. I even allowed Brian the privilege of spreading fresh straw on the floor while Barbara refilled the hay racks.

Once they had saddled up three fresh mounts, including the bad-tempered Blenheim Boy, it was back to work for me. This time, having learned from the previous three, I had finished the boxes well before they returned, and was contemplating going to the house for a mug of well-earned coffee when I heard the sound of a vehicle on the drive.

Curiosity, combined with the need to ease my aching back muscles, prompted me to walk to the top end of the yard. I was only mildly surprised to see the distinctive nose of a BMW that was parked behind my car.

If Trevor Matthews was mourning his recently deceased wife, it certainly didn't show in his apparel. His sports coat was a vivid check one that was loud enough to make me wonder where I'd left my sunglasses, and his multi-coloured tie was on the extreme edge of garish. It clashed violently with the coat – but then I think it would have clashed with anything. It put me in mind of those joke ones men wear at Christmas and I was tempted to ask Matthews to press it so I could hear what tune it played.

'Where's Mrs Lewis?' he demanded. 'I want a word with her.'

There was a distinct lack of old-fashioned courtesy in his abrupt manner. 'Exercising the horses,' I told him, adding, with some reluctance. 'Can I help?'

'That's what I want to talk to her about. She shouldn't be taking them to the gallops, and she shouldn't be using that path. She knows we've prohibited it.'

'You're rather jumping the gun, aren't you?'

'What do you mean?' Matthews was barely paying attention to me. He obviously thought I was one of Barbara's employees.

'You don't own the Rowandale estate. That means you have no right to permit or prohibit anything that happens on the land.'

He dismissed this with a wave of the hand. 'It's only a matter of time until we do. The paperwork is in the process of being drawn up. Once we get probate on Latimer's will, everything will go through on the nod.'

'That I very much doubt. If you're placing your hopes on the will Rupert Latimer signed eighteen months ago I'm afraid you're going to be extremely disappointed. I take it you haven't spoken to Norman Rhodes in the past couple of days.'

'I don't understand. Explain yourself.'

As he was speaking I heard hooves rattling on the concrete apron leading to the stable block. Perfect timing, I thought. 'I'll do better than that; I'll show you.'

I grabbed Matthews by the arm and steered him towards the stables. After a few strides he wriggled free and marched on ahead, walking as if he owned the place. The awakening would come soon, I knew, and it would be a rude one, brutal even. I was looking forward to witnessing it, which I suppose marks me down as a minor sadist. I greeted the returning riders. 'Barbara, you remember Trevor Matthews. He's back with some more empty threats.'

Matthews cut me short. 'You were warned before about using the gallops and the path alongside the forest, but you appear to have taken absolutely no notice. Once the sale of Rowandale Hall goes through we intend to seek to revoke the terms of Rupert Latimer's will and have you evicted from Linden House.'

The interruption was delivered quietly, which merely added to its effectiveness.

'There are a couple of problems with that statement. The first of these is that Rowandale Hall is not for sale. The second is that Barbara doesn't own Linden House, I do. As for that will, forget it. The document is no longer valid. Adam, would you mind explaining why and then escorting this gentleman from my property. I've a horse to attend to.' With that, Brian dismounted and headed for the stable.

Matthews looked at me for enlightenment, clearly stunned by what he must have considered to be a series of preposterous claims. I hastened to explain. 'If you read Rupert Latimer's will, the opening clause states that the document is only valid should there be no living relative, and if there is one, their claim nullifies all others. I'm quoting from memory, but I think I've got the gist of how it's phrased.'

'What's that got to do with anything? Everyone knows there are no living relatives. And who the devil is that?' He gestured towards Brian, who was now busy grooming Blenheim Boy. It was obvious that Matthews hadn't recognised him as the bearded tramp.

'Correction; everyone thought there were no living relatives. But they were wrong. And as to your other question, that's Brian Latimer, Rupert Latimer's son: the rightful owner of Rowandale Hall.'

'Don't be ridiculous; Brian Latimer has been dead for years.'

I sighed wearily. 'Not that Mexican nonsense again. Why don't you go talk to Rhodes? And whilst you're at it, get him to explain how the brown-eyed corpse from Mexico could be Brian Latimer, who everyone knows has blue eyes. Now I think you should leave, because I don't think Mr Latimer will take too kindly to your aggressive attitude to his fiancée.'

'Thank you, Adam,' Brian told me when I reported Matthews' departure. 'I was having trouble keeping a lid on my temper with the man; the way he behaved was intolerable.'

'You do realize who he is, don't you?'

'I heard you mention the name Matthews. Was that him?'

'Yes, Trevor Matthews to give his full name.'

'And he's the grandson of the man who was with my grandfather in Africa? Now it makes sense.'

'That's what we think, but the gravestone should tell us more when we look tomorrow.'

It was another early start for all of us the following morning. Once we'd completed the morning's work at the stables, which was a far more truncated version of the previous day's task, we loaded Blenheim Boy into the horse box, which I nicknamed the touring caravan, for the journey to Catterick racecourse. I say "we" but my involvement in the procedure was minimal, matching my knowledge and experience with horses. I'm not scared of them as a rule, but Blenheim Boy had a habit of staring coldly at me, as if to say, 'I'll sort you out' – though perhaps that was my imagination.

Once the gelding was installed, Brian and I prepared breakfast whilst the girls took it in turns to shower. Before they left, I handed Eve a small wad of banknotes. 'Let's see if The Boy can bring us luck,' I suggested. After we'd seen them on their way, Brian and I set off on our journey to the West Riding.

As we drove out of the village, my mind was occupied with the impending visit to the graveyard, and the hoped-for confirmation of the family connection between Trevor Matthews and the long dead soldier.

The subconscious mind works in strange ways sometimes – or at least mine does. It was this obscure process that gave me the answer to one of the clues left by Everett Latimer in his memoir. The catalyst was, of all people, Zeke Calvert. As we passed his cottage, I noticed the former gamekeeper standing by the front door, puffing on a cigarette. I thought he presented a rather forlorn figure, and wondered how he managed to fill his days now that he no longer had work to occupy them. I mentioned this to Brian, adding, 'The evenings are less of a problem, because he can always escape to the Admiral Nelson, away from his nagging wife.'

'Is she a nag? I never met her.'

'According to Henry Price she's always looking for someone to blame whenever anything goes wrong, and Zeke is usually in the firing line. Henry said she has a wicked tongue on her, and never gives Zeke a minute's peace. It's no wonder he told us he prefers quiet women.'

As I recounted Henry's words, I gasped aloud at what I'd just said.

'Something wrong, Adam?'

'No, but I've just thought of something. It could be important. Give me a minute to think it through, Brian.'

From my eye corner I could see Brian staring at me, his expression one of mild bewilderment. I concentrated on the road ahead, but my mind was elsewhere. We'd gone about ten miles before I spoke. 'You know the waterfall in the forest?'

'Of course I do. What of it? I didn't realize you did, though. Have you been there? Have you been into the forest?'

'No, but Zeke Calvert told me about it. Can you describe the surrounding area for me?'

'The waterfall isn't actually in the forest. Well, that isn't strictly true either. The falls, and Thorsgill Beck, split the forest in two. There's woodland to the north of the river, and also to the south, but the gill cuts right through the middle, running west to east. At the top of the falls the river is much wider, but the rock formations channel it towards what is really a force, or foss, I think the Viking word is.

'At the bottom there's a wide area of open land. The water tumbles into a huge, deep pool that is supposed to be bottomless. It was a favourite place for skinny-dipping when Babs and I were kids. Anyway, the pool forms part of a huge clearing that has never had trees in it as far as I can tell. That may be down to the stony ground, I'm not enough of a geologist to say. There are some depressions in the ground. When I was a kid, Zeke told me they were where people in the Stone Age or Iron Age excavated for minerals. I'm not certain what they were after, it could have been peat for fires, or flint for weapons or utensils, or iron, or coal even. Whatever it was, they dug down quite a long way. Some of the holes are twenty feet deep, maybe even more. Why the sudden interest in that part of the forest.'

'Remember the rhyme your grandfather composed? Think of the name of that waterfall.'

'Of course, the Silent Lady: *The maiden who seldom sings*. That has to be a reference to the falls, but what about the rest of the rhyme?'

'Those workings you mentioned, they would be more like open-cast mining than deep level, I guess?' Brian nodded agreement. 'And I'd also guess they would be roughly circular in appearance, if you looked from above, say from the top of the falls. Am I right?'

'Yes, but I still don't see –'

'If you'd paid more attention in class instead of daydreaming about Barbara you might have twigged it by now.'

He grinned. 'All right, genius; enlighten me.'

'Those excavations are known as bell pits. One of them has to be *the bell that never rings*, don't you think?'

Our excitement was tempered by a sobering reflection that arose from the remainder of Everett Latimer's rhyme. Brian gave voice to the disturbing thought. 'It's the other part that worries me. The bit about the gold *sleeping with those who are free from sin*. That sounds to me as if we'll find something else in that pit, along with the treasure; and I don't like the idea of what it might be. I don't like it one little bit.'

If anyone could be said to have a premonition into what secrets Rowandale Forest might conceal, I suppose it was only natural that it should be a member of the Latimer family, who had been associated with it for centuries. Nevertheless, I felt a slight frisson even as he spoke, and even now, when I recognize the accuracy of his words, my blood runs cold.

It isn't simply the violence of the events that had already occurred, or the tragic outcome of what was still to take place, nor even the terrible evil committed by those responsible. The sins of man, however bad, I can cope with. It is when I am faced with something for which there is no rational explanation; something way beyond my comprehension, that I confess myself beaten.

We were lucky, in that our journey time meant that we had

avoided rush hour, so after passing through Halifax with little in the way of a hold-up, we reached Luddenden well before lunchtime. We walked through the graveyard, keeping two rows of graves between us as we searched for the resting place we were seeking. Towards the upper end of the extensive plot we found what we were looking for. The grave was well kept, and although the lettering of the inscription had been weathered by time and in places was obscured by lichen, we were still able to make out the wording. I stared at it in total dismay. My carefully thought out theory was in pieces, destroyed completely by one simple phrase.

There could be no possibility of error, no chance that we were looking at the wrong grave. The epitaph was unmistakeable; 'Cpt Harold Matthews MC, 1882–1921, beloved husband of Frances and devoted father to Deborah'.

The obituary that Everett Latimer had pinned to his memoir had stated quite categorically that Matthews had left only one child. The accuracy of the newspaper might be called into question, but the inscription negated even that possibility. The fact that Matthews had only a daughter meant that Trevor Matthews could not be his grandson.

I glanced at the grave alongside Harold's and saw that it was that of his wife, Frances. And there was further confirmation, if any was needed, in the inscription, 'loving mother of Deborah'.

'It looks as if you were completely wrong, Adam,' Brian said quietly.

I walked away, too disappointed to respond. I'd only gone a few yards when I noticed another, much more recent grave, the stonework on the headstone unmarked by time. I read the message etched into the stone and turned towards Brian, signalling him to join me. I pointed to the inscription. 'What you said was correct. I was wrong, utterly and completely wrong. Tell me something, though; is it possible to be totally wrong and absolutely right at one and the same time?'

Not for the first time that day, Brian looked at me as if I'd taken leave of my senses, but my mind was whirling with the discovery and the connections it brought me. The reason for Trevor Matthews' curious phraseology; for the solicitor Rhodes's obstructive behaviour, were all explained by that short message carved in stone.

'I'm sorry, Adam, I don't follow you.'

I gestured to the stone. 'Read that carefully and I'll explain.'

Chapter Twenty-three

Although we had trouble finding a parking spot, we reached Norman Rhodes's office well before 3 p.m., the scheduled hour for Brian's appointment with the solicitor. Despite that, we were kept waiting for fifteen minutes or so. However, as things turned out, that time proved highly informative. Having left her post to inform Rhodes that we had arrived, the receptionist returned to her desk, where one of the lights on the small switchboard was flashing to signal an incoming call. As I examined the prints of Yorkshire scenes that adorned the walls of the waiting area, I listened to her half of the resulting conversation.

'I'm sorry,' she told the caller, 'Miss Moore isn't in the office today.'

There was a long pause, during which I heard some agitated squawking sounds filtering through her earpiece. The caller, it seemed, was upset at not being able to speak to their advocate. She spoke again, 'No, Miss Moore won't be in tomorrow either. Can one of the clerks help you?'

More distress sounds, following which she said, 'In that case, I suggest you leave it until after the weekend. No, she isn't on holiday. Family illness, I believe.'

She had only just ended the call with the dissatisfied client when the internal phone rang and we were shown into Rhodes's office.

The meeting was stiff and formal; Rhodes was dismissive of my presence until Brian insisted I remain. The arrogance he displayed at our earlier meeting at Linden House had not abated and it was clear from the outset that the solicitor was as suspicious of Brian as we were of him. The first hurdle Brian had to clear was the matter of the stolen driving licence, which had led everyone to believe he had been murdered in Mexico.

Brian attempted to explain. 'After I joined the American army I was sent to a training camp in Texas before being posted to Vietnam. We used to go into the local town and that's where my driving licence went missing. Either that, or one of the Mexican civilian workers on the base must have stolen it.'

The explanation convinced me, but Rhodes still wasn't satisfied, the element of sarcasm told me so. 'It seems curious that your driving licence should be the only item to have been stolen. I would have thought your passport would have been more valuable to a thief if he was thinking of selling it.'

Brian however, did not flinch and stated, as matter of fact, 'Passports are taken from you and held in a secure location whenever you are sent to serve overseas. It's a matter of routine, especially for servicemen who are travelling to a war zone. Identification is carried out via fingerprints and dog tags.'

Rhodes then spent a long time poring over the documentary evidence Brian had brought to confirm his identity, and eventually, when it seemed as if he had run out of excuses to block his claim, he announced with what appeared to be some reluctance that he was satisfied Brian was who he purported to be. His face took on a smug expression as he announced, 'However, there is still the question of your father's will to contend with. There is no bequest to you in it, and as the estate is not entailed, there must be some doubt as to whether you are entitled to any bequest from your father.'

In answer to Brian's silent appeal for help, via a pained look he gave me, I spoke for the first time. I reminded Rhodes of the opening clause to Rupert Latimer's will.

'That clearly states that if a living relative is found, the will is null and void. You know that, I know that, and Brian Latimer certainly knows that. So let's have no more shilly-shallying and get on with probate of the estate, which will mean that Brian is the sole beneficiary of all property and monies held by Rupert Latimer at the time of his death.'

I was quite pleased with the semi-legal terminology I'd used, and it seemed to sway Rhodes into a marginally more cooperative frame of mind. Perhaps it was at that moment he realized he had a potentially wealthy client in his rooms. 'I agree that it does seem to establish Mr Latimer's right to the estate and to other assets, which principally comprise a quite sizeable bank balance and a large portfolio of shares.'

He opened the bulky file in front of him and began sifting through the paperwork until he came to a sheaf held together with a paperclip. He passed these to Brian, a subtle but definite statement of capitulation. 'This is a list of the shares he held when he died, together with their value at today's market prices. I have received these quotations from a stockbroker here in Leeds. There is also a photocopy of the bank statements from each of Mr Latimer's accounts, both in his own name and the Rowandale Hall account. The shares cannot be disposed of, nor can the bank accounts be drawn on until probate has been granted, but I will be happy to advance you any reasonable sums you might need to tide you over. That disbursement would come from our office account and would attract interest as with any loan.'

Brian thanked him, but declined the offer. There followed a prolonged session of form-filling and form-signing, following which Rhodes promised to do all he could to expedite the granting of probate. 'If you are not in need of the money from the bank accounts, it can be used to satisfy the Inland Revenue's claim against the estate in the form of death duties.'

Eventually we left, and I was surprised to see that it was already well past 5.30 p.m. Our next task was to do battle with the Leeds city centre traffic. By the time we reached the car and inched out of the parking space it seemed that the whole of the city was gridlocked. The luck that had enabled us to avoid rush hour that morning had well and truly deserted us. I learned much later that a three-vehicle accident on the inner ring road combined with a fuel spillage from an oil tanker had exacerbated the normal problems faced by commuters.

'It's times like these that make me glad I live out in the wilds, not in a town,' I remarked.

'If you think this is bad, you ought to try New York or Chicago.'

'I've been to both. In fact, I used to work in New York.'

'I didn't know that.'

For want of something better to do, as we waited for the traffic to ease, I told Brian a little of my history before I met Eve; and for good measure related the events that had thrown us together.

He listened with interest, and after I finished, thought for a while before saying, 'You never know what life is going to throw at you next, do you? I certainly didn't expect to end up in the American army or be sent to Vietnam, or finish up as a prisoner of war. In fact, I had no clear idea of what I wanted to do with my life.'

'It's turned out all right in the end,' I pointed out.

Someday, I might learn to stop making such rash predictions.

We had arranged to be back at Linden House in time for dinner, but the delay getting clear of Leeds had thrown our plans into disarray. In addition to that, a glance at my fuel gauge told me I'd have to fill up before we reached home, or anywhere near it. 'I'm going to need petrol soon, so if we stop at a filling station with a public phone handy you could ring Barbara and tell her we're going to be late.'

We found what we were looking for close to the outer ring road. As we approached the petrol station, Brian pointed out a red phone box close by. 'Let's hope it hasn't been vandalized,' I muttered.

I had just finished paying for the fuel and was consulting the evening paper I'd bought in the shop when Brian returned. I looked up and noticed the puzzled frown on his face. 'Something wrong?' I asked.

'There's no reply. They should be back from Catterick by now, surely? It isn't that long a journey.'

'They're probably still celebrating.' I handed him the paper and pointed to the stop press column on the side of the back page, which displayed the racing results from that afternoon. Blenheim Boy had won the hurdle race by ten lengths. Moreover, at a price of 8/1, the hundred pounds I'd given Eve to back the horse would give them ample funds with which to mark the success in suitable fashion.

'Wow, that's great news! Babs will be over the moon. It isn't going to get us our dinner, though. Let's hope they're in a fit state to cook by the time we get back. Or at least, let's hope they've got home.'

With no reason to hurry, I took the drive back to Rowandale at a leisurely pace, so it was almost 8 p.m. when I pulled into the drive at Linden House. As I swung into the yard, the headlights picked out the squat, functional shape of the horsebox parked alongside Barbara's own car, but one glance towards the house showed us that something was amiss. No lights were showing, either upstairs or down. Brian and I exchanged puzzled glances. 'Perhaps they're down at the stables attending to the horses,' he suggested.

I gently inched the car forward until we could see down the yard, but as we peered towards the stable block, we could see that it too was unlit. 'Where the devil are they?'

I muttered. 'They can't be legless already, surely?'

'Even if they were, they would have put some lights on before passing out. No, there's something wrong.'

We got out of the car, concerned, but not alarmed. We set off towards the house, but Brian stopped me, putting one hand on my arm. 'Listen!'

The sound was like someone in boots marching to and fro. 'What is it?' I asked.

'I'm not sure, but I think it's coming from across there.' He pointed towards the horse box.

We moved forward, and sure enough, the sound got louder as we approached the vehicle. 'It's Blenheim Boy,' I exclaimed, 'he's still inside.'

Brian hurried to turn on the yard lights before he unlatched the tailgate. As we lowered it we could see the hero of the afternoon, whose temper was obviously not improved by being cooped up for so long. 'We'll have to get him out; we can't leave him in here.'

My mind was full of increasing concern as to what had happened to the girls. For the moment, however, the gelding demanded my constant attention. After Brian untied the halter that was securing the horse, I led the Boy down the ramp. It was the first, and hopefully the last time I'd ever been in charge of such a valuable racehorse. I began to realize the power these seemingly fragile animals commanded, and as I struggled to control him my respect for the stable lads to whom this was an everyday occurrence increased beyond measure.

The horse was fractious, tossing his head and moving skittishly to one side and then the other as he fought against my feeble attempts to control him. 'Steady, Boy,' I told him in desperation, 'we'll soon have you back in your box and eating your evening meal. You've earned it, by all accounts. Just settle down and follow me, there's a good fellow.'

Strange as it may seem, the nonsense I was spouting

seemed to calm him, and he ambled contentedly after me, entering the loose box that Brian had opened in advance. Soon, he was munching contentedly from the hayrack and we set off back towards the house. 'What shall we do now? I don't have a key.'

I remembered Eve putting the spare set Barbara had lent her in the glove compartment of the Range Rover. 'I have.'

We walked to the back door, only to find that the key wasn't needed. My alarm went into overdrive when we found the house was unlocked; memories of the grim discovery at Armstrong's cottage were still fresh in my mind. I tried to banish these images but without success.

We entered the house, cautiously, aware that danger could be lurking. Brian switched the light on; the kitchen was empty. At first sight, it looked exactly as we had left it that morning, but then I noticed three items on the table that hadn't been there earlier. One was an unopened bottle of champagne, the second, a small silver cup on a plinth. These were obviously the spoils won by Blenheim Boy that afternoon. Alongside these was a sheet of paper bearing only one word scrawled in what looked like felt-tipped pen. The word was 'Latimer'.

Brian snatched it up and turned it over. I saw more writing on the reverse. 'What does it say?' I asked.

He read the message aloud. It was short, stark and chilling. '"You have something of mine. Now I have something of yours. If you want it back wait there for instructions. No police or they die".'

I stared at him and I guess the horror on his face reflected my own. I swallowed a couple of times, and even when I spoke I barely recognized my own voice. 'What can we do?'

Brian shook his head, still in denial at the shocking message in front of him. After a moment or two he said. 'Nothing. We can't do anything. We have to wait.'

He didn't add 'and pray', he didn't need to.

We waited – although it was well past dinnertime, all thought of food had long since deserted me. The oppressive silence was broken only by the ticking of the kitchen clock.

The phone rang, startling me. Brian put his hand on mine, steadying my nerves. That didn't work. He crossed the room and lifted the receiver. I could hear Brian's half of the conversation; it was clear that he was being given instructions.'Yes, I think I know. I found out recently, but I can't take you to it tonight.' He paused to listen. It was obvious he was listening to threats.

'No, it isn't a trick. The place where the gold is can only be accessed during daylight; unless you want a broken neck.' Brian's expression implied he would happily break the neck or arms, or even legs of the person at the other end of the phone. 'It's deep in the forest, in a very tricky place to get to.'

I was to reflect later that it wasn't only me who seemed to have the gift of prophecy. Brian listened again; before saying, 'Very well, eight o'clock in the morning. I promise you; there will be no police. Just one more thing, if you harm them in any way I will kill you very slowly and extremely painfully. Do I make myself clear?'

How much of Brian's threat got through to the kidnappers, I'm not sure, because even from across the room I could hear the dialling tone before he had stopped speaking. He slammed the phone down. 'We have to wait here until morning when they phone with instructions.'

'Are the girls OK?'

His face was grim as he replied. 'They're alive. You heard me ask for proof that they had them. They made them squeal to show me.'

'What next? I can't wait here doing nothing.'

'You won't have to, but neither can we go off charging around in blind panic. We need to think and plan our every move. Luckily they've given us time to do that.'

'Where do we start?'

'Let's review the situation.'

We sat down at the kitchen table and as Brian began his appraisal of how things stood it was clear that his military training had merely accentuated a natural talent for leadership. I wondered what rank he had held in the American forces. I felt rather like a recruit being instructed in the art of guerrilla warfare by an experienced officer.

'The first, and by far the worst problem we have is that we don't know where they are holding the girls. However, thinking of what must have happened here today, they can't be that far away.'

'How do you work that out?'

'Blenheim Boy's race was at three this afternoon. After that the jockey would have to weigh in; then there would be the presentation of the cup, before they took him back to his box. He would need time to cool off, then they would have to load him and drive back. I can't see them getting back here much before six o'clock, can you?'

'I suppose not, and the kidnappers might have had some idea of when we would be home.'

Brian blinked with surprise. 'Why do you think that?'

'I'll tell you in a minute; continue with what you were saying.'

'OK, let's go over what we do know and try to work out what advantage that gives us, if any. First off, thanks to your detective work at the graveyard, we know who they are. Not, as we assumed, Trevor Matthews, but this other character.'

I had thought it must be Trevor Matthews until I read the inscriptions on the graves at Luddenden. The third headstone I spotted, for Harold Matthews' daughter, was the key. Deborah Matthews-Bartlett had died only three years ago, leaving a daughter and a son, Derek; grandson of Harold Matthews.

I explained the connection. 'Derek Bartlett is captain of the shooting syndicate at Rowandale Hall. Another member of the shoot is Ursula Moore, also his mistress. When she isn't shooting or copulating with Bartlett, she's a Leeds' solicitor – in the practice headed by Norman Rhodes. That explains how Bartlett knows so much about you, and why Rhodes was so obstructive. I suspect he was being manipulated by Ursula Moore. It could also explain how they would know what time we were due back here. All she had to do was instruct Rhodes to phone her as soon as we left his office.'

Chapter Twenty-four

Brian had taken full charge of the situation. 'OK, now we have a clear picture of who we're dealing with. You said earlier that you've only seen them in the pub so it's extremely unlikely that they would recognize you. Add that to the fact that they have no idea what I look like and that gives us another potential advantage.'

'What might that be?' I was curious where this was going.

'I'll come back to that in a minute. As for the main problem, how do we find out where the girls are?'

'If your theory about it being somewhere local is correct, the obvious place would be the cottage where Bartlett and Ursula Moore meet up for their dirty weekends. By what Zeke Calvert and Henry Price told me it's over at the far side of the estate, backing onto the moor.'

'I know the one you mean, but I'm not sure they'd use somewhere that could give their identity away. They've gone to some trouble to set Trevor Matthews up as the patsy; using that cottage could spoil that. But it might be worth checking the place out.'

'When are you thinking of doing that?'

'Tonight, of course. Before we do I need to think our strategy through. First, we need food. Food and lots of coffee. There won't be any sleep for us tonight.'

'Why don't I make sandwiches whilst you start thinking?'

By the time I placed the sandwiches on the table, Brian had more or less worked out our plan of action. I handed him a mug of coffee and as I ate, listened while he outlined his ideas.

'Let's start by stating our objectives. A lot of this might seem obvious, but we need it clear in our minds. Most important of all we need to ensure that Babs and Eve are released unharmed.' I nodded. 'We can't rely on bargaining to achieve that. They've already set up Matthews as the fall guy but the girls would be able to identify the real culprits. So unless we engineer their escape, the girls will be killed. We have to outmanoeuvre the killers and set Babs and Eve free ourselves.'

I felt a shiver run down my spine. 'Then how do we go about it?'

'It would help if we knew for definite where they are.'

'OK, again assuming it to be somewhere local and we discount that love nest of theirs, they would need somewhere that was remote, where they would not be overlooked. Ideally it would be somewhere that was –' I stopped in mid-sentence, staring at the house keys I'd put on the table earlier. 'Preferably somewhere unoccupied, remote, and moreover, somewhere Ursula Moore could have obtained keys for without anyone else knowing. Somewhere like Rowandale Hall.'

There was silence as Brian thought this through. 'You're right, Adam. It's the obvious place. That's genius. If that's the case, getting the girls free and clear should be relatively easy for me. However, we're going to need a diversion. Simply storming the place when both Bartlett and Moore are there would be highly dangerous. We must lure one of them, preferably Bartlett, away from the Hall and then deal with the other one. The question is how?'

'The answer to that is the gold,' I said. 'It's what this is all about. If we offer to take him to where the gold is, I bet he'd jump at the idea. I also think he'd leave Ursula to guard the hostages against his safe return and to prevent us invoking the police.'

'That's logical, but it would have to be you that makes the offer. Are you up for it? I'm not decrying your strength or courage, but I'm combat-trained where you aren't. Besides which, I think you'll have the more dangerous task.'

'I'm not worried about that. Well, not too worried.' I saw Brian grin. 'The problem as I see it is that they only want to deal with you.'

'I agree, but how would they know?' Brian asked.

'Sorry, I'm not with you.'

'How would they know if it was you or me? You said it yourself; they've never seen me, and they wouldn't recognize you again. If you present yourself as Brian Latimer, how could they prove otherwise? We're similar in age, height, weight, and build, even hair colouring. So if Norman Rhodes gave Moore a description of me, it could equally well fit you.'

'OK, I'll buy that, but there is one minor detail still troubling me. I've no idea how to get to the place where we think the gold is. That's one extremely large forest, in case you hadn't noticed.'

'Don't worry, by morning you'll be able to find your way there without problem. I warned you we were in for a busy night. One more coffee then we must get started. You make it, I'll nip upstairs to change. Back in a jiffy.'

He returned as I placed the mugs on the table. I glanced up. Brian presented a menacing sight, clad as he was from head to toe in black with the Ka-Bar strapped to his belt in a holster, and on the other side, an even more lethal-looking handgun. 'First stop is your place. You need to change.'

I selected suitable clothing for our trek in the woods and we headed back to Rowandale. Once we were clear of the village, Brian gave me precise instructions. 'As we near the Hall I want you to slow down. Not too much, just as if you were driving on an unfamiliar stretch of road. Don't speed up until we've gone well past. Remember, one of them could be watching.'

His last words prompted a chilling thought. 'What if there are more than two of them? Bartlett owns a big company. He could have got some of his workforce as hired thugs.'

'We'll deal with that problem if and when it arises. It's worth bearing in mind though, and all the more reason for us to be ultra-cautious.'

I did as he ordered, and slowed the Range Rover to no more than thirty miles an hour as we passed the Hall. Brian peered towards the building and once I was beyond the gates, turned to stare out of the rear window.

'Got it!' he exclaimed, triumphantly. 'You were spot on, Adam. There's a faint reflection at the rear of the building. Someone has left a light on in one of the rooms at the back of this side of the house; and it wasn't me. They must have thought because it's at the back that nobody passing on the road would notice. And they probably wouldn't have done, unless they were looking for it specifically, as we were.'

'What now?' I asked.

'Now we head for the forest. About a mile and a half up here there's a sharp left-hand bend. Slow down as you take it and don't accelerate afterwards. About three hundred yards beyond the bend there's a little track goes off to the left. I want you to take it.' He chuckled slightly, 'Anyone seeing the car will think we're lovers seeking a romantic rendezvous.'

'Much as I'm getting to like you, Brian, that was the last thing on my mind.'

He tapped me on the shoulder. 'That's the spirit, Adam. We've got to keep our morale up and jokes, even bad ones like that, are as good a way as any.'

Having left the tarmac surface, we bumped slowly

down the track which had been rutted by any number of heavy vehicles. I assumed these to have been tractors, until Brian explained. 'This is an old lumber trail. It was used to transport timber when the woods were being coppiced. For all I know it's still used, although as Zeke isn't managing the forest any longer, I doubt it.'

'You'll soon be able to find out now that the estate belongs to you.'

'That's true, I never thought of that. Somehow I still can't get used to the idea that I own all this. I suppose it will come, given time.'

'What's the plan? I mean, why are we here?'

'If you succeed in luring Bartlett away from the Hall, you bring him here. Tell him this is the most direct route to where the gold is. That's not true, but he won't know any different. It will give me time to do what I have to, and to catch up with you before you get to the falls.'

'You still haven't explained how I'm going to do that.' As I was speaking the lumber trail, which was hardly wide enough to take the Range Rover let alone commercial vehicles, broadened out into an area big enough to accommodate a dozen cars, I guessed.

'This is where they used to load the wagons,' Brian told me. 'We're on foot from now on. Follow me, and stay close. The first couple of miles will be straightforward enough, because you'll be going down the track they used to haul the logs to the wagons. Barbara's grandfather worked in this part of the forest for years, so I'm told, using his team of heavy horses to drag the timber out of the woods. After we leave this track it gets a bit more complicated, so I'm going to prepare a map for you.'

The night was bright but cold and occasionally, through the canopy of branches overhead, I could see a few stars gleaming brightly. Apart from that, all was dark. Dark but not silent. It takes some time for those unaccustomed to the countryside to appreciate and understand the sounds of the night in woodland such as this. That night was an education for me in more than one way. The soft savagery of an owl hunting for its supper I recognized easily enough, but when it was followed by a blood-curdling scream of pain, I feared that some creature was in mortal agony. Brian put me straight. 'That's a vixen having an orgasm. Sounds terrible, doesn't it?'

'At least someone's enjoying themselves,' I muttered.

Although the dense woodland provided almost as much shelter as a ceiling overhead, we could hear the sound of the wind blowing quite strongly. It rustled the few remaining leaves that had withstood the autumn shedding, and caused the limbs of innumerable trees to creak alarmingly. I felt extremely vulnerable, far from my natural environment. Brian, however, was quite at home, seemingly careless of any danger from falling timber. Likewise, although I stumbled several times when my foot got caught by low brambles, he seemed to be impervious to them. We must have been walking for the best part of half an hour before Brian told me to stop. By now, with no competing light to spoil my night vision, I was able to make out our surroundings – just about. I remembered something a rebel leader had told me long ago, when I was hiding out with his group of tribesmen in the Ethiopian mountains. 'No matter how dense the night, there is always light to guide those who know how to use it.'

Brian spoke, startling me slightly. 'Here's where you will branch off.' I saw his arm wave towards a gap in the undergrowth opposite us. 'Remember to take the fork to the right.' He made it sound like a road junction, which to him I suppose it was. 'Just to be sure, I'm going to give you a direction sign. Wait there and don't move.'

One second he was there alongside me; the next he was gone. The night was silent, apart from the faint rustling of leaves. Either we were in shelter or the wind was dying down. That would mean frost. I wondered if our footsteps would be visible next day, then told myself to forget about it. I had plenty of other things to worry about.

Into the near-silence came a new sound, an incongruous one, for all that we were in a forest. It was almost as if someone was sawing wood. Then the noise ceased as abruptly as it had started. Seconds later, Brian returned.

'Was that you making that noise?'

'Yes, I told you, I was making a signpost for you. As long as you know what to look for and where, you won't miss it. I've cut a square of bark from an ash tree a few yards down the track. I'll do the same again when we get to the next turn.'

'Isn't that a bit risky? What if whoever is with me notices it?'

'I doubt if they will. They'll be too busy watching where they put their feet to look upwards. I shinned up the tree and cut the piece from the trunk about twenty feet overhead.'

He made it sound like a simple, everyday task. Which I suppose for him it was.

After another half hour's walk – or so I guessed, during which we stopped twice for bark removal, I heard a tiny sound in the stillness of the night. At first I wondered if it was the rustle of leaves, but the wind had died away completely. I stopped to listen. The noise was only just audible. It sounded like a human voice, speaking in a whisper, as if keen not to be overheard. Brian too had stopped and seemed to be listening. 'Brian,' I spoke as quietly as I could, 'What's that?'

'That's the Silent Lady. There must have been more snow to melt than I thought; she's making more noise than usual. Come on, we're almost there.'

A few seconds later, we emerged from the woods. I looked up and could see the pattern of thousands of stars in the night sky. What light there was glittered on something in front of me, a broad band of silver that was continuously changing, and I realized we were standing on the bank of Thorsgill Beck, its water twinkling as it flowed swiftly past us.

'This way, Adam, we've a call to make.'

We walked for a few hundred yards, going slowly uphill; our progress slower as we had to scramble over rocks in places. I guessed we were close to the falls, but before we reached them I saw the outline of what appeared to be a building, its oblong shape jutting out slightly from the tree line. I gestured towards it. 'What's that? It looks like a small house.'

'That's exactly what it is. Welcome to my second home.' He approached the building and fiddled with something in front of him. I heard a creaking sound, reminiscent of all those haunted house films, before Brian said, 'Adam, turn your head away and look at the beck for a few seconds.'

I did as instructed, and, after hearing a scraping sound behind me, saw the reflected glow of light in the stream. 'OK, you can turn round now.'

I turned back and stared at the interior of a small log cabin illuminated by an oil lamp that hung suspended from the ceiling. The construction was superb; all the logs joined invisibly and even the furniture looked as if a craftsman had been at work. 'Who built this?' I asked.

'I did; it took me six months to make it weatherproof. Then I had to build the furniture.'

'Where did you get all the tools you needed?'

Brian grinned. 'I stole them from myself. I burgled Rowandale Hall and raided the workshop there. That gave me saws, hammers, screwdrivers, nails, screws, and even some glass for the windows.'

He gestured to each wall and I noticed the apertures for the first time. I walked into the cabin, which was generously proportioned, and examined the interior more closely. There was a double bed which had a mattress and bedding, all folded and piled neatly at the foot. In addition there was a table, two chairs, and a small work surface with a cupboard below. To one side of this, Brian had constructed a kiln-like oven of bricks, with a metal chimney that disappeared through the roof.

'That's clever –' I gestured towards it, '– where did you get the materials? Don't tell me, Rowandale Hall?'

'You got it. Now, how about a cup of coffee and I'll get what I came here for.' He opened the cupboard and took out a small Primus stove. He filled this from a tin of paraffin, before handing me a kettle. 'Go fill that from the stream, would you? I'm afraid I only have powdered milk.'

I returned a few minutes later to see that Brian had unearthed a couple of tin mugs and a pair of binoculars. We sat down to wait for the kettle to boil and he told me about the glasses. 'These are night vision binoculars. I thought they'd come in useful when we go back to the Hall. I want to do a recce before dawn.'

After our drink, Brian took me further upstream to the base of the falls where the beck had formed a deep pool. He gestured to the water. 'The legend is that this pool is bottomless, but I can't say whether that's true or not. I use it as a bath and shower combined. So did Babs when she stayed here.' He turned and handed me the binoculars. 'Focus on the far side of the beck. I think you should be able to see the bell pits from here.'

I did so. The binoculars gave everything a strange, green cast but I could clearly see the depressions where men had delved in ancient times. 'They look like huge bomb craters,' I told him.

'They do a bit, don't they? I'd never thought of them that way. Now, let's head back to the car. We've still lots to do before morning.'

Whilst he was tidying the cabin, I glanced at my watch. It was a few minutes after 1 a.m. As we emerged from the building I looked across the stream; then glanced up to where the Silent Lady loomed, dark against the night sky. Somewhere under that waterfall was the bell pit containing a hoard of gold; the value of which I could not begin to guess. 'One thing you haven't explained is, how do we get across the beck to the pits?'

He chuckled. 'I thought you were never going to ask. The answer is right in front of you, but you won't be able to see it until daylight. There's a set of stepping stones which are clear of the water at all times, unless there's been a torrential downpour. You'll be able to cross them in perfect safety tomorrow.'

'That's lucky.'

'Luck has absolutely nothing to do with it. I put the stepping stones there years ago, with Zeke and Stan Calvert to help me. It was better than having to walk two miles to the nearest crossing point.'

Within minutes we were back in the forest. Brian explained more of what he intended to do. I have to admit that his calm in the face of the danger threatening Barbara and Eve did much to settle my nerves, and as I listened to his scheme I realized that the planning was no accident. His military forbears plus the training given him by the US Army had prepared him for just such an event as this. Had Bartlett or Ursula Moore realized the calibre of the man they were up against, they would have stayed well clear of him. Brian outlined every detail of the plan, like a general briefing his troops before a battle, which in some sense I guess summed the situation up perfectly.

One aspect of the scheme caused me to stop in my tracks and stare at him in surprise. 'Say that again.'

'I think we should go to the police; but not until the girls are safe.'

'But won't that mean telling them about the treasure?'

'Of course it will, but not yet. Anyway, I've decided against keeping the gold. I don't need the money, and it was stolen to begin with. What I do want is to get Babs and Eve to safety and for the murderers to be brought to justice. But first we'll go and check out things at the Hall. I want to be sure the girls haven't been harmed. Your job will be to watch my back.'

Having seen him in action I doubted whether Brian needed anyone to watch out for him, but I agreed to what I felt sure would be a sinecure. When we reached the Hall, Brian instructed me to drive past the main gates and stop after a couple of hundred yards. I had visions of having to scale that wall and battle with the undergrowth again, but he headed straight for the heavy wooden door set into the wall that Eve and I had tried, without success. 'It's locked, Brian.'

He turned and held up a large key. 'One of the advantages of owning the place.' Once inside, I was relieved to see a narrow gravel path flanked by turf. 'Stick to the grass,' Brian ordered. Even I had worked that out.

We reached the building via a route that differed totally from the one I'd used previously. 'Stay here and keep your eyes and ears open. Don't move or make a noise. Remember, sound travels a long way at night.' Brian was speaking in a whisper, and as I strained to hear any further orders, I suddenly realized I was alone.

I'm not sure how long I waited, listening and watching, but it seemed an age before he reappeared. I was able to both see and hear him long before he reached me. That alone should have prepared me for bad news. 'They're gone,' he told me, his tone bleak.

'Gone? Gone where?'

'I don't know; they didn't leave a forwarding address.'

OK, so it was an extremely stupid question to ask, but I wasn't exactly thinking straight. I tried to work out the implications of this unexpected development. 'Are you absolutely certain they were here in the first place? Might you not have been mistaken when you thought you saw that light earlier?'

'No, I wasn't wrong. They were definitely here, and we only missed them by a couple of hours or so. There were empty mugs in the kitchen and the kettle was still slightly warm. In addition to that, I found the scarf Babs was wearing this morning in one of the upstairs rooms. She obviously left it as a signal for me.'

'This rather messes up your plans. Have you any idea what we should do now?'

'We're not beaten yet. Come on; back to the car. Let's go check out the enemy's lair. My bet is that they've moved Babs and Eve to that cottage. I'm not sure why; maybe they felt too exposed. They're expecting us to sit tight waiting for a phone call in the morning but maybe they were worried that we might come here instead.'

'They got that right. Perhaps the solicitor gave Ursula Moore some details about your military service, so they were concerned about the person they were up against.'

We jogged back to the perimeter of the grounds and a few minutes later we were en route for the cottage Bartlett had rented as a love nest: one we thought now had a far more sinister purpose.

Chapter Twenty-five

It was almost 4 a.m. when we reached our destination. The cottage was bordered on three sides by woodland, which made it easily approachable with little fear of detection. Brian pointed to one of the windows. The curtains had not been drawn, leaving a wide beam of light to flood out. 'That's careless,' he whispered. 'They obviously feel far more confident here than they did at the Hall. I noticed all the curtains there had been drawn.'

As we watched, a figure appeared. The man's features were clearly recognizable from our vantage point. 'Is that who you thought?' Brian asked.

'It certainly is. That's Derek Bartlett, grandson of Harold Matthews. And that,' I told him as a second figure joined Bartlett, 'is his mistress, Ursula Moore.'

'OK, I'm going to recce the building. You stay here and if you see or hear any sign of trouble you go crashing in via the front door. It's probably locked, but I want you to make as much noise as possible. Even hurl something through those windows. What I'm after is a diversion.'

'Aren't you going to rescue them now?'

'No, it's far too risky while there are two people guarding them.'

I witnessed again the speed and stealth with which Brian could move. Or rather, I didn't witness it. All I knew is that one second he was there, standing alongside me, issuing instructions, the next he was gone. I waited; eyes and ears alert for the slightest sound, the merest hint of trouble. I'd located a sizeable stone with my foot and picked it up, ready to send it through one of the windows should the need arise, but fortunately I didn't have to use it. Nothing disturbed the stillness of the night until a voice in my ear murmured, 'OK, let's go.'

'How do you do that?' I demanded when we were safely out of earshot. 'Moving so quickly and quietly, I mean?'

'Years of training and a keen desire to avoid being recaptured or killed,' Brian told me. 'Nothing I know concentrates your mind better than fear for your life.'

'What did you learn from your recce?'

'The girls are being kept in a bedroom on the first floor. I shinned up a drainpipe and had a look in through a chink in the curtains. There's no way we could have got to them and released them without risking their lives; not with two captors present. They're not only gagged, but they're fastened to a bed with chains that will take some undoing without a key.' Brian paused and gave a quiet chuckle. 'They don't look happy. Particularly Eve. I wouldn't want to be in the way when she gets free.'

'She's inclined to be a bit fiery,' I told him with just a touch of pride. 'It goes with the hair. What do we do now?'

'Go back to the Hall. I need a pair of strong bolt cutters and I know there are some in the workshop. After that, on to Linden House for you to swap clothes.'

'Why am I swapping clothes?'

'They might bring one or both girls to the rendezvous to identify whoever turns up. If Babs or Eve spot that you're wearing my clothes, they might realize that something is going on. At least that's the theory.'

Brian, it seemed, was leaving little or nothing to chance. That should have settled my nerves, which were growing ever more tense as dawn approached. The calming effect didn't work.

As the time for the phone call approached, I could tell that Brian too was affected by the tension. The call we were both hoping for and dreading at last came, and when the phone rang I looked at Brian. 'You answer it,' he said. 'If you've to meet them, they want the voice to sound the same. Say as little as possible, though.'

I picked up the receiver and said, 'Brian Latimer speaking.' Even saying the name felt strange, and I wondered briefly how I would manage to carry off the impersonation when I came face to face with the kidnappers.

'Go to the gates of Rowandale Hall at ten o'clock and await further instructions. Alone, and don't forget – no police.' The next second, I was listening to the dialling tone. I repeated the message to Brian. 'It was a man's voice, but I can't be sure it was Bartlett because I've never heard him speak. I've heard his laugh, but there was nothing funny in that call.'

'Latimer'. The single word was printed in large letters on an envelope. I stared at it, surprise and dismay mingled. I had arrived at the gates of Rowandale Hall at 10 a.m. prompt as per the telephone instructions. I had expected to meet one of the abductors there, but the area was deserted. I knew that someone was watching me. Brian, of course, but was he the only one? I had dropped him half a mile away a little earlier. He had told me to wait five minutes, and assured me he would be in position, concealed, before I reached the gates.

Having got to the meeting place I waited in the car, but when no one arrived, impatience and tension got the better of me. I opened the door and stepped out. Perhaps the sight of the man dressed in Brian's clothes would prompt someone to appear. It didn't. I can't remember how long I spent walking to and fro before I noticed the envelope, but it must have been several minutes. Eventually, I looked round; taking my eyes from the road for the first time and it was then that I saw the object. It had been wedged between the double gates, propped in position by one of the chains held in place by a padlock. I walked over and removed it, hoping it wouldn't turn out to be a flyer advertising double glazing or cavity wall insulation. It wasn't.

The envelope was addressed to Latimer, so I reasoned that as I was impersonating him it would appear natural for me to open it. I tore it open, still conscious that someone might well be watching me as I examined the single sheet of paper it contained.

The instructions were simple and to the point. 'Go to Brent Cottage and await further orders'. I read them aloud, hoping that Brian was close enough to hear me.

'Get back in the car, turn round, and pick me up where you dropped me off.' He had been close enough after all. I'd no idea exactly where he was hiding. By the sound of his voice he could only have been a few yards away, but so good was his concealment that I couldn't see him.

I obeyed instructions and seconds after I pulled to a halt further down the road, Brian dived into the passenger seat. 'Linden House, as fast as you can,' he ordered, his voice crackling with tension.

'Why Linden House? The instructions were to go to their cottage.'

'Because I made a dreadful mistake. A basic error any raw recruit would be ashamed of. Hopefully nobody was watching you collect that envelope, because if they were I might have blown the whole operation.'

'What mistake?' For my part I thought he'd planned everything down to the finest detail.

'I was supposed to be the one who kept that appointment. Alone, they said.'

'Yes, what of it?'

'I wouldn't have turned up in your car, would I? Not if it really was Brian Latimer at the gates of the Hall. I would either have been dropped off, or in Barbara's car, certainly not in your Range Rover. That would have been a dead giveaway.'

'Oh, I never thought of that, but you could have said you'd borrowed it.'

'You're missing the point. These people will be extremely nervous and highly suspicious of anything out of the ordinary. They've already killed three people and they have two more hostage. We can't afford to do anything that might cause them to act hastily; not until we're ready to make our move.'

'So, why are we going to Linden House?'

'We're going there for you to collect Barbara's car and drive to Brent Cottage in it. I will follow you in your car.'

I pulled up outside the cottage, where two expensive-looking cars were already in position. Judging from the personalised number plates on them, I assumed the Mercedes to be Bartlett's. The Porsche, I guessed, belonged to Ursula Moore. I smiled grimly. The fact that they were prepared to leave these pointers to their identity on display reinforced Brian's thinking that the couple were not intending any of us to survive once they had the gold.

The logic behind Brian's argument was strengthened by the fact that they had a ready-made scapegoat in Trevor Matthews. If their plans went ahead without a hitch, he would be convicted for the three murders they had already committed. Another three added to that wouldn't make a scrap of difference – to them. Nor would it add to Matthews' sentence. The only people to be affected would be the three new victims, Barbara, Eve, and Brian. Only it wouldn't be Brian, it would be me.

My objective was to put a spanner in their works. 'Here goes,' I muttered. I got out of Barbara's car and walked slowly across to the front door. There was no sign of life inside. I was uncomfortable; aware that we might already be too late. Had they moved the girls again? Simply because there were two cars outside didn't mean they hadn't used another vehicle. If they had moved, this would be only another round in their game of cat and mouse. And if Eve and Barbara weren't inside the cottage, all Brian's meticulous planning and preparation would be in vain.

I knew Brian was close by. I would have preferred him to be alongside me. In fact I would have preferred him to be here instead of me, or better still for neither of us to have to be in this position. The ordeal of the past few hours since we discovered that Eve and Barbara had been abducted was far from over. I only hoped it would end quickly and without adding to the torment we had already endured.

I knocked loudly on the door, aiming for bravado I didn't feel. 'Hello,' I shouted. 'It's Brian Latimer.'

There was no reply, not that I gave the occupants, if there were any, much of a chance. 'Hello,' I shouted again, and this time even louder. 'It's Brian Latimer. Is anyone there?'

Hopefully, either Eve or Barbara would have heard my voice shouting Brian's name and cottoned on by now. I dare not risk another repeat performance. I tried to ignore the flicker of movement I saw in my peripheral vision. Someone had peered out from behind one of the drawn curtains in the upstairs room. Short of yelling, 'do you want this bloody gold or not' there was little I could do but wait. At least I knew there was someone inside.

After what seemed an age, I heard a key being turned in the lock and the front door opened fractionally to reveal Derek Bartlett standing behind it. The fact that he made no attempt to hide or disguise his face was yet more confirmation of their intention to kill anyone who could identify them. The particularly unpleasant-looking revolver he was pointing at me simply underlined the immediacy of that threat.

'I'm Brian Latimer,' I told him. 'Who are you?'

'Never mind who I am. Did you come alone?'

'Of course I did. Those were your instructions.' My voice was raised in mock anger, to make it seem natural, as I added, 'Adam Bailey wanted to come with me but I wouldn't let him.'

'Where is my gold?'

'Hang on; first I want to know if Barbara and her friend are all right. If you've harmed them in any way …'

'Stay there,' Bartlett told me. He turned and called into the house. 'Bring one of them here for Latimer to inspect. Not the horsewoman, the other one.'

A few seconds passed before Eve appeared, her wrists bound in front of her. 'Hello, Eve. Adam sends you his love. He would have come with me if he'd been allowed.'

'Never mind that crap,' Bartlett interrupted. He turned to Eve. 'Who is this?' He pointed towards where I was standing.

'That's Brian Latimer,' Eve told him. 'He's engaged to Barbara.'

Bartlett nodded, and a split second later Eve was dragged out of my sight. Bartlett told his companion, who still hadn't shown herself, 'Take her back upstairs. I'll wait here. Come back and lock this door.'

He stepped outside and pulled the door to behind him. 'OK, you've seen one of the women. Now, what about my gold?'

'I told you, it's in the forest. At least I think so.'

'How do I know you're telling the truth? How do I know you haven't found it already?'

'Because I've only recently discovered my grandfather's memoir. It described where he hid the gold. I haven't had chance to search for it yet.'

'Your father might have found it years ago and spent the money. I heard the estate was skint until a few years back.'

'My father didn't believe the gold existed. He thought

it was only a fairy story made up by my grandmother. The money he used to turn the estate round came from his success in investing on the stock exchange and nowhere else.' I paused, before adding, 'The fact that you're aware of the gold's existence means that you must be descended from Harold Matthews who was with my grandfather on that expedition in Africa.'

'What does it matter if I am related to him? Did you know your grandfather tried to kill him out there in the wilds so he could keep all of the gold? I bet he didn't put that in his memoir.'

'He did, but the way he told the story, it was Matthews who tried to kill him.'

Bartlett waved a dismissive hand. 'That's all ancient history now. I'm more concerned with the present day.'

'If you're descended from him, you must be Trevor Matthews. Barbara told me you were desperate to get your hands on my estate. Now I understand why.'

'That's correct; but don't get too excited. It isn't knowledge that you're likely to be able to share with anyone else.'

Bartlett had made another basic error. By hinting at their intentions, he had confirmed what Brian and I had guessed. The knowledge that we'd been correct brought absolutely no comfort.

I hoped I had managed to convince Bartlett that I was indeed Latimer by my intimate knowledge of Everett's memoir. I also hoped I'd persuaded him I thought he was Trevor Matthews, despite the evidence to the contrary from those number plates.

Once he heard the key in the lock, he gestured towards Barbara's car. 'Drive.'

I climbed into the driving seat and started the engine. I deliberately made a hash of engaging reverse gear. 'Sorry,' I told Bartlett, who was alongside me, 'I'm a bit out of practice at driving.'

We reached the main road and as I glanced right and left to make sure there was no traffic, I noticed that Bartlett had relaxed. This should have been good news, but I realized that the revolver, which had been pointed at my heart, was now aimed at a very sensitive part of my anatomy. Eve wouldn't be at all happy if I got wounded there, I thought.

Chapter Twenty-six

When we reached the clearing in the forest, I stopped the car with its front end facing the woodland. Bartlett ordered me to get out of the car first. I did so and began walking towards the rear of the vehicle.

'Where the hell are you going?'

I turned and stared at him coldly. 'I'm going to get a couple of shovels out of the boot. You surely don't imagine my grandfather would have been stupid enough to leave the gold out in the open, for any Tom, Dick, or Harry to discover by accident, do you? Have you never heard the expression, "money doesn't grow on trees"? That's bound to be true in this case. Only an idiot would believe we could find it without having to work for our reward.'

I tried to put as much arrogance and contempt into my voice as I could. That, along with the insults, I hoped would rile Bartlett. I wanted him angry. The risk was small. He needed me, or Latimer, as he believed me to be, at least until such time as he got his hands on the gold. After that I knew it would be open season on me. Before then I hoped to provoke him into making a mistake. Not yet, but as soon as I was certain that Eve and Barbara were safe.

I held a shovel out for Bartlett to carry, an offer he declined. His refusal came in the form of a gesture with the gun that was unmistakeable. I stared at him coldly. 'And how do you think you're going to find the gold without me to help you?' I gestured towards the woods. 'If you don't have me along to guide you, I reckon you'd be lost within half an hour of going in there.'

'Yes, and if I don't return safe and sound with the gold, that woman of yours and her ginger-haired friend will be dead meat, so get on with it.'

I led the way into the forest. On my previous trek I'd lost track of time, but Brian hadn't. Earlier that morning he'd told me how long it would take to reach the various markers he'd carved for my guidance.

After we'd been walking for twenty minutes or so, I judged it to be time to stir Bartlett up a bit. Apart from that, the story I was about to tell him might make him stop and reconsider before acting rashly. 'Have you ever been in the forest before?' I asked him as an opener.

'Shut up and keep walking.'

I glanced back over my shoulder. Bartlett was obviously out of condition. The walk wasn't exactly a forced march because the terrain didn't allow for rapid progress. Despite that, he was already perspiring freely. That gave me the perfect excuse to mop my face, and by pretending I was sweating too, I had chance to check my watch without arousing suspicion.

'Did you know the forest has a very bad reputation? The locals believe these woods to be haunted.'

'No, I didn't, I told you to shut up.' It seemed that conversation wasn't his strong point.

I ignored the instruction. 'I'm not saying I've seen the ghosts myself, but I do know others who have. They say they're the spirits of three dead children who were murdered in these woods. Either that; or they wandered in here, got lost, and were devoured by wolves, or bears. Yes, it wasn't that long ago that this forest was home to both bears and wolves. According to the legend, the ghosts of the dead children roam the forest for all eternity looking for a way out. The most sinister part of the legend is about their uncanny ability to foretell death. I'm told they appear to someone close to the person who is about to die, and to nobody else.'

'Superstitious claptrap,' he growled.

'That's as maybe. The story of the children might be no more than a myth but I remember something else that happened in here when I was a small boy. Two ramblers who were part of a walking party got separated from their colleagues in the forest. They were unable to find their way out, and although the others raised the alarm and search parties were sent out, they didn't find the bodies until over two weeks later. Of course, there wasn't a lot left of them by that time. If I remember it right, they never could tell whether they died of starvation or whether they were killed by predators. Animals,' I added cheerfully, 'there are plenty of carnivores in this forest. Did you know there's a herd of wild boar in here? They're extremely dangerous. Then there are the foxes and badgers, to say nothing of the eagles and crows. And of course the maggots. No, it's hardly surprising they couldn't tell which was the man and which was the woman.'

I looked at Bartlett again as I finished spinning my preposterous yarn. There was little doubt that he believed every word of it. Proof of how well he'd been taken in came via his pale expression and the nervous glances he kept casting towards the dense woodland that was all around us.

He was obviously trying to remember where he was, but any attempt to fix your bearings in such thick cover was impossible; certainly without a signpost. As I turned back to concentrate on the track ahead, I noticed the first of the carved pieces of trunk a short distance ahead. I was confident that Bartlett wouldn't see it, let alone realize its significance, because had I not been on the lookout for it, I would most certainly have overlooked the bare rectangle where the bark had been removed.

'We turn off here,' I told Bartlett confidently when we reached the fork in the track. 'The trail we were on was part of the old logging route. From now on it gets harder.

This bit has only been used by deer, and possibly wild boar,' I added, to remind him of the creatures he might encounter.

I think my intimate knowledge of the forest, as he perceived it, must have dispelled any lingering doubts he might have held regarding my identity, and I began to feel more comfortable. Apart from the shirt I was wearing, that is. It was of a thick weave that was uncomfortably hot and itchy. I made a mental note to have a word with Brian about his taste in clothing.

Always at the back of my mind during that long trek was concern for how he was faring with his mission to rescue Eve and Barbara. I felt a degree of confidence from the fact that he would be taking Bartlett's partner in crime by complete surprise. That, along with Brian's undoubted military prowess, bolstered my hopes, but there was always a degree of concern that something might go wrong. At least our little charade at the doorway of Brent Cottage had made Eve aware that something was about to kick off, and I knew that the girls would be ready to assist Brian if the need arose.

Quite how Brian had intended to carry out the rescue bid, I wasn't sure. However, as I'd been changing into his clothes at Linden House I'd glanced out of the window in time to see him loading various items into the back of the Range Rover, one of which looked suspiciously like a petrol can. The significance of this became more apparent when I'd been chauffeuring Bartlett towards the forest. When we'd been travelling about a mile or so, I'd glanced in my rear-view mirror and seen a plume of smoke rising from near the cottage where the girls were being held. Had Brian torched the building, I wondered?

Although he hadn't let me into his confidence about the rescue bid, Brian had given me clear instructions as to what to do when I reached the falls. 'Cross over the beck using the stepping stones and as soon as you reach the other side; look up towards the Silent Lady. If I've been successful, you'll know straightaway.'

'How?'

'Because either Barbara or Eve will be standing there, on the right hand side of the falls as you look at them. She'll only be visible for a second or so, in case Bartlett looks that way too.'

Eventually, we reached the clearing, and I was able to appreciate how clever Brian's handiwork had been. Even in daylight, the log cabin he had constructed was barely noticeable, camouflaged as it was by the surrounding trees and the dense undergrowth of briars, brambles, and bracken. To distract Bartlett from seeing the cabin rather than imparting information, I told him, 'We need to cross the beck. The place where the gold is hidden is on the opposite bank somewhere.'

I gestured towards where Brian had told me the stepping stones had been placed. Bartlett stared at the steep banks of Thorsgill Beck. 'How are we going to do that?' His tone was weary, and as I glanced at him, I noticed how pale and tired he looked. That cheered me. Tired men make mistakes; their reflexes are slower, and they fail to take in minute details, which was exactly what I wanted.

Bartlett's question should have been easy to answer, but in truth I wasn't sure. Although Brian had assured me the stepping stones would be clear, when seen in daylight, Thorsgill Beck appeared to be in full spate; leading me to wonder if the stones would be clear of the surface. 'Follow me,' I told him, my tone reflecting confidence I didn't feel.

'Don't worry,' he snarled, 'I'll be right behind you.'

The crossing was clear, I could tell as soon as I reached the bank. There was about six inches between the surface of the beck and the top of the stones. However, their surface was damp, and the growth of moss on them could have made the crossing tricky. In the event, I made it in perfect safety, and as I reached the far side, I risked a glance towards the Silent Lady. Sure enough, exactly as Brian had promised, I caught a quick glimpse of a figure standing on the edge of the escarpment to the right of the falls. It was only momentary, but before they vanished from view I was able to recognize them, and my heart rejoiced. There was no mistaking that red-gold hair.

Bartlett had kept pace with me, two stones back to ensure I didn't misbehave during the crossing, and once he stepped onto dry land I gestured towards the falls. 'We go that way. From what Grandfather wrote, I believe the gold is in one of these pits, but as to which one, I've no idea.'

Reaching our destination took longer than I'd anticipated, as I insisted on descending into each of the bell pits to inspect them for signs of the buried treasure. Bartlett remained on top, prowling the rim of the crater, his eyes never leaving me. It must have seemed to him that I was as keen to discover the gold as he was, whereas the reality was that I was playing for time, to enable Brian to reach a place where he could launch an ambush.

None of the excavations yielded any clue that might suggest treasure within, until we came to the final one. It was close to the edge of the cliff that housed the Silent Lady, and here the waterfall at last belied its name. Although the sound was barely noticeable even after we crossed the beck, when we were nearing the falls the volume increased. It was by no means deafening, but loud enough to mask other noises. This was to my advantage, I thought.

As I stared into the bell pit, I noticed something unusual on the side facing the Silent Lady. It was a pile of rocks that appeared to have been left in purely haphazard fashion, but as I stared at them I was able to make out the shape of the two letters E and L picked out in stone. Unless someone was concentrating on that heap of rock, they would never have spotted the hidden sign, or thought it anything more than a random chance that had left them like that.

I gestured towards the pit. 'The gold must be in there,' I told him. 'I think we should remove those stones and see what's behind them.'

As I spoke I was thinking, where the hell is Brian? Why hasn't he shown his hand before now?

'Get down there and start digging, then.' Bartlett's order was curt, but then I was getting used to his abrupt manner.

'I take it that means you're not going to help?'

'Do as you're told.'

I looked at him. The trek had obviously taken its toll. It had been tiring for me, coming after a long day and a sleepless night combined with a lot of physical activity, but I was younger, much fitter, and more used to exertion, I guessed. Despite the cold weather, Bartlett was sweating profusely, his face grey and etched with weariness, or pain, or both.

I began my climb down to the base of the pit and after ordering me to go to the far side, close to the stone cairn, Bartlett followed suit. I watched him, but my eyes were trained on a spot behind and above him. There, all but hidden by the rim of the crater, was Brian, clearly assessing the scene below, judging the right moment to attack. It came, faster than any of us could have anticipated.

My attention reverted to Bartlett. At first I thought he was staring at me, but then I noticed that his gaze was at something behind me and to my left. I looked over my shoulder, but all I could see was the cliff face. I turned back towards Bartlett. He was still looking towards the same spot, his face a mask of indescribable horror. He raised his hand, the one not holding the revolver, and pointed to where he was looking. I saw that his hand was trembling and his face was ashen, the last vestige of colour drained away. 'They're here! The children. They're here. Can't you see them? Three of them, just as you said. All covered in blood, like the legend.' His voice trembled.

I looked again, but still couldn't see anything but the cliff, the pile of stones and some wispy grass. 'I can't see anything.'

'You must see them. Right there.'

I shook my head. 'You're imagining things.'

Above and to his right I could see Brian poised, as if about to attack. Bartlett made it easier for him by backing away towards the far wall of the bell pit, desperate to get away from whatever apparitions only he could see. 'No, no, go away. Look, they're pointing at me. They're telling me it's me they want. Can't you see? Can't you understand?'

From being in total command of the situation, Bartlett was now a hysterical, quivering wreck. I stepped forward, hoping to keep his attention focused on what was happening within the pit rather than what was about to take place above.

'Go away, I tell you. Leave me alone.' Bartlett's plea was my cue to risk a second pace forward. As I moved, something hit me very hard in the small of my back. I felt a violent thump on my head and then everything went black.

Chapter Twenty-seven

'He's coming round.'

I recognized the voice and I know I was smiling even before I opened my eyes. Eve was cradling me in her arms, but as I struggled to sit up I could see we were still in the bell pit, which had become very crowded. To my right, Bartlett was seated, still staring towards the falls, but he no longer held the revolver. His wrists were secured with handcuffs, which I assumed had been provided by John Pickersgill. The constable was standing a couple of yards away from his prisoner, talking to Brian whilst making notes in his occurrence book.

Barbara was also crouched alongside me. I looked back at Eve, staring into her beautiful eyes as I asked, 'What happened to me?'

Eve gestured beyond me. You were hit by a low-flying solicitor.'

I turned my head cautiously and noticed the limp body of a woman stretched out on the floor of the bell pit, gagged and with her hands tied. 'Is that Ursula Moore? Is she ...?'

'Dead as a doornail,' Eve replied cheerfully. 'But don't let it worry you, Adam, she's no loss. She murdered three people and bragged that she was going to do the same to us. What's more, she tried to, even though Brian had left her tied up.'

'What happened to her? How did she die?'

'Babs was standing on the cliff top, watching Brian, who was about to ambush Bartlett. The idea was that she could distract Bartlett's attention long enough for Brian to overpower him. Suddenly, Moore ran at her and tried to knock her over the edge. Luckily I saw her in time. I stuck my foot out and tripped her up. I sent her flying, but I didn't expect her to crash-land on you. Whether it was the fall, colliding with you, or hitting her head on the floor of the pit, we'll probably never know, but the result is she's got a broken neck.'

'How did Pickersgill get here?'

'We called at his place en route to here, but he was out, so we left a message with his wife for him to follow us. Brian borrowed a lot of those traffic cones from the police house and left them to mark the route. We brought Moore along as a possible bargaining chip, but we never expected her to take up diving.'

'What happened down here?' Barbara asked. 'One moment Bartlett was threatening you with the gun, the next he looked terrified and when Brian got to him he took the gun from him as easy as anything.'

Eve was watching me as Barbara spoke, and her words brought back my memory of the events leading up to Bartlett's surrender. 'Are you all right, Adam? You've gone quite pale.'

I shook my head, partly to clear the memory of what Bartlett had said; of what he had seen. 'I'll explain later. First of all, I have to try and understand it myself.'

The bell pit became even more crowded once DI Hardy and the young DC arrived, accompanied by four uniformed officers. I gathered that Pickersgill had summoned reinforcements before setting out in pursuit of Brian and the girls. They too had been given instructions to follow the traffic cones.

Two of the uniformed men departed, taking Bartlett with them and with instructions to call the pathologist and coroner. As they left, Bartlett, who as far as I could tell hadn't spoken a word since Ursula Moore's death, stopped alongside where I was sitting watching events unfold. He looked at me, his eyes haunted as he pleaded. 'Did you see them? Please tell me you saw them?'

I shook my head. 'Sorry, I didn't see anything. Only the rocks.'

His shoulders slumped wearily, as if this was the final defeat, and the light died in his eyes.

As we watched him go, Eve asked, 'What did he mean? Who was he talking about? What was it he thought you saw?'

'Leave it for now, Evie. I'll explain later, but not here. Not in this place.'

At that moment Brian came across to join us. 'Hardy's got the gist of what happened here and earlier, but he wants to talk to everyone concerned. I suggested we adjourn to the cabin and he can join us there later when he's finished sorting things out and supervising the removal of the body and so on. Anyone fancy a cuppa?'

We went across the beck and entered the cabin, where Eve and Barbara insisted I sit down whilst they helped Brian prepare our drinks. Once the kettle was on the gas, Brian looked across the room. 'How are you feeling, Adam?'

'I'm OK; just a bit of a sore head, that's all.'

Eve, who hadn't been inside the cabin before, was looking around her eyes widening with surprise as she saw just how comfortable it was. 'You did all this yourself?' she asked Brian.

He nodded, before revealing his plan. 'Actually, it's given me an idea. I'm thinking of building some more, along the banks of Thorsgill Beck. This part of the forest is rarely seen by anyone apart from perhaps me and Barbara, or Zeke Calvert, and it's so picturesque I thought it would be a great location for some holiday cabins. I could rent them out for campers, or for adventure expeditions, anglers, birdwatchers, you name it.'

'That sounds like a great idea,' Barbara agreed.

Once the kettle boiled, Brian brought me a mug and sat down alongside me. 'Are you ready to tell us what happened back there? It seemed very odd, the way things turned out. One minute Bartlett was threatening you; the next he was a gibbering wreck. And that was before the woman died. I know he was talking, but I couldn't hear a word of what he said because of the noise from the waterfall. So what exactly did go on?'

I took a deep breath, gathering both my thoughts and my courage before launching into what many would regard as a preposterous tale. I'd known all along I would have to explain sooner or later. It might as well be sooner, before my nerve failed me and I bottled it up.

'I now believe I understand the final part of Everett Latimer's cryptic rhyme,' I told them. 'When he went to bury that gold in the bell pit he discovered something else. Something that had been buried there since long before the gold had been created. Something that had lain undisturbed for centuries, possibly millennia.'

I watched them exchange glances, and smiled as I interpreted their thoughts. They were obviously wondering how much damage the blow to my head had caused, for me to be talking so wildly. I hastened to reassure them. 'It's all right, I'm not wandering. What I'm about to tell you isn't the result of concussion. The problem is that events in the bell pit have been difficult for me to come to terms with, let alone describe to someone else. If I hadn't been given advance knowledge of the subject, I don't think I could even begin to explain it. Understanding what lay behind what Bartlett saw, or thought he saw, in there doesn't help me to come up with a rational explanation, because I don't believe one exists.'

I paused and took a sip of my tea before continuing. 'Bartlett was threatening me with the revolver, but suddenly his attention was distracted by something in front of that heap of rocks where I believe Everett Latimer hid the gold.' I hesitated for a second. 'What he saw was the children.' I looked at the disbelief on their faces but continued, 'He knew the story, because I repeated the legend to him as we were walking through the forest. I was only trying to scare him; to put him off his guard, nothing more than that. I had no idea it would seem like a prophecy come true such a short time later. I even explained that the children only appear shortly before someone dies, and that they usually only appear to somebody closely connected to the victim.'

'You're saying that Bartlett saw the three children?' Brian's voice reflected his obvious surprise.

'He did; and I had no trouble believing him, because he described them almost exactly as you had done. He mentioned their torn clothing, the blood that was spattered all over them, the piteous, haunted expression on their faces. He pointed them out to me, but when I turned to look, all I could see was the heap of stones, some wispy grass and the escarpment alongside the falls. What really spooks me is that within minutes of the apparitions manifesting themselves to Bartlett, his partner in crime had been killed in a very sudden and violent manner. How you explain that? I've no idea, because I certainly can't find a logical explanation for it.'

'You believe that Bartlett actually saw the children; the ones described in the skipping rhyme?' Eve asked. I nodded. 'But I thought they only appear to locals, or people with local connections?'

'Perhaps Bartlett's quest for the gold qualified him as having a local connection,' I told her. 'Or maybe it was the location that overrode the normal rules.'

'What do you mean?' Barbara asked.

'I mean that I believe that when the stones that Everett Latimer carefully piled up so they spelt out his initials are removed, we will not only find the gold there, but also the bodies of those three dead children. Remember the rhyme? The location of the gold was described as "sleeping with those who are free from sin". I believe the children lie behind that wall of stone.

As the others dwelt on this, I asked Brian, 'How did you rescue Eve and Barbara?' I thought it was time to change the subject before I was asked any further questions for which I had no answer, and for which, as far as I could tell, there was no logical explanation.

'It was all fairly simple. It went even better than I'd hoped. I knew the cottage had two entrances. In addition to the front door, there's another one round the back. So I waited until you had been gone a few minutes and then I sneaked up to the front door and poured petrol over it. I set fire to the door and then waited by the rear entrance. Sure enough, the Moore woman came dashing out a few minutes later. She was going too fast to spot the danger before it was too late. I knocked her out, tied her up and dumped her in the back of your car; then went inside for the girls. Once I'd freed them and got them out of the cottage, we set off for the police house. Oh, by the way –' Brian smiled apologetically, '– I owe you a fire extinguisher. I used the one from the Range Rover to put out the blaze on the front door. Fortunately, the door's made of oak, so it should repair easily enough.'

Barbara took up the story. 'After we'd explained what was going on to Mrs Pickersgill, Brian brought us into the forest after you. We had to frog-march the woman between us. We must have looked really odd, with Eve and me dragging the woman along, and Brian toting a collection of traffic cones. However, we made really good time.'

'That's right,' Brian added, 'so good that we were watching you even before you reached the stepping stones. And the rest of it, you know.'

Chapter Twenty-eight

A week passed, during which little happened beyond a spate of interviews with DI Hardy and his colleague, interspersed with the tedious but necessary process of making statements. During the first of these, Brian showed Hardy his grandfather's memoir and we explained the connection between Bartlett and Harold Matthews. It was then that Hardy insisted this particular item be omitted from any statements. 'If word got out about the possible existence of treasure and the media got hold of it, there might be the biggest gold rush since the Klondike. The forest would be overflowing with prospectors.'

In a later interview, Hardy revealed that they had sent the revolver to a ballistics expert for checking. 'It was manufactured by Webley and Scott and is quite old. Judging by the date, I'd say it could have been issued to Bartlett's grandfather when he received his commission.' He grinned and added, 'The ironic part is that Bartlett couldn't have harmed you with that weapon unless he'd clubbed you over the head with it. The firing mechanism had been disabled.'

Hardy also provided the answer to a question that had been puzzling me ever since the dramatic events in the forest. 'Why were Bartlett and Moore prepared to reveal their identity?' I asked. 'I can understand that they intended to kill us, but supposing we'd left a message for someone giving details of where we had gone, and who with? They only had three of us under their control. How did they intend to silence the other one?'

'The answer is that they had no intention of hanging

around for anything such as that to become a problem. Bartlett has been talking freely, and from what he's told us it seems that they started out with the intention of their identity remaining secret. That was why they went to so much trouble to set Trevor Matthews up as the scapegoat. However, events over which they had no control overtook them. I'm not speaking of Latimer's dramatic reappearance after everyone believed him to be dead, although that certainly didn't help.'

Hardy sipped the tea that Eve had made, and after setting the mug down carefully, leaned forward in his chair. 'Bartlett's company was already in serious financial trouble before they started this. The firm had been hit very badly by the property slump in the mid-seventies and had been teetering on the brink of collapse ever since. In order to dig himself out of the mess and stave off the threatened insolvency, Bartlett took on a contract that should have been extremely lucrative. If that had worked out, perhaps none of the rest of this would have happened. We'll never know. Unfortunately, the contract that should have saved Bartlett's bacon had quite the opposite effect. There were severe penalty clauses written into it, and when he failed to meet the completion deadline these were invoked. My colleagues in Leeds went to Bartlett's business address at my request, only to be greeted by the receivers who had been put in by the company's creditors.'

'That explains why he was so desperate to get hold of the gold,' Eve remarked, 'he wasn't interested in the estate at all. But it doesn't explain the motive for Charles Lewis's murder.'

'Eve's right,' I added. 'Nor does it explain why Ursula Moore was so keen to go along with Bartlett's scheme.'

'Lewis's murder resulted from his own greed more than anything. He wanted money, and Ursula Moore was his preferred source of income. In other words he was blackmailing her. Not only over her affair with Bartlett, but because she'd represented a series of clients who she got acquitted of all sorts of crimes There were assault cases, robberies, and biggest of all, a property swindle which involved grants, amongst other things. There were forged planning consents and a lot of other financial irregularities, and she managed to secure the acquittals by bribing or threatening witnesses and jurors alike. The person she chose as her intermediary to pass the money to the people she'd suborned was Lewis. To be fair, I don't think she could have made a more disastrous choice. That flash car Lewis drove was supposed to be part of his reward for services rendered, but from what Bartlett told us, Lewis only considered it to be a down payment. Eventually, his demands got too exorbitant for them to pay.'

Hardy took another swig of his tea. 'According to Bartlett, they met with Lewis on the day of the murder to try and reason with him, but the argument got heated and when Lewis threatened to go to the Law Society, Moore stabbed him. Unfortunately for her, Armstrong and Veronica Matthews witnessed the murder whilst they were having a little afternoon delight in his cottage across the beck. Instead of silencing a witness to the bribery allegations, Moore laid herself open to blackmail because of the murder. When Armstrong approached her for money; he and Veronica Matthews had to die as well. We found the murder weapon, hidden at Brent Cottage. It had blood that matched all three victims on it, and the only prints were those of Ursula Moore.'

Hardy drained his mug before concluding. 'With Bartlett's company about to go bust, and Moore likely to be disbarred, or worse, there was nothing to keep them in this country. We discovered documents in Moore's flat that showed they intended to disappear and set up home in South America. That's what's known in police circles as "doing a Ronnie Biggs". What they didn't bargain for was coming up against you two and Brian Latimer. As a result of what Bartlett told us in his confession, our colleagues in Leeds have already made several arrests. I think the detectives want to adopt you.'

He looked at me, then at Brian, before asking, 'What can you tell me about this other matter Bartlett has been on about? He keeps asking if we've found the children. The ones covered in blood.'

Over a month had passed since the death of Ursula Moore and the arrest of Derek Bartlett. I was working on a new manuscript, whilst Eve was wrapping Christmas presents. My thought processes were disturbed when the phone rang. Eve answered it, and then told me, 'It's Brian on the line. He wants to know if we're busy tomorrow. I said I didn't think so. They're going to excavate for the gold, and he'd like us to go along.'

When we arrived at the waterfall the following day, it seemed that Brian wanted more than merely our presence. I glanced around the bell pit after helping Eve down the steep side. If it had seemed crowded the last time I was there, it was even more so now. Brian introduced a string of officials from various government departments who all had a vested interest in the treasure, plus several archaeologists. 'They want me to begin removing the stones to start the dig,' Brian told me, 'but I've decided that the task should go to you.'

'Me? Why me?'

'Because you deciphered the rhyme. If you hadn't worked out where the gold was buried, we'd not be here today.'

'There's no proof the gold really is here,' I pointed out. 'It's only guesswork. Everett could have been playing an elaborate prank.'

Brian grinned. 'That's the other reason I want you to do it. I've told everyone you were the clever clogs who worked out the clues, so if it proves to be a hoax you'll be the one with egg on your face.'

'Oh, thanks, Brian. Thanks a bunch.'

I began work, conscious of my audience which included several cameramen. I removed a few stones, passing them to willing assistants who stacked them at the far side of the bell pit. As I worked, I became aware of the musty, slightly unpleasant odour from within the recess that lay behind the wall of rock.

After I'd taken about a dozen small boulders from the pile, one of the archaeologists suggested we should take a look inside before continuing with what might prove to be a fruitless task. He held out a torch, and I scrambled up the cairn and shone the light inside.

There, as I'd hoped, were the stout wooden boxes I knew would contain the treasure. The torch beam moved as I straightened up to inform the others of my discovery and I stared in horror at what it now revealed. Beyond the crates, in a neat line, there were three sets of skeletal remains, their skulls propped against the rear of what was a small cave, as if they had lain there to go to sleep. The small stature of the skeletons told me all I needed to know.

Expert analysis would later confirm that the remains were those of three children who had been between the ages of eight and twelve years old at the time of their death. The tests also established that the remains dated from somewhere in the region of a thousand years ago, which would have placed them at around the time of the Viking incursions, or possibly the Norman conquest of Britain. Although all flesh and tissue had long since gone, post-mortem examinations revealed that all three had been murdered, their throats cut with such violence that the marks of the blade were visible via notches on their bones.

St Mary's Church in Elmfield was packed to overflowing long before the service was scheduled to start. After Eve and I took our places in the front pew alongside Brian and Barbara, I took the opportunity to look around the building, which I'd never been inside before. I'd seen it when driving past of course, and had frequently marvelled at such a large church being built to service so small a community. It was typical of many constructed by the Normans following the invasion of 1066, although St Mary's was on a grander scale than most. Equally unusual for a country church was the fact that St Mary's boasted a lady chapel.

It was to this building that Barbara and Brian had been brought when they were christened, and here that they worshipped as children. It seemed appropriate that the adventure in which they had been so closely involved should end here.

Many of those attending that day were locals, but they would not have filled the church, let alone caused some to stand, or to remain outside. Their numbers had been swelled by the hordes of media representatives and those merely curious to observe proceedings.

The events within our little community had gone from local headlines to national and then to international, and the focus of the media's attention was centred on the most bizarre aspects of the case which had swept us all along with it.

I'm not sure which of the reporters it was who had latched onto the story. I suppose any of those prepared to stand in the bar of the Admiral Nelson and buy a few rounds of drinks might have been rewarded by it. However, once the strange tale was backed up by the discoveries close to the Silent Lady, there was no holding the media back.

The story of the Kaiser's Gold, as the press dubbed it, was fascinating enough in itself. The return of Brian Latimer and his subsequent decision to donate his share of any wealth found on his land to charities working in Africa made for more sensational headlines. However, even these paled into insignificance once the greatest mystery became known.

My thoughts as I looked around the church centred on the insoluble puzzle of the children whose remains were now shielded by three simple coffins that had been placed at the front of the church. The vicar, a young and enthusiastic parson, walked slowly forward to commence the ceremony. He had approached Brian beforehand to request his input regarding the content of the funeral. The resulting service was simple but immensely moving. When it was over, Brian and I assumed our positions along with the funeral directors to act as pallbearers for those poor unfortunate souls as we carried them to their final resting place.

After the coffins had been lowered into position alongside the flowing waters of Thorsgill Beck, and the vicar gave the Benediction, we moved away. After leaving the churchyard, I looked back. Beyond the throng of mourners, media, and onlookers, I could see the three graves, illuminated by the pale winter sunshine. I shuddered, still affected by my encounter with things I could not explain.

Less than a week after the service at St Mary's, Eve and I returned to Dene Cottage from our morning stroll, a habit we had begun to enjoy. A car was parked in the lane by our house. Not just any car, but a huge, gleaming Rolls-Royce. I was still wondering if this was someone who was lost, or if not, why they might be at our house, when the driver's door opened. As the driver stepped carefully out of the vehicle, Eve recognized him. She introduced me, before asking the visitor what had brought him to Laithbrigg.

'I came to see you,' he told us, glancing from Eve to me. 'I needed to see you both; to ask you a favour. I know it might be a bit presumptuous, especially after what you've just gone through, but I wanted to ask you to find someone for me. I want you to find a dead man.'

But that's another story …

END

Postscript

Although several years have passed since the children's bodies were discovered, to my knowledge, the apparitions have not been seen again. Perhaps those poor little innocents really are at peace now.

The Eden House Mysteries

For more information about **Bill Kitson**

and other **Accent Press** titles

please visit

www.accentpress.co.uk

Printed in Poland
by Amazon Fulfillment
Poland Sp. z o.o., Wrocław